THE HEARTLESS PRINCE

Geneva Cerrato

This book is dedicated to the younger version of myself, the girl who lived in her head, loved to write, and dreamed of someday sharing her characters and stories with the world. You did it Geneva.

contents

Before you Begin...

I wrote this novel with an older teen to an adult audience in mind. It contains language and mature subject themes. If you're ready to meet the characters and the exciting world of Wisteria...please dive in...

1

"Corinthia!"

I dug my heels into the ground at the shout of my family name, wanting to fall through the floor, into another time and place–anywhere but here. For a moment I imagined a little cottage surrounded by lush greenery and colorful wildflowers, a small stream flowing by, and deer nibbling at the bark of the trees. Birds chirped in the breeze and my sister and I sat inside reading by the warm light of a fire. Alone. Safe. Home.

I opened my eyes and my sister's met mine and held on–the same caramel shade as mine. Her chest rose and fell and her eyes widened reminding me we were not in an idyllic cabin in the woods–more like a prison.

I squeezed her hand, my thumb resting over her quickening pulse and gave her a smile. "It will be fine."

Internally I screamed *shit. How are you going to get out of this one?*

She swallowed and nodded, her mane of brown hair falling over her shoulders. We were twins, and though we looked so much alike, I always took pride in being the older one–the first born, arriving minutes before her. At least, that's what my father always said, but he always told us lies and half truths and not a word could be trusted out of his mouth.

All activity stopped in the common room of the conscription lodge where my sister and I lived. Joshua raised an eyebrow and ceased drying the clay bowls we ate our measly helping of soup out of every night. The bowls were cracked and worn; we were in desperate need of new ones—well new everything around here—but they were expenses the empire wouldn't waste on us.

Avery dropped the basket of laundry she carried, the white linens spilling out; bedsheets and blankets with holes, socks beginning to unravel, and clothing that either fit too snuggly or too loosely.

The rest of our housemates hurried out of the room, scurrying like cockroaches, wanting to avoid the confrontation awaiting my sister and me.

To the overseer we might as well have been cockroaches. He wouldn't hesitate to stomp us under his boot. Or throw us out for whatever he'd found upstairs. And there were *many* illegal things hiding in the shabby room I shared with my sister. The question became: what did he find?

"Get up here now!" My sister flinched as the shout came again, the walls shaking with it. Joshua dropped one of the bowls and it shattered into small pieces all across the wooden floor.

My sister coughed into her handkerchief, no doubt aggravated by the stress of his shouts. I pretended not to be overcome with dread when she pulled it away and small drops of blood showed. She'd always been sick and I always pretended it didn't make a difference in her survival; because she had me. And I would *never* let anything happen to her.

"It will be fine Danielle," I said again. But we both knew it would not.

I headed up the rickety stairs first, my sister's meek steps falling behind, the wood groaning with every step.

I saw Hawthorne's back first towering over the broken object on the floor. He clenched his fists and slowly turned, his dark eyes burning a hole in the both of us.

"Whose is it?" I heard the threat in his voice as my eyes fell to the broken guitar, wood splintering just like my heart the first night we came here two years ago, sold by our own father into conscription for the empire at sixteen. And now we were forced to rent this room in the conscription lodge, barely able to scrape by or afford better lodgings. We paid for everything the empire gave us in blood, sweat, and tears. The coins they gave us weren't worth shit; not when I couldn't afford to buy my sister medicine or buy undergarments without holes in them.

I didn't hesitate. "It's mine."

A hand cracked against my face. My head whipped. I tasted blood. But I raised my chin and steeled my eyes in return. He would not break me. Ever. Let him try. Let him beat me black and blue. He could kill me even; it might be a mercy.

I touched my fingers to my lips and they came back red. An echo of a memory flashed in my mind. Red like the robes the emperor wore. The empire's signature color. Red like fire. Red like blood.

I looked at Hawthorne and smiled.

Let's see how you like that.

He grabbed me by the shirt collar, heaved me down the stairs and practically threw me out the door into the cool night air. I landed, my hands and knees scraping into the rough gravel. "You'll be sleeping with the horses tonight. This is your last warning and your rent is increasing by 2 silvers after your little stunt. If I find any more contraband you will hang."

I couldn't afford any extra silvers. I couldn't afford to hang either.

I thought of the bodies I'd seen in the town square that very morning. Two men and one woman. I recognized one of them; a man passing out bread and blankets to children in the streets of Sageburn. I shuddered at the memory, blinking my eyes until it vanished like smoke.

Somberly I headed toward the stables, resisting the urge to kick rocks. My feet were bare, there was no sense in breaking my toes. Instead I picked one up and hurled it as far as I could into the woods with an aggravated scream. I rubbed my hands against my arms. I wore only a thin shirt and pants a size too small, hardly enough to keep me warm in the brutal cold. Despite the cold and the promise of hay poking into my skin, I smiled at the fact I'd protected my sister again and managed to piss off Hawthorne in the process.

It had always been that way between us. My saving her. Protecting her.

The guitar was hers. A birthday gift I painstakingly saved up for months ago, even bartering doing chores in exchange for silvers from my housemates. I procured it while on one of my merchant runs in Sageburn, on one of the busier days when I knew no one would be paying attention to me.

"You know what the consequences are?" An old merchant named Van asked me the day I approached his stall with my precious silver coins. My determined stare answered his question as he wrapped the silver package with a whisper and slid it secretly into my delivery cart. "Don't. Get. Caught."

3

There were pieces of our history I wouldn't give up, despite the consequences, and I knew how much my sister loved music. Buying the guitar and having it in my possession was as illegal as playing it, but I told myself if my sister were ever caught, I would take the blame.

It didn't matter that I'd watched her painstakingly learn how to play, her fingers calloused and sore from the strings, on the days when Hawthorne went into town and we wouldn't get caught. Few in the lodge harbored *distractions*, as the emperor liked to call them, but we all lived with a code; we would turn a blind eye as long as it didn't threaten our own survival.

Music was outlawed by the empire, only certain songs approved, and that went for the creation of music as well. All forms of creative expression were subject to whipping, conscription, or even death, including reading, writing, or drawing anything the empire deemed a distraction.

A woman reciting poetry in the market lost her tongue a few weeks back. She'd been warned, fined, whipped; and stubbornly she kept defying the empire–four times to be exact. A part of me envied her resolve, the backbone she must have to take a stand again and again. But what could one person do against the empire? Could *one* make a difference?

The Arias empire craved control and sworn loyalty from everyone.

I saw it in the way Dean Carmichael was dragged out of the lodge only a week ago when discovered he was Gifted, a fire elemental, and I remembered the shot that rang out; the blood that stained the cobblestone sidewalk a reminder of the price paid for defiance. Being Gifted made you an enemy of the empire–there were no warnings, no chances of redemption; only execution.

And I wondered why Dean didn't fight back? Why didn't he use his powers to save himself?

I saw it in the way everything the citizens of Sageburn worked hard for belonged to the empire. You could be on your last loaf of bread and the empire would still demand it from you, watch your children starve and cry with no mercy.

I saw it in the way young men were taken from their homes and forced to enlist in the empire's army. How the sweet mannered boys of my youth became ruthless gun and sword wielding tools of war that oppressed their own people while owing the empire their undying fealty.

My sister and I were not conscripted into the army, but into labor. We both worked as mules for merchants–thankless and tiring work, and we paid a good portion of our wages for a room in the lodge and a bowl of soup at night. Five years we were indebted to the empire by our father's hand–the selfish bastard. Three more years and then we would be free, but in wishful thinking only. Freedom did not exist in the empire, but it didn't stop me from dreaming about our idyllic cabin in the woods–the future home my sister and I would find.

I reached the stable and led one of the horses over to a quiet brook; one of my favorite places on the estate. I caressed his back as I looked past the tall towering pine trees and into the inky darkness of the night sky, small stars scattering around carefree like glistening specks of sugar.

I wondered what it would be like to be a star as I felt the familiar pull and lull of the woods whispering to me. A whisper I mastered ignoring.

I never walked into the woods.

There were times I thought of running. But the empire did not take kindly to dissenters. I owed my time and service. And I knew the instant I made a run for it the empire would put a bounty on my head. And the people were desperate for coins–some even making a living off collecting bounties for the empire.

Past the trees jagged mountains rose up with snow peaked on the tips of them. On the other side of the mountain lay Wisteria, where the Gifted reigned–the sworn enemies of the Arias empire. There were creatures and magic the empire would kill to get its hands on: Firebirds, Unicorns, Dragons.

We were told as children to never cross the mountains into Wisteria, where the Gifted lived, and only the army was allowed to do so, after the plague, after the emperor declared war eleven years ago. A war I could never see the end too.

"Do you still think about Dean?" My sister asked me earlier that day by this very brook. And then more hesitantly, "Did you *know*?"

"Of course I didn't know." My cheeks had reddened at the accusation. "We were hardly anything." We'd fooled around in the stables a few times, but nothing substantial happened between us. He'd been a distraction, a way to pass the time.

"If you knew, would you have said anything?" My sister always asked introspective questions; questions I'd prefer she didn't ask.

Anyone with a Gift was mandated to report their power to the empire. Anyone hiding their power or harboring knowledge of someone else with a power was punishable by death. For those in the Arias empire - humans - were not born with power.

"No," I'd told her and I meant it. Dean may have been Gifted, but to me he was still Dean; no malicious intent in his body. He'd appeared no different than me. Perfectly normal. I would have no way of knowing he was an Elemental–those born with the gifts of either fire, ice, earth, or lightning magic.

I stared off again into the allure of the dark woods.

If you knew you were an elemental why didn't you run away Dean? Why didn't you fight back?

I didn't know what lay beyond the mountains and would never dare to wander in the woods, but there were days when I became curious about the pull and call. Curious about a place where few humans would dare venture. And to me – that sounded like peace. A place others feared could be a place I could find solace. One thing I knew - if my sister and I stayed here we might as well sign our death warrant. It was only a matter of when.

Three years couldn't pass soon enough.

I turned my attention back to the horse. "Would you like to hear a story?" I whispered. He turned, nudging his snout into my face in response. "Well then...since you asked so nicely." I chuckled. "This is the story of The Heartless Prince."

I felt devilish even saying the words, sharing the story. I couldn't recall where I'd first heard it or what forbidden book I'd read it from, but I always found it intriguing. And repeating it could get me whipped or worse, but I supposed a horse would not tell on me.

I patted his mane as I began. "Once upon a time, a man fled the empire and went to Wisteria to join the Resistance. Some say he was kidnapped, some said he did it to spite his father, but others said he fell in love with a Gifted. He ran away with her, forsaking his duty, and his empire to be with her; lured by her magic against his own will."

The horse whinnied in response. "Oh you like this story do you? So do I. Can I tell you a secret? They say it's about the emperor's son. But please don't repeat that."

I couldn't recall the emperor ever speaking of his son. I knew anyone caught spreading rumors or stories about his son would be promptly dealt with. Hard to say if he even existed or was merely a story told to warn us of the dangers of falling in love with a Gifted; how they could lure even the most loyal to the empire. And a warning to stay far away from the woods.

"And don't tell anyone, but I don't think he was lured against his will. I think he wanted to be with her." A small secret hope bloomed in my chest at the words. I would not consider myself a romantic by any means, but perhaps in another life I could allow myself the idea of finding someone who would choose me over everything else. A fantasy no doubt for those with the luxury to dream of such things.

With a sigh I ignored the familiar caress on my skin, the quiet voice in my ear, coaxing me into coming closer to the trees, and I headed back to the stable, feeling it slip away.

I told myself–three more years. Hold on for three more years.

Then you will be free to leave.

***

I'd fallen asleep on the hay when my eyelids fluttered open at the screams ringing out from inside the lodge. I leapt up, straw flying everywhere as I ran inside, blood pounding in my chest and ringing in my ears.

Hold on Danielle.

I bounded up the steps, my knee smashing into one as I lost my footing.

I reached the room and braced myself.

Danielle sat on the floor holding a hand up to her face, her nose bloodied and a bruise blooming on her cheek. Her eyes met mine, a sort of pleading in them, and it reminded me of when we were young.

Books were strewn all about the room, pages ripped and crumbled, black words torn like jagged pieces of a puzzle littering the room like confetti. He'd found my stash under the mattress.

Shit.

"I suppose you better get the noose ready." I said it to watch his face grow red and contort, and to focus his attention on me, not my sister.

"I know this isn't all yours Cora."

My intentions were not so secret apparently.

"You can't protect her anymore. She will be punished the same as you." He went after my sister again, grabbed her from the floor and hit her across the face. Her screams were all I needed to fuel me forward.

"Leave her alone!" I grasped at his shirt to pull him away and he turned, his fist flying across my face. I fell to the ground in a heap. Slowly, but surely I got back up and turned my eyes toward Hawthorne. He towered over me, angry jowls and bloodshot eyes.

"Perhaps if you pay double this month I will be willing to let this indiscretion go." His lips formed into a cruel smile. There was no way in hell I could pay double and he knew it.

My fingers went to the pulsating pain at the side of my head and they came away bloody. I stared, my vision spotted, and for a moment I looked in on myself from farther away. I stood, so still, skinny, bruised, and broken. And I willed her to fight back.

Save your sister.

No one else would save us. Silence fell over the lodge, everyone else in their rooms staying far away from the confrontation. Everyone looked out for number one. That was the only way to survive in the empire.

Hawthorne's hands dug into my shoulders, holding me tight against the wall when he realized I wouldn't take him up on his proposition. I slammed back into my body. "Who did you get the books and the guitar from?"

"No one," I choked out.

He slapped me. Hard. The sound made a crack like a whip against my face. I tried not to cry out. Not to let him have the satisfaction. Instead – this time I met his eyes feeling that voice in my head again as my sister looked on helplessly.

Fight back.

This amused him. "What are you going to do?" His mouth curled into a cruel smile. "Perhaps it's time I separate you and your sister due to insubordination. I hear the madam is looking for a few new whores."

Something in his words broke me further. To threaten my sister. Visions flooded my mind of tucking her into bed at night as a child, tending to scraped knees, telling her stories, and teaching her how to read in secret. All the nights I spent staying up with her when a coughing fit would overtake her, afraid she might not wake up in the morning. For him to hold me against this wall. To hit me. To bruise my body. To follow the empire's orders. It boiled my blood.

I cried out, something feral even to my ears. A woman possessed, I pushed him forward with foreign strength. He backed away, shock coloring his face.

Instinct fueled me.

Primal.

I lifted my hands to his face, fingers landing on his temples and I felt a thrum of energy flow through them.

Everything blurred. His eyes widened. His hands fluttered to my hands, a feeble attempt at prying them away from his head, powerless against me.

Blood. So much blood.

It poured out of his ears, his eyes, his nose, his mouth.

He reached for me, his bloodied hands finding my thin shirt.

"Cora! Run!"

My sister's voice echoed in my head as I pushed him away and ran.

Down the stairs and out of the lodge.

Down the gravel path, no plan, no thoughts, only sounds and sensations. Hard gravel beneath my bare feet. Then darting off past the little brook and into the pine covered forest, into the woods I said I would never enter until my time was up.

My feet screamed in protest as I scaled the ground.

Survive. Survive. Survive.

Get as far away as possible.

Keep running.

And so I did.

Until everything went black, and the only thought that echoed in my mind was-

Silencer.

***

When I awoke darkness flooded my vision.

I sat on metal, my feet planted on the ground, but I could barely move them in front of me. I tried to move my arms and met resistance. Cold cruel metal shackled my arms to the sides of the chair. I realized with sickening dread that the metal also shackled my ankles, keeping me in the chair.

I remembered running in the woods.

And then nothing.

I squinted my eyes in the dark and a shadow moved across the room.

"Ah you're awake," the voice said creeping across the room faintly. I recognized that voice. I heard it so many times over the years ringing out over the PA system–thanking us for our loyalty to the empire, asking us to give more, do more, keep fighting until we were safe again from the threat of Wisterian takeover.

Light suddenly flooded the room, my eyes burning from the impact. When I opened them again I took in my surroundings. A small, cold looking room. 4 concrete walls. Concrete floor. And me sitting in a large throne made of the same cold concrete.

I wore a blood red nightgown now, but I couldn't remember changing.

My feet were bare.

"Do you know who I am child?"

The emperor stepped forward, every bit as handsome as they said. Tall, well muscled, even hiding behind his blood red suit I could see his strength. His eyes were a piercing blue, a calculated coolness to them. His hair, a dark blonde, swept back, not a piece out of place. The echo of his boots sounded as he stepped closer to me.

I felt a strange pull to keep looking at him, as if I knew him in a deeper, more intimate way. There was a familiarness to him. A recognition. Mentally I didn't understand it, but physically and emotionally I responded to him.

"You're the emperor," I managed to say, my throat chalky. "Emperor Arias."

He smiled, but it didn't quite reach his eyes. "Very good." A pause. "And do you know why you are here?"

I felt my breath hitch as the memory of what I'd done to Hawthorne came flooding back. And with it so much confusion. So much shame.

What had I done?

Why did he die when I touched him?

He took a step closer, that same cruel smile on his face.

I instinctively tried to free my arms, fighting helplessly against the metal biting into my skin.

He stood in front of me now.

"All will be as it should again..." he said, his eyes taking on a hazy glow. And it was only then that I noticed what he held in his hands. A small gold circlet. Intricate designs of leaves and vines etched into the shining metal. Subtle in its beauty.

And when he placed it on my head, everything went black again.

2

Does time matter anymore when it is stolen from you?

Do memories matter if you cannot remember?

3

Where am I?

I sat up, dazed as if coming up from a long deep sleep. My vision blurred and I held a hand up to my head. I needed to remember something important. I caught flashes of warm hands hurrying me down a passageway...in the castle? That couldn't be right. A flash of turquoise eyes. A panicked voice telling me to flee.

I will always find you.

An explosion sounded in the distance, fire erupting into the dark sky, orange flames licking up straining for the stars.

I sat outside the gates of Sageburn, the capitol, sprawled on the ground in a heap.

People ran. Screams filled the air. Smoke filled my lungs and stung my eyes. Adrenaline coursed through my veins as I tried to untangle my thoughts.

Were we under attack?

In the midst of mayhem no one paid attention to me, even though soldiers were among the civilians trying to maintain the peace. I needed to go back for Danielle and figure out what was happening. But I couldn't go back right now, not with the soldiers.

If I went back what would I be going back too? Surely I would be imprisoned or hung for murder. The fact of the matter was I murdered someone with my bare hands *after* being found with multiple forms of contraband.

Hanged for sure.

I needed time to gather my wits, formulate a plan, and then save her. And I would need help. Someone stronger than me. Perhaps someone with magic.

The Resistance.

I bolted for the trees, wanting to get out of sight.

Tears and dirt streaked my face and vines and brambles tore at my skin as I ventured deeper into the forest, my thoughts slowly catching up with my primal need for survival.

As I ran I racked my mind, my memories, trying to dredge up anything that would help me remember how I got here.

I remembered the emperor. A cold concrete room. I remembered killing Hawthorne.

You killed him with your bare hands.

I couldn't allow myself to let the truth sink in. The only ones who went around killing others with their bare hands were Silencers. And I was *not* a Silencer. Silencers possessed one of the most rare forms of magic–the ability to kill with their touch alone.

And I'd never killed anyone with my touch before! How could it be possible?

As a human I barely survived the plague that spread across Sageburn as a child. Many died during the plague, and many were weakened, still suffering from chronic fatigue and coughing fits, like my sister Danielle.

The plague of course, like most of our suffering, was blamed on Wisteria and it was all the cause the emperor needed to declare war.

The morning light peeked through the trees filtering the forest floor around me as the full moon descended. It made the forest no less ominous, but held a strange beauty. Leaves crunched beneath my bare feet, freshly fallen off the trees for the fall season.

Gods Danielle I hope you ran away. Or told them the truth. Tell them it was me.

I couldn't let myself filter through all the different scenarios of what may happen to her. Despite her sickness, Danielle possessed the heart of a survivor. And she was smart. No one would think her capable of killing Hawthorne.

By some miracle, as if it were meant to be, the trees opened up and the mountains came into view, tall towers striking up against the sky. And between them, a sloping path beckoning me forward.

This way, it seemed to call. A familiar whisper.

I realized I could go back the way I came and take my chances in Sageburn, or I could continue forward and find out the truth about Wisteria. Find out if it were a place my sister and I could be safe. Free.

Find the Resistance and ask them to help me.

A gamble. But everything in my life was a gamble.

I continued along the winding steep path, the jagged edges of the mountains on either side of me, until my feet were cracked and bleeding and the cold air filled my lungs in short gasps. I couldn't fathom a measure of time as I walked, only one foot in front of the other, every aching inch the sun crept higher in the sky; when I finally passed the threshold into Wisteria.

Once on the other side a new forest of trees came into view, wispy and willowy, a light fog settling over the area. The air shifted; a familiar caress on my skin like the wings of a butterfly. This place held a haunted quality. I imagined any moment skeletons might emerge from the mist with broadswords and strike me down. These woods held secrets, but what would be the cost to unravel them?

Did I make the wrong choice?

As the cries of foreign birds filled my ears and the dim glow of fireflies lit the way, I searched for a source of water. My throat burned with the exertion of crossing the mountain.

Before long a beautiful spring came into view, encircled by weeping willow trees, their branches fanning out like silky threads. The trees gave me the illusion of safety, rest. I didn't trust it. But the water sparkled; clear and blue, inviting.

Entirely too thirsty to resist, I approached the spring, eager to clean my face and drink water until my stomach hurt, when a voice stopped me.

"I wouldn't do that if I were you." The words a warning fading into the sound of crickets chirping in the tall grass.

I paused and jerked my head up from the water. He leaned against one of the weeping willow trees, his arms crossed against his chest. His arms were tan, the color of warm sun and well-muscled leading up to broad shoulders, the planes of his chest barely showing as the top button of his black shirt was undone.

He looks like he could break me in half.

Most striking were his eyes, a dark green fringed by dark lashes, and two dark brows arching over them. His hair a mop of light brown curling lazily above his eyes. Those eyes appraised me now the way a predator might assess their prey.

He held a dangerous allure as if under any other circumstances he would be doing his best to make me laugh or doing his best to charm me.

Dean had been charming too.

Any other girl would have swooned, would have thought him dashing. But seeing him only made my spine stiffen and my fingers reach for a weapon I didn't have. Would he kill me? Were Wisterians as bloodthirsty as the empire said? Would he give me a chance to explain myself?

"I have no interest in harming you," he said, taking a small step away from the tree – and I wondered if my thoughts were said out loud. His eyes rolled. He appraised me again and this time there was no mistaking that look – pity or disgust.

Of course he thinks you're disgusting. You're a human.

"Unless you give me a reason too," he amended, his voice sharp with irritation. Clearly my presence massively inconvenienced him. "Why don't you go back where you came from." An order, not a suggestion.

"I'm not going back," I said firmly. My voice sounded so small, so quiet, but I meant it. I stood my ground even though my legs were beginning to shake - no doubt the adrenaline and shock that propelled me through the forest wearing off. "Not yet."

I owe it to Danielle.

"Why not?" His lips curved into a crooked smile, more mocking than friendly. "There's nothing here for you human."

A tired wisdom rested in his eyes. I recognized it the way only two people who have been forced to grow up entirely too fast would. He'd endured pain and loss. Once you did - you learned to recognize it in others. I saw it in so many people these days.

"Is this Wisteria?" I asked at last. One thing at a time. If this was Wisteria I could move on to finding the Resistance. I blinked, the exhaustion hitting me. I needed water. Dehydration loomed making my head spin. I was of no use to my sister when I couldn't think straight.

The man watched me curiously, his hand going to his dagger hilt.

I bent down again to get some water and relief, when something gray and fleshy sprung toward me from the water, bones protruding from it grotesquely, black gaping holes for its eyes, and gray hair stranding down its head. As it sprang I heard the man shout "NO" and before I knew it I fell in the water, and so did he.

A flash of steel cut through the water and red rippled everywhere. Blood.

His hands tried to pull at me and I thrashed away, unwilling to let him touch me.

"Let me help you!"

I climbed out of the water sputtering, now fully soaked, water dripping from my hair and into my eyes. "What was that thing?" My eyes darted to the spring where blood rippled out in waves, evidence I didn't imagine the ghastly creature.

"Figures – in the first minute you enter Wisteria something wants to kill you." There was nothing but disdain in his voice. "Typical for a human."

I balked at the man beside me. His soaked clothes clung to the muscular ridges of his body. He ran a hand through his wet hair and those deep green eyes met mine again. From up close I could see the smattering of light freckles that lay under his eyes and over his nose. Similar to my own. Twin daggers lay beside him, clearly the source of my rescue.

His eyes trailed down my form for a moment and then looked away in irritation. My soaked red nightgown clung to my skin, leaving nothing to the imagination. I crossed my arms across my chest instinctively. The red bled into my memory and the vision of the emperor in his red suit flashed before my eyes.

What happened to me?

He got up and appraised me again with that same kind of pitiful but curious look and he held out his hand.

I hesitated.

The last time I touched someone it killed them. And I didn't know why. How. I didn't trust myself.

Unless I imagined it. Did it really happen?

I shook my head.

His brows furrowed. "I can always let the nymphs have you if you prefer."

I looked up and met his eyes. "You shouldn't touch me."

He didn't argue again.

"Why are you here?"

I considered my options. Find my way alone and hope nothing else tried to kill me or ask him for help.

I let out a shaky breath. "What can you tell me about the Resistance?"

4

Time felt unimportant as we walked, slowed down to the weary beat of a failing heart. It felt eerie, a dormant power pulsating through the grass, the willowy trees, and the misty fog settling over us like a soft blanket.

It whispered to me, asking me to wander deeper into its clutches. The same pull and call I'd experienced in Sageburn now embraced me, wrapping its arms around me like shadows that would never let me go. I heard the rustling of creatures I couldn't see in the grass and felt as if I were being watched with every step. Birds flew and cawed above the trees. A green frog leaped over my bare feet.

An odd sense of deja vu danced in my mind, unnerving me.

"Careful," the man spoke, his voice soft music in the mist. "You can't trust anything here. You're essentially a fly tempting a venus fly trap." He paused as he waited for me to catch up to him. "Stay close to me." I watched nervously as his fingers went to the dagger sheathed at his side, lingering there. "Who knows you're here?"

His question confused me. "Nobody."

"Where did you come from?"

"Through the forest and then a pass in the mountains," I said simply. "From the other side." I let the words linger hoping it would prompt him to tell me where exactly we were in Wisteria. No human was oblivious to the magic of this place. I could feel it pulsating in waves, rippling through the trees, whispering in the wind.

He stopped and the forest seemed to stop with him as if reacting to him. "Obviously," he said. He was frustrated or just being an ass – I didn't know him well enough to tell but he'd been nothing but annoyed with my presence from the beginning. "Why did you ask about the Resistance? You know the Gifted don't take too kindly to humans—especially those from the empire."

"I ran away."

He turned to look at me and the closeness of his body, the intimacy of his eyes, stirred something within me. Something foreign. My hands trembled at my sides. It wasn't safe to be this close to me, I still didn't understand what I did to Hawthorne; or what I could do.

Can I ever touch anyone again?

He seemed to register the panic in my expression and once again he said, "I'm not going to hurt you." His green eyes explored my body in a clinical way, landing on my bruises, and taking in the thinness of me. "At the very least you need to get cleaned up. Get some food in you. And rest."

Perhaps he would help me.

His eyes slowly trailed my face, the dirt and tear stains, then down to my arms and legs coated in dried blood from the scratches of the vines, before firmly meeting mine, as if he were looking at a wounded animal.

"What the hell happened to you?"

I tried to find the words to speak, but only stared at him numbly.

He let out a whistle and something small and bushy came bounding out of the woods. I stumbled back and his eyes rolled in amusement despite the fact he'd told me not to trust anything in this forest.

A jackal, cream colored with tipped ears, and alert green eyes stood in front of me. They assessed me curiously waiting for an invitation to say hello. He wagged his bushy tail in approval as the man bent down to ruffle his head.

"This is Cyrus. He's with me."

I regarded him curiously. The jackal came closer to me, sniffing, still waiting. "Will he bite me?"

"He won't hurt you. Unless you attempt to hurt me." He raised his eyebrows in warning. "I wouldn't underestimate him."

18

Cyrus pushed his snout into my hand before I could protest and I sighed in relief as my hands went to smooth the fur of his head and behind his ears. My touch did not harm him. Thank the Gods for small mercies.

We walked a bit longer before the man paused and drew out a piece of cloth. I looked at it questioningly. "I'm afraid for the rest of our journey you will need to be blindfolded. Unless you'd prefer to turn around and go back to the human realm."

I took the cloth and hastily tied it around my head. "Satisfied?" I took a step forward. "I will follow the sound of your footsteps. Don't touch me."

***

The trek to the location he didn't want me to know about lasted hours. I knew he was walking slower than normal to let me keep up and I took every step without complaint, letting my senses guide me.

We stopped twice along the way and he removed the cloth so I could see enough to drink water. The sun hung high above the trees like a dangling orb, creating playful streaks of light through the tree branches and forest floor. Reluctantly I put the cloth over my eyes again.

This guy better be taking me to the Resistance.

At long last I sensed we reached our destination. I could hear the click of a door, and then the crackling of a fire. I heard the soft steps of boots on the hardwood floor. Another click of a door and finally the blind fold fell away from my eyes.

We were in a small room. Twin sized bed. A bay window with the last rays of the day filtering through. It was unassuming and reminded me a bit of my room back home on the farm. Bitterness tugged at the thought. The farm was *before* the lodge and I didn't often think of my past life. The days I spent feeding chickens, picking ripe fruit, and planting vegetables; helping my father on the farm.

Before the bastard betrayed you.

"I'm sure you'd like some time to get settled. There's a washroom through the door there," he motioned. "The tub is already filled with hot water. And you will find a change of clothes in the wardrobe there. Anything you need." He hesitated and his eyes skimmed over me again like he wanted to say more, but thought better of it. "We will be back soon to ask you some questions."

We?

Perhaps the mystery tub filler.

After he left the room I went into the washroom to clean up. I caught my appearance in the oval mirror hanging on the wall and I did a double take, my hands hesitantly touching my face.

Gods I look awful.

Not only awful, but I didn't look the way I remembered. I looked *older*. My dark blonde hair tumbled down my front in waves, much longer than I remembered, making me appear more feminine. Zero bruising appeared near my caramel colored eyes even though one of the last memories I had was of Hawthorne hitting me. My skin glowed; sun kissed and lightly freckled from all my time working in the streets of Sageburn. I scrunched my dark brows together, and my stomach tightened as I racked my memory. All I could see were patches of black with nothing in between.

Why couldn't I remember?

The memory of the emperor flashed behind my eyes again. His red suit. The cold metal biting into my skin. Him placing something on my head.

And then nothing except for waking up outside of Sageburn.

I took off the red nightgown, and again did not recognize the woman standing in front of me. I did not appear as skinny and underfed as I should be eating only bowls of soup every night for dinner.

You have curves. When did that happen?

I climbed into the tub, hissing in relief as the steamy water met my flesh. As much as I longed to soak my tired muscles, I began scrubbing all the dirt and grime off my body, and washed my hair with a bar of soap that smelled like jasmine. The bath water now a murky brown and red made my stomach churn and I quickly got out.

When finished I found, as promised, a pair of black pants and a blue shirt in the wardrobe. I felt relieved that the clothes were not red. And then I reminded myself that these people hated the empire. And they hated me by association.

Lucky for them - I hated the empire too.

And if everything worked out according to plan–I would find the Resistance, and they would help me save my sister. I only needed to figure out what I would give them in return. What did I have of value?

I braided my hair and tossed it over my shoulder when I noticed a cup of tea sitting on the table by the bed. Steam rippled from the cup continuously. I smelled it curiously before taking a small sip and sent up a prayer it wasn't poisonous.

It tasted rich and sweet, hints of honey and vanilla.

Did poison have a distinct taste?

All my life I was taught to be afraid of the Gifted.

All my life I was taught that we needed their power to protect ourselves, and the notion that the empire would do anything to get it tugged at the back of my mind.

I didn't even know what caused the plague, only that the Wisterians were blamed for it. The emperor said magic caused the plague. If we possessed magic we would be stronger, able to defend ourselves. I wondered if the emperor would ever find a way for humans to use magic, or if a truce could be formed between the warring lands.

A soft knock and the clicking of the door interrupted me. I scurried back against the bed as a woman entered.

She stood tall and lithe, a cascade of dark hair falling down her back and curling softly at the ends. Her brown almond shaped eyes landed on mine intently. She had a heart shaped face and full lips. The fighting leathers and dagger at her hip gave me the impression her beauty was a boon, and I sensed she'd best any man in a fight.

"I didn't mean to scare you," she said. Her voice sounded gentle, but even I learned early on that the sweetest voices were lures, traps, and not to be trusted. "I will let him know you're ready." She smiled. "I'm Lex."

I didn't bother trying to smile back.

She closed the door and I wondered if by "him" she meant the man that helped me in the forest who I clearly inconvenienced. Sure enough she did. Before I mentally prepared myself a knock sounded and he came in after Lex.

He wore a white shirt this time, the sleeves rolled up above his elbows and a pair of black trousers with daggers at his hip. His brown hair was slightly damp and curling above his eyes. Freshly bathed. His green eyes found mine betraying no emotion.

He approached the foot of the bed, Lex trying to keep her distance. She leaned against the wall near the window crossing her arms over her chest. I could tell she wanted to feign disinterest in me, but I saw through it.

"Are you ready to answer our questions?" The suspicion in the room felt palpable, both their eyes fixed on me.

I stared him down not wanting to feel like a small animal he just found in the forest and raised my chin. "Are you part of the Resistance?"

They silently exchanged a glance, obviously well trained in the art of masking their emotions. I couldn't read them. His eyebrows furrowed together and Lex stared at me unblinking. Neither acknowledged my question, their silence and reaction enough to confirm they didn't trust me yet. I didn't blame them; I felt the exact same way.

"Why are you asking about the Resistance?" Lex asked, her eyes narrowing. I took note of the way her fingertips pressed slightly into the skin near her elbows, how her heels leaned back slightly. Defensive.

I said nothing.

"We need to know who you are and why you're here," the green eyed man inserted.

He sat on the window seat and leaned forward contemplating. I watched as his fingers intertwined together one by one and his hands folded together. His eyes wouldn't leave me and the way they watched me felt intimidating.

"What's your name?"

"You wouldn't prefer to call me 'human'?" I said it just to see his hands tighten and the way his lips pursed in contempt. Lex smirked from beside him.

"We have ways to find out your name if you're going to be uncooperative." As soon as the words were out I saw a hint of regret in his eyes. Did he think I was fragile and I would break at the threat of violence? I wouldn't let it get to me–even if it did–I wouldn't let him see.

"Cate," I said, feeling the lie fall out of my mouth. I gave him my mothers name. I didn't yet trust these people with my name. Whoever they were.

"Cate," he repeated it and it seemed believable enough. His green eyes grew hazy and his brows furrowed. "Cate what?"

"Just Cate." I wasn't about to give him my family name.

"And what are you doing here *Cate*? I know you said you were running away, but-" he brushed away a few brown curls that fell into his face, "Most humans don't enter Wisteria willingly unless they have no choice."

His eyes were laced with accusation, looking for a tell, a chink in my armor, something to give me away and prove I was nothing more than a threat and a liar. I might be both.

"I chose to come here," I replied, crossing my arms across my chest. His eyes darkened in response. "And I will choose to go back. When I'm ready. On my terms. I need to find the Resistance."

"You're not going to find the Resistance," Lex said, her nails tapping against her forearm. "And why would a human seek out the Resistance?" Her dark brows arched curiously.

"So you're saying you can't help me? I wasted my time coming here?"

The two exchanged another glance before the man stood up and indicated for Lex to leave the room. She did, but he stayed. "Do you know how many soldiers the emperor sends into Wisteria trying to weed out the Resistance? And you thought you could come here and find them yourself or that we would take you to them willingly?"

"I get it. You think I'm an imbecile. But I didn't have a choice."

"Why not?"

I pursed my lips. I didn't know how much information I should give to anyone outside of the Resistance. Would he laugh in my face if I told him I needed to save my sister? Would he consider it a cause worthy of taking me to them?

You're a human. They will never help you.

"I can't help you if you refuse to answer my questions." He opened the door to the room. "And don't bother trying to run away from here. You won't last two seconds out there by yourself, *human*."

***

I'm in a beautiful garden. A large fountain stands in the center, surrounded by rows upon rows of beautiful flowers. Lilies, roses, chrysanthemums, carnations. The early evening sky turns a purple pink as the sun sets.

Strong stone walls surround the garden. It appears empty at the moment, the solitude feeling natural to me. I am meant to be alone.

I can't recall why I'm here. Only that I am walking, wandering. And although the flowers are beautiful, I don't feel anything looking at them. No desire to touch them or smell them manifests. I look at everything with a clinical sense.

I approach the fountain and sit on the edge, letting my fingers skim over the surface of the cool water. I look at my reflection. A young girl. Maybe ten.

I wear a long dark red robe, my blonde hair falling down around my shoulders in waves. And on top of my head is a gold circlet. I look like someone of importance, royalty perhaps.

I move and the girl in the reflection moves as well. I touch the circlet atop my head, and slowly take it off and set it beside the fountain.

All at once the world comes to life in full color.

I take in the brightness of the purple pink sky.

I feel an urge to touch and smell the flowers.

I reach my fingers up and gently touch my hair and then my cheeks, the feeling making my skin tingle. Warm. Alive.

I am feeling for the first time, aware of every sensation, thoughts flowing freely in my head, the beauty of being able to think and feel stirring my heart awake.

I walk around the garden taking in all the different flowers. I touch them gently, awed at their colors and shapes. I lean close and smell their sweet scent. I feel tears brimming my eyes when I realize across the way from me, a young boy peers at me through the cover of the flowers.

His eyes are piercing, fixed on mine. They are the kind of eyes that I can't decide if they are blue or green, seamlessly weaving into both. He appears to be a little older than me, but he holds himself with a maturity he shouldn't know at his age.

"Why are you crying?" He asks quietly. He looks at me as if he's never seen tears before.

"I don't know," I reply, wiping my eyes with my sleeve. "The flowers are just really beautiful, you know?"

He grins, a dimple showing in his right cheek. "Do you want to see something more beautiful?"

I nod.

"This way," he says and I follow him, weaving in and out of the pathway through the flower beds, keeping my eyes fixed on his blonde head.

We reach the far corner of the garden and he stops. He stands in front of the most beautiful flowers I've ever seen. They are tall and varieties of color. Some are a deep purple, some pink, some deep dark red, but he reaches for the dark blue one and turns, holding it out to me.

"What is it?" I ask, taking the flower gently in my hand and twirling it, admiring how the colors are a kaleidoscope of different shades of blue bleeding into one another.

"An orchid," he says, his eyes watching my every move. His eyes are blue now, shining.

My eyes fall back to the assortment of orchids. "Why not this one?" I ask my fingers absentmindedly touching a blood red one. I feel a pull to it. The back of my mind reminds me of where my loyalties lie. Red means something important.

He shakes his head and his eyes narrow. "When it's just us...you can pick any color you want. You don't have to choose red."

I marvel at his words and the way he looks at me. As if he knows me. As if I know him. I want to know his name.

The sound of footsteps approaching meets my ears and I feel panic. I am suddenly aware that I am not supposed to be here. I shouldn't be talking to this boy. Or choosing the blue orchid. Or feeling. Or thinking.

"I will always find you," *the boy whispers.*

I sat up in the bed with a jolt. My chest heaved, my breath came in gasps.

A dream, I told myself. *A strange dream.*

But the dream felt so real.

I closed my eyes and saw the blue eyed boy holding out the blue orchid to me, letting me choose. *Choice.* It felt so far away that of course the only place I'd find it would be in my strange dreams given to me by a strange boy.

When I got my bearings I threw the covers off. The light of the moon poured into the room. I put my ear up against the doorframe and heard nothing; only quiet.

He said don't try to leave on my own–whoever "he" was–I still didn't know his name. But I wasn't about to listen. And anywhere I went would be of my own choosing. Anywhere I would stay would be of my own choosing. And if these people weren't going to help me find the Resistance, I would find someone else.

Surely there would be a town nearby where I could find a tavern and gather information. Not all Wisterians were so difficult, were they? Surely one would help me.

I'm going to find help Danielle and then we will be free and make a life of our own, far away from the empire.

I wouldn't let it have me. Not anymore.

I climbed out the bay window, seeing it as my best option. The air was humid, and an owl hooted distantly in the trees. I felt the familiar caress of the wind whispering at me to stay.

Once out the window I got a better view of my surroundings. The window I came out of belonged to a quaint looking cottage made of brick; and I found it ironic as I always dreamed of having a cottage someday.

Not far in the distance I could see a small fire recently burned out, large logs sitting around it as seating, and a few enclosures for sparring with bows, swords, daggers, chainmail, and helmets hanging around the circular wooden ring.

I approached the ring slowly, my boots crunching against the ground. My fingers skimmed the weapons, landing on a dagger. Small enough to not feel intimidating and easier to yield. I put it in my boot.

I'd never used a weapon in my life; not for fighting or defending myself.

What are you doing Cora?

I ignored the more pragmatic voice in my brain and grabbed a canteen I spotted near the sparring ring, and headed toward the lake behind the cabin.

The lake spread out like inky fingers in the darkness and I shuddered at what might lie beneath its depths. I hesitated to get near it after my encounter with the grotesque water creatures earlier in the forest spring, but I determined it worth the risk. I would need water.

I knelt down beside the water and lowered the canteen, the cold seeping over my fingers. My other hand went to my boot, ready to draw the dagger at a moment's notice. After it was filled, I breathed a sigh of relief that nothing tried to attack me, put my dagger back in my boot and made my way into the trees wanting to stay hidden.

If I could find someone to help me rescue Danielle she and I could charter passage on a ship and sail to a land far away. The thought fueled me and my resolve to find help. I would need coin to barter with or something of value. Again I racked my mind, before my eyes trailed down to my hand and the sapphire ring resting on my middle finger.

Where did you come from?

I couldn't remember receiving it, finding it, stealing it; nothing.

But there it was as if the Gods granted it to me in my hour of need.

I can sell it. Surely these people value coins as much as humans do. It must be worth a small fortune.

Perhaps I didn't *need* the Resistance. Not if I could find someone willing to take coin in exchange for helping my sister get out of Sageburn.

I must have walked an hour, my feet still cracked and sore despite the boots I wore. No sign of life greeted me, no sign of a town, simply forest that stretched on and on. The trees here were not willowy like when I first entered Wisteria. They were birch, their bark white as a ghost. There was no mist either.

More unnerving was the silence that fell around me. No creatures. No crickets. Only a bleak heaviness that seemed to suck any trace of life. Was it this quiet before?

I heard a noise from behind me at long last–too careful–but meant for me to hear. "Who's there?" I called, my hand shaking as I cautiously removed the dagger from my boot.

Pitch black. Only darkness. The rustle of the wind in the trees and the bright stars up above me were my only source of comfort. I got lost looking at them for a moment. My throat tightened and I fought the urge to cry.

Don't cry, I told myself. *There will be time soon.*

A twig snapped in front of me and a figure came into view. For all intents and purposes he seemed like a man, but with distinct eyes, they held a red glow around the rim and there were inky faint lines of blue and black trailing from his eyes outward around his eyes and down his cheeks.

"Stay back!" I held out my dagger in front of me.

The figure chuckled and took a step closer. "What's a pretty little human doing out here?"

It clearly wanted to play with me. So human aside from the glowing eyes and faint traces on his skin. It grinned and fangs flashed in the light of the moon. I didn't have a name for this creature, but I knew those fangs were not just for show.

"Don't come any closer," I warned, but my voice shook.

In a burst of speed it jumped on me, fangs flashing. It held my arms down above my head, the dagger clattering from my hands and I watched as those fangs came closer clearly wanting my neck. I screamed and kicked, managing to get my knee in its gut, but the thing didn't budge.

Is this how it ends? Are you so weak Cora?

Suddenly the thing was hoisted off me. I took deep steadying breaths. I sat up and watched as two figures battled it out in the near distance. There was no mistaking that head of curly brown hair or the ease of which he used the dagger to dispatch the demon. One plunge into its neck and it squealed, falling to the ground. He leaned down and made quick work of his blade til the thing's head was severed and thrown away from its corpse.

He stood, turned to face me and the relief on his face was quickly covered with displeasure. His green eyes flashed. Ichor streaked his face and his white shirt, which he now lifted up and used to wipe his face. His muscular abs flashed as he did so and I averted my eyes. I was no stranger to the male form, but there weren't many men in Sageburn who looked like him.

He could definitely break you in half.

"Did I—or did I not—tell you *not* to try and leave?" His words were clipped. Precise. Filled with frustration.

I stared at the ground before slowly lifting my eyes to his, feeling like a scolded child. He held out his hand to help me up from the ground and I took his hand in mine, only because he wore gloves. "Sorry?"

"I don't think you are," he replied. "You would have been dead."

"I suppose you followed me then. I thought I heard someone behind me." I tried to shrug it off, but I knew he could see right through me. "I could have handled it—you gave me no time."

You're weak. You can't save your sister.

"If I waited another second he would have ripped your throat out." His eyes flashed again before they rolled at me. "Why are you such a pain in the ass?"

I glared at him. "If I'm such a pain in the ass then let me go. Let me escape. Let me die. What do you care about what I do?"

"You would like that wouldn't you? If I just let you off yourself. You humans are terrible at staying alive."

"I'm not trying to 'off' myself," I retorted. "I took a bath and ate some food. *Just* like you wanted. Is there something else you want from me or can I be on my way?"

He ran a hand through his brown curls. "Why don't you let me take you back to the other realm. I'm sure there are plenty of places for you to go be a pain in the ass there."

"Fine," I shot back. Now that I had a new plan for how to help my sister I didn't see what it mattered if a human or a Wisterian helped me. I would sell the ring and pay someone to help me, perhaps even bribe some of the empirian soldiers if it came down to it. He seemed to relax at my response. "Not the answer you were expecting?"

"No it wasn't." His eyes narrowed suspiciously. "But I'm not going to argue. The sooner I'm rid of you the better. You shouldn't be here if you can't stop asking so many damn questions about the Resistance." He looked back into the woods. "Cyrus! Come!" He whistled and Cyrus came bounding out of the woods to join us, his bushy tail swishing.

"Great, then let's get rid of me." I took off walking and I could feel his eyes shooting daggers at the back of my head.

Fuck the Resistance. And fuck him.

"You're not going the right way. And you forgot your dagger. I don't see how you can possibly survive in the human realm either."

"I know a thing or two about survival." I leveled with him. When I turned to face him he was closer than I expected. I nearly touched his chest. I flicked my eyes up to his own and his expression hardened. "The only way to kill someone isn't physical."

"I know that." His words came out with a sigh. He didn't bother countering with a smart remark. His eyes held mine before his gaze fell to my mouth and then seeming to catch himself ire replaced the softness in his eyes.

"Before you dump me in the human realm I suppose I should know your name. Who shall I thank for escorting me back?" I knew being cheeky would only irritate him further and I relished the thought.

"Lockwood," he said. "You can call me Locke."

***

"Are we there yet?"

"Trust me," Locke said, Cyrus trailing right behind him, "you would know if we were there."

We'd been walking for what felt like hours. The sun rose high in the sky now, the light filtering down. Despite the shade it provided sweat clung to my skin beneath my clothes. I smelled like the merchant streets of Sageburn.

The trees changed again as we walked from the birch to the wispy willowy ones with mist settling over us. Despite the humid mist, the air here felt less heavy. Less threatening.

Thoughts of my sister plagued my mind. I needed to get back to her. I needed to find out what happened in Sageburn. But of course Locke took the opportunity again to drill me with questions, determined to figure out anything he could about me.

"So tell me," he said with a curious lilt to his voice. "What were you running from? Most humans want to *stay* in the Arias empire. Haven't you been spoon fed scary stories about our kind your entire life?"

I didn't want to talk about my reasons for running away. I wanted to get away from Hawthorne, away from a noose, but I suspected there was something else entirely I was running from. Even if I couldn't remember.

Perhaps he sensed he overstepped because he changed the question. "Why didn't you go to Alexandria? I've *heard* their leadership is more progressive than Sageburn's. That the empire hasn't totally gotten its claws in them yet."

It was true. The neighboring kingdom of Alexandria still operated from its own policies separate from Sageburn's. A King and Queen ruled Alexandria, much like the old world, but there were whispers that the empire desired to have one kingdom to rule the entirety of the human realm. And not a King, but an emperor.

The only reason I could fathom the emperor waited to move against Alexandria was because of the resources, protection, and soldiers they currently provided for the empire. It was a mutually beneficial relationship for the time being.

"I don't wish to talk politics with you," I snapped. "At the time I didn't have the liberty of time to decide where my best choice of direction to run was. If I did - it wouldn't have been to you."

Locke's shoulders tensed and his hands clenched into fists. I knew how to push his buttons already. It amused me how much power I could wield with my words alone. How every phrase out of my mouth irked him. Despite my cheekiness he began a new onslaught of questions, refusing to let periods of quiet linger too long between us.

"Is there anyone waiting for you back home? Do you have a family?" I didn't miss how his eyes fell to the sapphire ring on my middle finger. My new ticket to saving my sister. Self consciously I began to twirl the ring on my finger.

Another wrong question.

"I don't have a home," I replied. I hated the way it sounded. So pathetic, but true.

Only the one you've crafted in your delusional lonely mind that doesn't exist.

"I have a sister," I admitted at last. I figured it made no difference now that I would be leaving. "And I need to go back for her."

I could feel his eyes on me, scanning my face as if I were a puzzle meant to be solved. It made me feel unnerved when he did that - as if he managed to find a chink in my armor it would be my undoing.

"I once had a sister. Two in fact." He said the words quietly and I sensed the subject sore for him. I averted my eyes and quickly changed the subject, not wanting to make our situation more intimate than it needed to be.

Intimacy is dangerous.

"If you're Wisterian..." I asked changing the subject, but also to gauge what kind of predator Locke might be, "What power do you have? And what was that thing that attacked me back there? A vampire?"

Perhaps he was a Shadow–able to alter one's perception or turn invisible, or maybe even an Empath–able to read my thoughts and sense my emotions, but more likely than not he was an Elemental.

His eyes flashed at me. "Oh so now you want to be friendly." He paused and I sensed the next subject was also unpleasant for him. "We call those creatures *the cursed*. That's what happens to us when our magic is manipulated. Ask your emperor." He tacked the last part on for good measure.

I felt heat flood my cheeks. "He's *not* my emperor."

He knew how to push my buttons as well. "Surprising. Maybe you are cut out for the Resistance after all. If you weren't a useless human."

I turned to him. "So they do exist?" I thought of the emperor's son then. The story of the Heartless Prince. "Has anyone from Sageburn ever joined the Resistance?"

He laughed. Literally laughed. But it was full of condescension.

Asshole.

His amused eyes met mine, but I didn't return the sentiment. "There are no humans in the Resistance. And you're the only human who's ever come here searching them out. You still haven't told me why."

"I thought it would be obvious after I told you about my sister."

"And you...what?" He crossed his arms over his chest. "Thought the Resistance would help you *save* her?" Genuine disbelief laced his tone, his eyebrows drawing together in puzzlement.

31

I lifted my chin. "Do you know what it's like in Sageburn? What we live with every day?" I took a shuddering breath. "Nothing belongs to us. Everything is taken from us. We have no future. No freedom. So yes," I sharpened my gaze, "I *did* hope the Resistance would help me save my sister. Because delusion is *all* I have to hold onto."

And it terrifies me I might be too weak to save her by myself.

He rubbed his jaw and stared at the ground.

We were silent the rest of the trek.

You're a damn fool. Why did you come here?

I'd wasted two days with my half assed plan. I saw the Resistance as a magical entity that dared to defy the empire. I even filled my head with stories about the Heartless Prince who joined them. But perhaps my perception of them was wrong; a lie concocted to give me hope while I survived in the empire. The sooner I could get back to my sister the better. And I would find someone to help me.

"It should be here." Locke paused as we came to where the edge of the forest met the mountains, the winding mountain path in the distance.

But looking out we could see that a sea of red and black soldiers stood around the pass, fanning out on all sides of Wisteria, a mass of metal armor, swords and shields, and guns. Whether they were standing guard or looking for something I couldn't be sure.

How am I supposed to get back to Sageburn?

Cyrus let out a low growl in response.

"Shit." Locke put his hands in his hair clearly exasperated. And then he lowered his hands and looked at me strangely, trying to analyze me again. I felt a strange sensation again when he looked at me with such intensity, tugging at a string, willing it to unravel and reveal all my secrets.

"What now?" I asked, ignoring the feel of his eyes on my skin.

"Now I figure out what I'm supposed to do with you. Because you can't leave Wisteria and there are Empirian soldiers crawling all over the place. And that...is very dangerous for you."

Inside I fumed. I panicked. How long before I could get back to my sister? What was I supposed to do now? But I turned to Locke with a smirk, not wanting him to see my distress. "I suppose you will just have to endure my lowly human existence for longer than you anticipated."

5

Locke and I headed back to the camp I fled the night before. I did so apprehensively and he grudgingly. Thoughts of my sister swirled in my mind, the anxiety eating away at my stomach. What if something already happened to her? Did she stay at the lodge or run away? I tried my best to hide my emotions and screwed my face into stone despite my anxious thoughts.

On our way to the camp Locke stayed silent, not one for chit chat. He dispatched a few creatures along our way I'd never seen before. One wolf like with shaggy fur, drool dripping from its teeth. Another a large bird that swooped down out of nowhere with a magnificent shriek.

He ended them in swift blows, clearly well practiced with a sword and dagger, and also a bow and arrow. He remained alert, his senses keen. He moved with the art of a dancer, flowed like water, and struck like lightning. I trusted in his capabilities to defend me, but I knew he could as easily kill me. If I made another smart remark I wouldn't put it past him.

After dispatching the creatures he knelt beside them, laying a hand gently on them and spoke words quietly in a foreign language. It sounded like a prayer. I watched curiously. "What are you saying to them?"

His eyes shot up as if I were invading a private moment and he had forgotten I stood there. "Offering my thanks - and my sadness. The creatures of this forest were once far gentler. They have been driven mad."

"Because of the emperor?"

He nodded - solemness in his face. "Magic is not meant to be yielded by humans. It offsets the natural balance of the world. And as a result it warps and corrupts our land." His eyes met mine. "You humans called it the plague."

"You're saying the plague was caused by humans? Not Wisterians?"

"I assume they teach you something different in Sageburn."

We trudged along as I pondered his words. The sun towered above us, the humidity bearing down on us despite the cover of endless forest. Tiny drops of sweat fell down the side of my face.

If the plague happened eleven years ago—did that mean the emperor found a way to use Wisterian magic then? And it was the empire's fault it happened?

I pictured my sister. Once upon a time she was perfectly healthy—until the plague. Until the emperor's greed spread sickness not only to our land, but to the creatures of Wisteria as well. The very war he started and we fought...could it be caused by him?

Of course it could.

"Why is it that the day after you show up here the border is crawling with Empirian soldiers?" His green eyes found mine again.. What was it in me that brought out such contempt in him?

"I don't know."

"You don't know?" His eyes flared as he stepped into my path. My hands clenched at my sides and I braced myself. "You *better* start answering my questions."

I raised my chin and tossed my braid over my back, knowing I had no good answers for him. "Why? Perhaps if you stop talking to me like I'm shit on the bottom of your shoe I'd be more inclined to answer your questions. Eager even."

"You won't live much longer if you can't learn to trust me," he said it with such factualness I found myself taking a step back. He didn't understand the gravity of what he asked me. Trust him? The only man I ever trusted betrayed me, my own father. Other men sought to use me, exploit me and overwork me while beating me if I stepped out of line.

"And why should I trust you? I don't even know you." My eyes swept down his frame bitterly. "And you clearly harbor hatred toward me for simply existing."

"I have saved your life twice now. What does that tell you?"

34

I stared back at him, my hands relaxing a bit. I couldn't deny the truth of his words. Danger oozed from him and I didn't fully trust him. But his intentions were clearly not to kill me or let me die. As much as he might hate me, he had saved my life twice. Making it back to my sister in one piece likely required his help.

Someone's help.

Cyrus sat beside Locke, his green eyes anxiously darting between us. He let out a low whine. He did not like our heated exchange. Locke looked down at him and his eyes softened. He ruffled his head and sighed.

After a moment Locke held out his hand, a question. A truce. "Why don't we make a game of it? A challenge? How many times will I need to save you before you make it back to the human realm?"

I met his eyes. "Does your ego really need that much of a boost?"

A small smile cracked at the edge of his lips. He cleared his throat. "It doesn't hurt. Simply adds to my reputation."

"If your reputation is being an unbearable asshole."

He fought the curve of his lips into an amused smile and a dimple showed in his cheek.

"Why do you care about keeping me alive? I'm just a human."

"What can I say? You've piqued my interest." I rolled my eyes and he cleared his throat. "There's something...*curious* about you. It's not every day humans come waltzing into Wisteria asking about the Resistance."

I hesitated before putting my hand in his, his glove warm. He would keep me alive. He would get me back to my sister. Hope bloomed in my chest. He was my best bet to survive for now.

He held my hand for a beat longer than necessary, the forest becoming infinitely smaller as all my focus faded to the two of us, hand in hand. "I don't suppose you're going to explain the no touching rule?"

I took my hand from his and shook my head.

Tell him you're a Silencer and see if he still wants to keep you alive.

"But you can touch Cyrus." So he'd noticed. I nodded.

We continued walking, stopping at a small stream to gather water and clean the sweat off our faces. I hesitated, the memory of the nymphs fresh in my mind, but Locke's confidence bolstered my own.

"No nymphs here?" I asked.

35

"Not all nymphs are cursed. The more magic the empire steals from the land, the worse it gets. The curse spreads and seeps into the land." His eyes dimmed. "They can't help what they are."

"Is that why my sister is still sick?"

He seemed taken aback by my question. "Humans are affected as well?"

I nodded. "She's been sick since the plague happened."

I sat beside the stream and filled my canteen. I took greedy gulps of water, the coolness settling in my stomach. I could feel the heat of Locke's eyes on me again, stealing a glance when he thought I wouldn't notice. I paused and he cleared his throat turning away from me.

Gentle noises from the forest rang out around us, birds chirping curiously, the wind rustling the long willowy branches of the trees, and I felt a strange sensation of being watched by other things in the forest. I suspected not all of them were friendly–driven mad just as Locke said.

I looked up at him. He didn't sit. I watched as his eyes roamed the trees around us, his ears perking at every sound, his stance ready to leap into action if necessary. Perhaps he sensed what I did as well.

"Doesn't being so vigilant exhaust you?" I dared to ask.

His eyes lowered to mine, his mouth tense. "I thought you wanted me to keep you alive?"

I wrapped my arms around my legs, hugging them tightly. I watched as a few fish swam down the stream, flashes of orange and green. "Humans don't often survive here then?"

"They didn't," he said in a clipped tone. "Not until they started coming here with large numbers, weapons, and stolen magic. The whole balance of things is offset thanks to your empire."

They must hate us. I could feel the hate emanating from him in his words, but I didn't blame him if the emperor indeed stole magic from Wisterians and caused the plague. It only added to my list of growing reasons to hate the empire. And once again I wondered at what magic Locke might possess.

"What powers do you have?" I asked the question hesitantly. I'd always been curious to know and see the magic they possessed, but I also carried a healthy fear of it. What I was really asking was...how many different ways should I be aware that you can kill me?

"We may not make it back to the camp before nightfall, not with so many soldiers patrolling right now." I got to my feet and at first thought he was going to ignore my question, but he continued. "I'm an Elemental. Earth magic." He said it as if it were nothing special. And it was true that elemental magic was the most common Gift Wisterians were blessed with - but that didn't make it any less incredible to me.

He continued walking and I hastened to keep up with him. "I knew someone that was a fire Elemental in Sageburn, but he...died." *Why did I bring up Dean?* "So what can you do?" I kept my voice neutral, hoping he'd dismiss my admission.

The look he gave me was incredulous, as if he didn't believe me and knew I had ulterior motives for asking, but he simply said, "You shouldn't be so curious, human. The less you know the better. Wouldn't want to scare you."

"I could say the same for you," I shot back thinking of how he continued to question me. "And I don't scare easily." I rolled my eyes and kept walking but stopped at the piece of stone that rested in front of my foot. My eyes followed a trail of broken pieces, curiosity getting the best of me - despite his earlier remark.

"What are..." my voice trailed off as I bent down to better look at the two farthest pieces. I picked them up, each stone heavy in my hands and watched as I joined them together and they made out the face of a young girl - her eyes and mouth forever etched in horror. "Is this...?"

"Don't touch it," he said quietly. I could feel him behind me - standing as still as the very stone I held in my hands.

A brief image of a girl who looked similar to me flashed in my mind. She reached out a hand, and the instant she touched the person in front of her, they were consumed in stone–frozen forever in time.

The image faded, but my heart pounded in my chest. I set down the pieces gently and stood slowly, turning to face him, trying to hide how much the vision disturbed me.

His eyes hesitated to meet my own. I could see his hands clenched tightly at his sides. His chest rising and falling in measured breaths. His lips in a tight line.

"Silencer," he said at last. "An abomination to our kind if you ask me."

I'm not a Silencer. I'm not a Silencer.

I didn't realize until this moment there were varying ways a Silencer's touch could kill. Apparently one of those ways included turning someone to stone. Based on Locke's words–Silencers seemed as hated as humans were.

I can't catch a fucking break.

His eyes finally met mine and they flickered. I tried to identify what I saw in them. A momentary flash and then it was gone. "Come on - let's keep going. By the looks of the sun it's late afternoon."

***

We kept walking, but twice needed to change direction or wait out a cluster of soldiers appearing on the forest path. We stayed hidden in the cover of the trees, avoiding the direct path. I marveled at the soldiers riding through the forest on horseback, the familiar insignia of a firebird on their uniforms. Firebirds were not native to Sageburn. Another warped way for the emperor to lay claim to what did not belong to him.

We hid behind trees and bushes everytime we heard the thundering sounds of hooves or saw the flash of a red uniform on the path. Locke whispered under his breath and I watched in rapt fascination as vines whorled and danced together, providing a cocoon of greenery around us, keeping us well hidden.

"You can wield vines and shrubbery. I'm impressed." I whispered the words as we leaned against the greenery. We were awfully close in the small space. I could barely see him in the dark the cover provided, but I could hear him breathing, and smell his scent. Fitting he smelled like the earth.

"Why do I get the feeling you don't mean that sincerely?"

I didn't need to see him to picture the way his lips would curve in amusement.

"I suppose I was expecting something a little more...*extravagant* when you revealed your power to me. Although this is rather useful."

"Trust me my vines have *many* uses."

Grateful he couldn't see the way his words elicited a blush creeping up my neck and over my cheeks, I peered through the bush, itching to get out of the small space. "It looks clear."

The greenery retracted and we headed off again, but our detours cost us daylight. The sun faded on the horizon. I could sense Locke's unease as he walked faster and I tried to keep up with his long legs. As night began to fall the mist grew thicker, the whispers in the trees louder, and that same creeping feeling I experienced alone in the ghost like trees returned.

"We need to stop for the night," he decided, his lips pursed into a concerned line. "I can't risk making it back to the camp." His eyes scanned our surroundings with increased foreboding.

"I can feel it too," I said, surprising myself.

His green eyes met mine and he nodded, his throat bobbing. "These woods are no longer safe. The Empirian soldiers don't typically patrol so relentlessly. And you never know when the Red Reaper will show up." His eyes were up in the sky now, trained on the moon.

"The Red Reaper?" My eyes dimmed.

He opened his mouth to speak and hesitated. "There are few things I'm afraid of. She is one of them." I couldn't imagine Locke being afraid of anything. I could only imagine the monster this creature was. Worse than a Silencer?

"Where will we stay?" I asked quietly.

He motioned for me to keep up with him and we kept walking. "There is a town a few hours from camp. I often go there to get supplies, food, whatever we need..." his voice trailed off.

I thought of the woman at camp with him and my curiosity got the best of me. "Lex? Is she...your...?" I trailed off not knowing the best word and suddenly feeling self conscious for even wondering.

Locke threw his head back and laughed. It was the most beautiful sound I'd heard come out of him. Loud and generous. I averted my eyes - feeling suddenly shy and wondering what I said that was so funny.

"Lex is one of my most trusted friends," he explained. The smile no longer reached his eyes as he reigned himself back in. That careful semblance of self control. "Her and Xander live with me at the camp. I imagine you will like Xander." His voice grew soft and faded as he looked away. But then, as if sensing an in, his eyes fell to the ring on my hand and I dreaded his next question.

"And what of that?" He gestured to the ring. "Is there a special someone?"

I shook my head. "It's just a ring. It means nothing."

His eyes dimmed. He searched my face, that same perplexion in his expression. "It's a rather fancy ring to mean nothing."

I couldn't seem to pull my eyes away from him; they lingered too long on the strong cut of his jaw, creeping up to his curving lips, and then to the light freckles beneath his eyes, and I wondered what it would be like to lay my fingers on his sun touched skin and count them.

My eyes met his, dark green, fringed by dark lashes and he didn't look away. Something sparked between us, subtle, but undeniable.

You can't possibly be attracted to him. Or touch him. If you touch him you will kill him.

I shut my eyes and stepped away.

"Everyone has a past," he said. "Yours doesn't matter to me."

It sounded like something the men in Sageburn would say to get into your pants, but I didn't tell him that.

He turned again and indicated for us to keep moving. I couldn't decide what his words meant. His tone was simple; factual. But there was something within me that craved deeper meaning. To matter.

"Welcome to Loom."

And sure enough in the distance I could make out a sea of red and green brick buildings with thatched roofs and stalls in the middle of the courtyard, the makings of a small town. Small wall sconces lit up the night, but there were few people out in the street, no bustle of activity.

"Pull your cloak over your head," he told me. "It's better if no one gets too close of a look at you." I wondered at his words, but I listened, carefully concealing my head the best I could. Perhaps they didn't take kindly to humans in this town.

We entered the town and I admired the signs proudly on display above the shops. They were written in cursive, flowery script, green flowers and trees etched into the wood of the signs.

We passed an apothecary, strange colorful herbs and plants on display in the window shelves. And then a weapons shop, a great big axe hanging proudly on the door. When I saw the books so casually displayed in the window of the next shop–I paused–my fingers skimming the window of the shop as if I could feel the worn leather spines of books.

My mind flashed to the books ripped to shreds in the shabby room back at the conscription lodge. I'd memorized some of the text; poems that I recited in the dead of the night when I couldn't sleep.

One of my favorite lines I recited often in my head was: *Let them try to cage you; for they may cage a bird, but they cannot force it to sing.*

Behind the main heart of the town were rows of houses, accessible by small alleyways weaving in and out. I saw a light flicker out in one of them and a curtain close.

I imagined during the day the stalls brimming with activity as everyone sold fresh bread, clay bowls, soft silks, and hard to find herbs. I could picture children laughing and running through the streets. But for now, the only sounds were coming from the tavern.

A man stood outside the tavern door banging on it loudly. The door opened for a brief moment and there was a flood of light from inside, but then the door was promptly shut in the man's face. He wandered off in defeat.

"Why didn't they let him in?"

Locke drew closer to my side. "It's the hour. He could be a Cursed, or a soldier, or if we're really unlucky a Silencer, but more often than not, they stop letting anyone inside after sun down. Unless you're a citizen."

"Then how are we-?"

He cut me off with a knock on the door. I could hear voices inside, music, laughter. A stark change to the quiet ominous energy outside. And a moment later, the door opened.

An old woman met Locke's eye with recognition. She was short and wore a long dress, the hem dragging on the ground. Her white hair was pulled into a bun at the back of her head and she possessed sharp blue eyes, withered with time, but wise all the same.

"Lockwood," she said in surprise. "What brings you here at this hour?" And then her eyes turned to me. "Who's this?"

"We need to stay for the night." I noticed he didn't answer her question. "Too many soldiers are patrolling right now."

She nodded. "I can only spare a room. But you are welcome to it." Her eyes fell on Cyrus at Locke's feet. "I suppose you'll be staying too then. As long as you behave yourself."

"He always does." Locke winked at her as she let us in. Her eyes carefully scanned the outside perimeter as she shut the door and fastened lock after lock on the door.

"Thank you Beatrice," Locke said with a relieved sigh.

I was distracted by the warmth and commotion happening inside the tavern. A bar stretched across the back of the room and the floor was littered with round brown tables and stools, most of them taken up by patrons drinking mugs of ale and glasses of wine.

41

A small band played in the left corner of the room by the soaring fire and some of the patrons danced in tune to the beat. I'd never seen or experienced anything like it and it made me wonder if Sageburn used to be filled with music like this; before the plague and before the war.

Locke's eyes were on mine, curiosity in them. "Do you like the music?"

I nodded, unable to turn my eyes away.

"Sit and listen for a moment," he told me, pulling me to the corner of the room where we could watch without drawing too much attention to ourselves. We sat at a small round table. Despite his attempt a few patrons came over and looked at Locke with recognition, bowing their heads in respect before leaving. *That was curious.*

I found myself lost in the speed at which the violinist drew the bow across the strings back and forth, or the way the drummer kept a steady beat, and let the frenzied notes of the flute fill me as someone placed a large mug of ale in front of me. I took it and sipped it curiously, trying not to make a face as I did so. I rarely drank alcohol. I liked to keep my wits about me and it was hard to procure in Sageburn. Another method of control.

Locke's eyes watched me as I sipped my ale and listened to the music, studying me, trying to put the puzzle pieces together that would complete me. But what he didn't realize was the puzzle would always be incomplete. I didn't even know how to put them together.

I thought of my sister then. Danielle with her big brown eyes and big heart. I pictured her strumming the strings of her guitar, her voice ringing out as she sang. And then the memory faded as I saw the guitar splintered and broken on the floor.

To hear music played so freely now was surreal; visceral. I wondered if someone would emerge from the shadows and punish me for such an infraction. My eyes watered in response. I placed my hands under my legs to stop them shaking.

"What is it?" Locke stretched out his legs in front of him, his arms crossed against his chest. Did he have to watch me so intently? I couldn't even hide the damn tears threatening to spill from my eyes.

I cleared my throat. "The music. I..." how did one put into words how truly evil the empire was? "Music is outlawed in Sageburn. I'm not used to hearing it so openly."

He swallowed and didn't respond, but his eyes dimmed in quiet understanding and contemplation.

As the night continued on, more and more of the townsfolk showed recognition and respect to Locke, some of them looking at him with tears in their eyes, others coming forward and bowing before carrying on their way.

I finished my ale, my eyes feeling heavy, when Locke indicated for me to get up and follow him. We headed up the stairs of the tavern, the music becoming more faint and part of me wondered if I'd imagined the whole thing. I didn't want to forget it. I didn't want to go back to not knowing what live music sounded like, or miss the bitter taste of ale on my lips.

We entered our room and Locke secured the bolt to our room. He waited a moment before looking at me over his shoulder and I realized I was staring at him, the curve of his back, down to his strong legs. His dark green eyes met mine and I felt my breath hitch and I stepped back.

It was instinctive, but I didn't want him to get the wrong idea. I shouldn't be looking at him. I didn't even trust him. And being alone in this room with him made me feel even more like prey.

Locke regarded me carefully, his movements measured. "You can sleep on the bed," he said quietly, his expression giving nothing away. "I will sleep there," he indicated a chair sitting by the window. And then his eyes met mine again, a quiet understanding in them. "I meant it when I said I wouldn't harm you."

I wanted to believe him. And I didn't want him to think me weak or scared, especially not of him.

We took turns cleaning up in the washroom. I scrubbed my face, still awed by the mature years in my face. I hesitantly touched my fingers to my face, tracing them lightly over the freckles sprinkled down my nose, curving down to the cupid's bow of my lips. I stared into my caramel eyes in the mirror, admiring the way my lashes fanned against my cheeks and my dark brows arched over them like the wings of a bird.

I'd never had much time to spend looking in a mirror or considering my appearance. But looking at myself now–I decided I was not a lost cause. Pretty even. At least to the human eye.

Locke probably thinks you're hideous.

I frowned at my reflection before leaving the washroom. I didn't need to spend any time thinking about him. Unless he would help me save my sister or lead me in the direction of someone who would—my time spent with him would be wasted.

When I exited and sat on the bed, I glanced around warily, wondering where he'd gone too. Only Cyrus occupied the room with me, sprawled in a heap on the bed.

"Oh you're going to sleep here are you?" I reached out a hand and scratched his ear gently before turning my attention to yanking the boots off my feet.

I removed my socks, wincing at the pain—and at the same time Locke came back into the room, closing the door carefully behind him. He held a small bowl in his gloved hands.

"I hope that's food," I said, wincing again at the state of my bleeding, cracked feet.

He paused in front of me, holding the bowl in front of my face. It looked like a sludge of green paste and smelled vaguely of aloe. "For your feet."

I met his eyes, taking in the stoic expression on his face.

"I would help, but I know you don't want me to touch you."

I swallowed the lump in my throat and took the bowl from him, mildly touched by the gesture—that he'd cared enough and paid enough attention to know. "Thank you," is all I could muster as I took the bowl from him.

6

My dreams were unsettling. Flashes of panic. Fighting. Running. I was back in the lodge feeling Hawthorne's fist connect with my face, his sneering words as he referred to my sister as a whore, and then my fingers were at his temples, watching in slow motion as the blood poured.

Running through the woods.

Being chased by wolf-like creatures until I fell down, their fangs dripping intensely close to my throat as I tried to reach for the dagger in my boot and failed.

And then I fell down into a deep pool of water, the bony hands of the water nymphs dragging me down.

And all I could think of was Danielle. How she would never know what happened to me. She would be all alone if I didn't make it back to her.

Then there were the piercing blue eyes of Emperor Arias. So cold. His red suit dark as blood. His echoing steps on the concrete floor as he made his way to me. And his hands held a gold circlet he lifted up, up and placed gently on my head.

I sank into darkness.

I woke up gasping for air, forgetting where I was. The moonlight filtered in gently through the window now and I clutched the white sheets tightly to my chest as my breathing slowed.

Locke sat on the chair across the room from me. His head slumped into one of his hands as he leaned back into the chair, but his eyes were open now, alert. He stared at me like seeing a ghost.

"Are you alright Cate?" He asked in the darkness.

I nodded numbly, but then wondering if he could even see it I replied back quietly, "Yes."

We didn't speak again and I laid back on the bed, closing my eyes and focusing on my breathing. In and out. In and out. I heard Locke settle in the chair, but from the sound of his breathing he remained awake.

Cyrus laid on the bed curled at my feet. Feet that already felt immensely better after I applied the soothing salve Locke brought me.

Why did he do that for me?

It made me uncomfortable. The last thing I needed was to feel indebted to him, to somehow owe him because he helped me. After growing up in the empire with an every man for himself mentality–his kindness unnerved me.

I finally dozed off for a few more hours before the sound of Locke shuffling around the room awakened me. I rubbed the sleep from my eyes, rays of sun peering into the room as I sat up. I scratched Cyrus's head as he let out a wide yawn and then leapt off the bed.

"Get changed and come downstairs," Locke said. His eyes fell to the pair of clothes on the end of the bed. They looked worn, but they would do. I wondered if the tavern keeper brought them for me. "Don't forget your cloak."

I took my time changing. The clothes were surprisingly easy to move in, comfortable. I washed the sleep out of my eyes in a small basin and brushed my long blonde hair out, before my fingers skillfully weaved together a braid.

I put on my cloak, careful again to conceal my head and face the best I could. I wondered what was so dangerous about me being seen. Why did he want to hide me?

Because you're human and you don't belong here.

When I went downstairs the tavern was much quieter than the night before. A few patrons were already drinking of course, but most of them were enjoying breakfast. It looked like porridge. My stomach rumbled.

"Seems to be more patrols happening than normal," I heard two of the patrons whispering to each other quietly at a table. "The soldiers were in the woods again last night. I could see the light from their torches."

"They're looking for something. Or someone." The other patron chimed in and I felt a strange sensation at the back of my neck, their words chilling me. "Wonder if it's related to the commotion that happened in Sageburn this week?"

I felt Locke's eyes on me and spotted him sitting at a table in the far corner of the room, Cyrus laying at his feet. Two bowls of porridge were already on the table waiting.

I tried not to look too eager as I sat down and began to eat. He watched me curiously, his eyes trailing my body in that clinical way he did.

"How are you feeling?"

I paused mid bite, the spoon stopping before my mouth. "What?"

His eyes sparkled in amusement. "Your feet?"

I set my spoon down, feeling my cheeks heat. Why did his question unsettle me so? I supposed I wasn't used to others asking about me; nevertheless how I was *feeling. Or doing nice things for me.*

"Better," I said. "Thank you. Again."

His hand rested on the table and my eyes were drawn to his fingers laying elegantly sprawled against the table. "You don't have to thank me."

"I do." My eyes flashed to his, green and unyielding. "I'm not sure what you want in return but-"

"Cate," he stopped me, his eyes dimming. "It was nothing. I expect nothing from you. Except maybe a little less attitude." I didn't miss the crooked smirk that played on his lips.

I begrudgingly took another bite and felt a sense of relief when his eyes left me and he focused more on his own porridge. "So what now? Will you take me back to the pass?"

"I will. Once the commotion on the border dies down and the patrols lighten. It seems the empire is looking for something. Until then–I'd like you to come back to my camp with me."

Why?

But I didn't ask him why. Not yet. Instead, I swirled a clump of porridge in my bowl with a spoon. "How long before the patrols lighten?"

"Hard to say. It could be a few days. It could be a few weeks."

Weeks? I didn't have weeks.

I thought of my earlier plan to sell my sapphire ring and find someone to help me get back to the border and free my sister safely from the conscription lodge. My plan didn't seem as feasible with so many soldiers patrolling the woods and border. Perhaps I did need to wait.

"Fine," I said. "I will go with you. But not for weeks."

He nodded. "Let's go then."

Before we left Beatrice joined him and took his hands in her own. I stepped outside, not wanting to intrude. I couldn't hear what she said to him, but their faces were serious. She patted his hand once and smiled at him before he joined me outside.

The market stalls were filled to the brim today with townspeople buying and selling. It was just as I imagined it would be. Stalls were filled with smoked meat, warm doughy bread, herbs and spices, and even fruit tarts. Other stalls were filled with embroidery, handcrafted jewelry, and wooden carvings.

The little wooden animals transfixed me. My fingers skimmed over a fox, then one of the magnificent flying creatures I saw Locke strike down, then a unicorn, and lastly a small bird. A dove.

Cora. *My name.* It meant dove.

I closed my eyes and saw myself as a child, holding the warm hand of an adult as we perused market stalls, my small eyes taking in everything with wonder. Small hands wanting to touch and feel and experience. The world still a safe place worth exploring, people still worth trusting.

"Don't dally love. I've got other customers waiting," the voice of the stall owner rang out as I realized I'd been staring a little too intently at the wooden figures.

Locke stood beside me watching as my fingers retracted from the small bird. "Do you like it?" he asked, his eyes fixed on mine curiously. Why did he care what I liked?

I paused, my voice caught in my throat. I shook my head and stepped away from the stall. "We should get going. Lex is waiting for you. She probably wonders where you've gone."

"She knows exactly where I've gone," he said quietly. I felt the familiar whisper of the woods on my skin and I shuddered.

His eyes followed me curiously as we headed through the bustle of the courtyard, past all the sights and smells of the stalls, past the laughing children, some who stopped to give Locke a hug before running off. The children liked him and did not fear him. I was trying to wrap my mind around the reverence this village held for him.

We made our way out of the village, the sound of the market and the people slowly dying out the farther we traveled. Not far from the village the trail wrapped around in a circle and within it stood a beautiful fountain. Or at least it once was beautiful.

It was made of green polished stones, the water it housed now a dirty mossy green. In the middle stood a large stone statue, its likeness now covered with moss and vines. Curiosity got the better of me and I took a step forward, wondering what was beneath the vines.

Locke hesitated.

"What is it?"

There was trepidation in his gaze. "Let's keep going."

I nodded and followed him away from the fountain and down a more treacherous looking path away from the main path of the road.

I recognized the look in his eyes. He was hiding something from me. I understood what it meant to have secrets, to have a past, and the fear of being found out, but I needed to find out more about him if only to better protect myself.

Survival, I reminded myself. *It's about survival.*

"The people in Loom seem to know you," I said as we walked on. I dangled the words like bait, hoping he would bite.

The path winded like the shape of a snake, sloping downward. I could hear the sounds of birds in the trees and I let myself relax a little. Or perhaps my relaxation was due to the fact that Locke's eyes were always trained on the woods and his fingers rested close to his dagger.

Cyrus walked ahead of us, occasionally darting off the path to chase a squirrel or rabbit that caught his attention before he'd come back to the path again, his tail swishing contentedly behind him.

"Everyone knows everyone around here," Locke shrugged. "Loom is the only town around these parts. It's small."

I sensed bullshit.

"Why do you stay at the camp and not in Loom?"

"I value my privacy," he said, his eyes narrowing. "No one comes to the camp."

"But you brought me there." I tried again. "How long have you lived there?"

His eyes flashed, the familiar guise of annoyance back. "I see what you're doing."

"Can't I be curious about you?" I gave him the most innocent look possible.

He rolled his eyes. "You expect me to answer your questions, but you refuse to answer mine?"

"How do you expect *me* to trust *you* if you tell me nothing about you?" He stopped in front of me and I nearly stumbled into him, digging my feet into the dirt to stop.

He turned, his eyes narrowing as they met mine. Dark and deep. "Tell me something about you. What were you running from? I get it, the empire is terrible. But why now? Why did it take you so long to leave?"

Why *did* it take me so long to leave? I supposed I would have stayed and put in my time, but then what? Danielle and I would have left without a bounty on our heads, without giving the empire reason to pay attention to us—and we would have made a home of our own somewhere far away. I wanted to do things the *right* way. The *acceptable* way. If it meant she would be safe. But none of it was right to begin with. And now neither of us were safe.

I shook my head. It felt impossible to make Locke understand why I waited so long. And I couldn't tell him about Hawthorne. How I killed him with my touch. He'd already made it clear how he felt about Silencers. "I thought you said you didn't care about my past."

He came closer, his fingers reaching up, barely to my arm, as if he wanted to touch me, and I held very still. He was so close, our chests barely inches apart. I could feel my heart shuttering in my chest, not as stone as I thought.

"You can't touch me," I reminded him. "You're not wearing gloves."

His eyes held mine, but then his fingers hesitated and he pulled them away reaching into his pockets to retrieve his gloves and put them on.

I was grateful for small mercies. In that moment I didn't think I had the strength to resist letting him touch me. My body craved it if only to prove to myself that I imagined the entire thing. That there was nothing wrong with me. Now my hands felt foreign to me. Deadly.

What if you really are a Silencer? What if you're not human?

"What happens when people touch you?"

"They get hurt."

He contemplated my words. I could see the wheels working in his mind. And then he pulled out the cloth again. "I'm going to need to blindfold you again before we make it back to camp."

***

We made it back to the camp a few hours later, the rest of our walk in silence. And mine in darkness. There were a few times I nearly stumbled down the winding path, but Locke grabbed my arm with his gloved hand, guiding me gently the rest of the way.

I didn't want to admit I liked his hand on me, even if I couldn't feel his skin. It comforted me somehow, became familiar to have him there.

You can't afford to get attached to anyone.

I understood the point Locke wanted to make, he wanted me to trust him and open up, especially if I were going to question him. And that was fair. But it also made me wonder what he wanted to be so secretive about. Not just with the camp, but in Loom, with not wanting to draw attention to me.

The camp looked as I remembered it, but more vibrant in the daytime; a different aura than at night. A quaint brick cottage surrounded by the glimmering lake and lush trees, all different shades of red, yellow, and green. The sparring ring and the small campfire in front of the house where I could imagine sitting by the warmth of the flames at night with a rich cup of tea. An idyllic place in the woods where Locke could have all the privacy he wanted. The kind of place I yearned for Danielle and I to find.

Danielle...

I thought of her and my heart constricted in my chest. How many days had it been since I ran away from Sageburn?

From the distance I could see Lex and another man sitting on the logs by the campfire, the smoke rising lazily into the sky. Cyrus ran to them, reaching them in three short bounds. They greeted him and then stood up the instant they spotted us, concern and then relief spread on Lex's beautiful face. The man next to her smiled like a coy fox.

"Took you long enough," the coy looking man declared. "You had this one going crazy. She was about to light the forest on fire looking for you." He gave Lex a teasing smile.

"She seems to be in one piece," Lex smiled at Locke as her gaze fell on me. "But she didn't make it back to Sageburn?" Her tone was imbued with another undertone. Disappointment.

"Empirian soldiers swarming it," Locke said. He gave her a lingering look—the kind someone makes when they want to share something they can't say out loud. More secrets. "We'll try again."

"This is Cate," Lex said, introducing me to the man beside her and I felt a twinge of guilt at the fake name again. "And Cate - this is Xander." Xander was much taller and more lithe than Locke, easily over six feet; his skin muscular and dark brown. He had a dark head of hair and matching eyes, but there was a soft twinkle in them that matched his coy smile.

"Nice to meet you kid."

I supposed 'kid' was better than 'human', but I wrinkled my nose at the nickname. I was far from a child and not tiny by any means, but standing next to Locke and Xander my five foot six frame made me appear smaller.

"How long are you sticking around for?" Xander asked, crossing his arms, his smile fading into a more serious expression. I didn't miss how his question seemed more directed at Locke than me.

"I need to make it back to Sageburn..." I trailed off. "As soon as possible."

"I'm glad you're here kid," Xander said with a wide grin. "The rest of these pricks have a stick up their asses about humans, but I don't," he proudly declared.

I thought I might like Xander.

"And why is that?" I asked.

"Cause I'm half. A halfling."

My eyes widened.

"And obviously he's very proud of it," Lex chimed in with a roll of her eyes, but I could sense the bond between them; all in good fun.

"Why wouldn't I be? My parents taught me everything I know. My family is proof that this war can end and we can find peace."

Locke rolled his eyes now too. "As you can see Xander is an idealist."

"Don't we all start off that way?" I asked. I didn't mean for it to sound so pitiful, so full of resentment, but being idealistic never served anyone in the empire. There was nothing one person could do to change things, and most were too afraid to speak out or take action.

I thought again of the woman in the courtyard–her tongue removed for reciting poetry; the man hanged for handing out blankets and bread to children. The message from the empire was clear; those who defy us will pay the price.

What price are you willing to pay?

The implication of my words fell around us amongst the crackling sound of the fire we stood around.

If my words bothered Xander he didn't show it. "The world is a cruel place, kid. But that doesn't mean you have to let it make you cruel. Whatever happened in your past...you get to take and create something better for the future."

I fought the urge to tell him to take his ideals and shove them up his ass–only because I sensed he meant it genuinely. He genuinely believed what he said. But how could I imagine a better future when I didn't even know if my sister would be in it?

"Shall we sit for the sermon?" Lex rolled her eyes again. Xander retaliated by grabbing her by the waist and throwing her over his shoulder as he ran off with her.

A moment later she vanished from his arms into thin air as if she'd never been there at all. Xander looked around with a grin. I did too.

She's a Shadow.

She reappeared a moment later, jumping onto his back and knocking him to the ground before vanishing again. The two howled with laughter.

I watched them with a kind of wonder, feeling slightly jealous at the ease at which they could tease and touch, feeling captivated by Lex's power–until I realized Locke was staring at me intently.

"Don't mind those two," he said with a small smile. "They're always messing with each other. But when it comes down to it...they're the most loyal friends I could ask for."

Friends? I tried the word on. Did I have any friends? Besides my sister?

A friend sounded like a liability. A luxury.

I didn't even consider Dean a friend. Only a distraction.

"You must be tired? Do you want to go inside and rest?" He arched his eyebrows in question, waiting for my answer.

I shook my head. "I think I'd like to sit out here a little longer." To assess the situation and these two new possible threats? Friends? I didn't know what to call them yet.

He nodded. "I'm going to gather wood for the fire. I will be back soon."

I watched him walk into the confines of the woods and my eyes turned back to Lex and Xander who were walking back now. Lex went into the sparring ring and I watched as she wrapped her hands and then began punching a wooden dummy in the ring. I marveled at the way she moved with cat-like grace, her punches landing fluidly with a crack each time. She didn't even flinch. She turned her body gracefully and launched a high kick into the dummy's head and the wood cracked again.

Xander sat on the log beside me. "She's something else right?" Even sitting he towered over me. He folded his hands together and gave me a beaming smile full of perfectly straight white teeth.

I decided to take the friendly approach. "You two are close?"

"We grew up together practically. Lex is the daughter of...someone very important." I didn't miss how he carefully chose his words, omitting information. "And my parents are the leaders of Frostblight."

My eyes widened, intrigued. "Frostblight?"

"It's a land to the northeast. And as the name implies it's very very cold. Snows all year round. But it's so beautiful. Damn gorgeous. It's where I grew up. The castle is made of ice. And...we have dragons." I realized I didn't want him to stop talking–his enthusiasm and love for his home contagious. He seemed much less guarded than Locke and he didn't seem keen to interrogate me like Locke, which made me soften a bit towards him. Or perhaps the fact he was also human like me, although half, made me feel like we were kindred spirits. "And so when our parents would gather for important meetings Lex and I would always play together. And get into trouble too."

"It sounds amazing."

"It is. You should see it someday. If you stick around - you might."

"I have to go back to Sageburn for my sister," I said softly. "I can't leave her behind." I once again felt guilt for leaving her behind in the first place.

Understanding lit his eyes. "Family first. Always. You and I share that value. You know...if your sister and you ever come back to Wisteria together - you would be more than welcome at Frostblight. It's more safe from the empire than any other part of Wisteria. The blizzards keep the soldiers away."

"Thank you." I was genuinely taken aback by his kindness. My throat grew dry and I cleared it before I spoke again. "Are Lex and Locke like family to you? Did Locke also grow up with you?" If Locke weren't willing to share about himself, perhaps Xander would be more willing.

He shook his head. "Locke's a wild card. Village kid. We met a few years ago. But I love him like a brother."

My eyes were drawn back to Lex sparring in the ring again. She kept throwing punch after punch. She stopped after a moment and turned, eyeing us curiously as she stretched out her arms across her chest, one after the other. She was barely winded.

"Don't mind her," Xander said following the trail of my eyes. "She comes across cold and unfeeling. And she is," he laughed, "But she can't help who her father is." Before I could say anything he clapped his hands together and changed the subject. "You want to throw some punches?"

"I don't know how. I wouldn't know where to start."

He grinned in response. "Then you'll have to learn."

I considered his words. Perhaps I should.

"It would be a pain in the ass to teach me. I'm stubborn."

He grinned again and I couldn't resist smiling back. "Lucky for you, stubborn students are my specialty."

"If you say so." I thought of Lex and Locke's powers as I regarded the man in front of me who strangely felt like he could become a friend. "Do you have a Gift?"

He seemed more willing to share than Locke was. "I do. It's boring, but it serves its purpose."

"What is that?"

"I can find things. People. Objects."

My ears perked up. "You're a Seer then. Do you also have visions?"

"I try not to - cause trust me - it's all fun and games until you see shit people don't like." He blew out a breath. But the wheels in my mind were already turning...if he was a Seer, perhaps he could find my sister. He could tell me if she was still in the lodge. "What about you? You're really just a boring ass human?"

"Yep. Sorry to disappoint."

Silencer, the voice at the back of my head taunted me. *Your touch is deadly.*

"Huh," he regarded me curiously. "I was kind of hoping for another halfer like me. Not many of us, you know." His eyes swept to the ground with disappointment.

"They don't treat you the same?"

"Wisterians are very purist. I have my place. And despite the fact my parents are in a position of power, there are those that disrespect them simply because of the fact my father is human."

I frowned. "I'm sorry. I don't think it should be that way. Everyone deserves to be treated equally."

He smiled and his eyes lit up. "I knew I liked you."

7

"I will always find you," *the boy whispers.*

The footsteps approach faster now. I turn and a man stands in front of me wearing a red suit, his blonde hair is swept back meticulously, his blue eyes narrow in my direction. And then they narrow in the direction of the boy and I see the resemblance between the two of them.

"Cora," *he says much the way one would speak to a dog.* "What are you doing out here?"

I shrug my shoulders. "I don't know."

"Where is your crown?"

I shrug again.

His eyes turn to the boy. "Did you do this?"

The boy shakes his head. "She did."

"That's not possible."

The man holds out the gold circlet in his hands. His questions are clearly a test. He doesn't trust me. He doesn't like my non answers. He wants to put me back where I belong.

"I told you to never take this off. Never let anyone take it off you. It's the only way I can keep you safe."

Safe, the word echoes in my mind.

My eyes meet the boys again as the man places the crown on my head. I feel his words again echoing in my mind.

I will always find you.

I will always find you.
And then everything fades to black.

***

In the morning I stepped out of my room and into the heart of the cottage. A small kitchen with a large wooden table sat on one end. A large vase of wildflowers adorned the table along with a strange set of wooden carvings. They were animals I realized as I picked one up and turned it in my hands. A fox. And it looked identical to the wooden carvings I saw in the stall at Loom.

On the other end of the quaint room a brick fireplace cascaded up the wall, a fire burning warmly within it. And in front of the fireplace and on either side were settees. Atop of the settees were cushions made of wool. More of the curious wooden carvings lined the mantle of the fireplace - I spotted a wolf, a bear, and a deer, along with various books on herbology, history, and poetry.

You can read a book here and no one will stop you.

The realization floored me and my fingers curiously touched the worn spines of the books, and then they retracted with guilt. I didn't have time for reading. I needed to go back for my sister.

I pulled back the light blue curtains on the windows at the front of the cabin, letting more sunlight filter in.

Outside I could see Lex and Xander sparring within the ring. And to the right of them Locke sitting on one of the large logs by the campfire.

When I stepped outside the quiet and calm soothed me. The sun peeked out from the horizon and the leftover night air danced on my skin. The birds chirped harmoniously in the trees. The fire crackled in the distance, the flames licking toward the sky.

This place is beautiful.

Locke stood beside the fire, roasting meat on a spit. He wore a pair of black trousers and a green shirt. He rolled up his sleeves and I watched as he rotated the meat, unable to pull my eyes away.

I felt my eyes drifting up toward the planes of his chest, over his collarbone, and then up to the curve of his jaw. My eyes settled on his lips for a moment, and then I felt flustered when I met his eyes and they were on mine.

I broke my gaze as I sauntered over to him. "Good morning," I said quietly. And then a little more boldly, "When are we going back to the mountains?"

He rotated the meat again letting me soak in the silence. "Can't wait to leave huh? First, you're going to learn to defend yourself. Starting now." He gestured over to the sparring ring. "Lex and Xander will teach you."

"Defend myself?" I let the words hang as if he'd told me to jump in the water with the nymphs. "Did Xander put you up to this?"

I ignored the rumbling in my stomach at the sight and smell of the meat - but Locke did not miss it. "Sit," he told me, indicating the log next to him. I sat obediently and a moment later he handed me a plate. I looked at the meat curiously–as good as it smelled.

"I've kept you alive and well so far yet you don't trust my cooking?" His lips were in a tight line, but his eyes were warmer today, a playfulness to them. "It's a rabbit. And perfectly safe I promise."

"Did you pray over this one too?" I asked as I plucked a piece of the meat and popped it into my mouth. I didn't mean for it to sound condescending but Locke did not seem to take offense.

"I pray over every animal," he said matter of fact.

I let the silence fall over us again as I plucked at the meat and he did the same. It was good. It felt warm in my belly and I realized how hungry I'd been the last few days. I felt his eyes on me as I ate–that same "trying to figure me out" stare.

"I don't know how to use any weapons," I said. The fact was I didn't know how to use a weapon - but that didn't mean I'd never killed anyone. The memory of Hawthorne filled my vision and I clenched the plate in my hands tighter. I was a *murderer*. Maybe even a Silencer.

"You'll learn," Locke said from beside me. "You need to if you have any hope of surviving here and making it back to your...realm. It takes nearly a day to get back to the pass. Plenty of time for something to kill you."

I set the plate down on the log beside me, noticing the shake in my hands. He saw it too and his brows furrowed together. *There he goes again trying to figure me out*, I thought.

"What if I don't want to learn how to fight?" I countered even though I knew it was a lie. I did want to learn. I did need to learn. But becoming more indebted to these people felt like a mistake. It felt like I was giving my power away. And how long would it take for me to learn? I couldn't afford to waste time.

"Do you really want to rely on me to keep you alive?" He raised his eyebrows. "I will do my best - but you must know that I can't always protect you. And consider this a parting gift - one you can take back with you to the human realm." He folded his hands in front of the fire and paused, more serious than mocking. "If you're going to help your sister...you need to be able to fight." He didn't meet my eyes.

I swallowed a lump in my throat.

He knew I was running. And he knew I needed a way to defend myself.

My two choices were to accept this gift and hope I didn't look like a fool in the sparring ring...or reject it and remain defenseless.

I glanced down at the sapphire ring on my finger. I could still sell it. I could still find someone to help me. But if I knew how to fight - my chances of saving her would be even better.

"Thank you," I surprised myself when the words fell out of my mouth. His green eyes were unreadable, despite the small sign of kindness, and he nodded towards the ring indicating for me to join Lex and Xander.

But not before handing me a pair of black gloves. "For the touching."

I took the gloves gratefully, feeling my chest tighten at the gesture.

The morning was spent making me stretch and then run the expanse of the encampment in circles until my legs felt like jelly. As I ran, Xander and Lex sparred in the ring seemingly oblivious to my exhaustion, but at one point Xander did shoot me a grin as if to say, "I told you".

Locke sat by the campfire still, one hand holding a small knife and his other a wooden trinket. He carved at the wood in small intentional strokes and I wondered if the carvings at the stall in Loom were his. But I felt his eyes on me watching as I ran myself ragged.

When I felt like I couldn't take anymore and I stopped to lean forward resting my hands on my thighs panting he said, "That's enough running for today. Get some water and cool off and then go into the ring to spar with Lex."

I shot him a glare before heading toward the glistening water. "Nothing is going to jump out and try to eat me?"

"You're safe," was all he said, still carving away.

Safe.

The word came back to haunt me.

"I told you to never take this off. Never let anyone take it off you. It's the only way I can keep you safe."

The strange dreams and visions lingered in the back of my mind, along with the vision of the girl I'd seen turning someone to stone. What did they mean?

I scooped water into my canteen and drank greedily, before dumping the rest of the water over the top of my sweaty head. I turned and headed back to the ring to spar with Lex.

And still – I could feel his eyes on me.

When I went into the ring Lex instructed me to begin with stretching. She showed me how to go through the motions. She then taught me how to properly punch, making sure my thumb was not tucked into my hand, how to hold my stance, and where my legs should be placed. And then she made me practice the motion alone against the wooden dummy without actually hitting it.

"What's the deal with the gloves?" She asked me at long last.

I didn't know what Locke had told her. "I don't like touching people."

I left it at that and although I saw the wheels turning in her eyes she gave me a nod and left it alone.

***

The next few nights my dreams were restless. The same scenes replayed in my mind of fighting, running, feeling panicked and out of control–my sister always out of my grasp. In between the panic I caught glimpses of my family farm, the memories too painful to remember; remnants of a good life.

And then there was the day in the middle of dinner when a knock sounded at the door and my father somberly stood from his chair and told me I needed to leave with the gentlemen outside and that there were no other options available to me. No one was coming to save me. And I went and walked into a nightmare.

I thought of these memories and dreams every day that I trained. The thought of becoming strong, becoming someone that no one could control – fueled me. The thought of being able to protect my sister. Of freedom. And yet I felt like a mouse running on a wheel - running, but getting nowhere.

And each day that slipped by filled my heart with guilt. Each day I spent away from my sister felt like a day too long.

In the mornings when I woke Locke was always the first one awake. Often I would see him coming back from the forest with wood for the fire, or sitting beside the lake deep in thought, a knife carving skillfully at the wooden figure in his hand.

I would watch him for a few moments before Lex and Xander would come out of their rooms; Xander always laughing and ready to take on the day, Lex more stoic and sound, her cat-like eyes always searing into me as if she could see my secrets.

Some days Locke would leave early in the morning and wouldn't return for hours and I wondered where he went, what he was doing. The only town I knew of nearby was Loom.

Every morning I ran. Miles and miles. I ran until my lungs burned. Until the sweat stung my eyes. And over time it became easier. My legs felt less jelly–like and my breathing became more steady–accustomed to running.

In the afternoon Lex and Xander sparred with me in the ring. I was finally able to throw a punch and now we were moving on to working with long swords and daggers. Swords were incredibly heavy and hard for me to wield.

The daggers were my favorite. The only disadvantage with daggers was needing to get much closer to my target, but I found my body limber enough to do so with a cat-like ease. It didn't feel like my first time wielding a weapon; my body knew what to do as if in another life I'd trained with weapons.

"Not bad," Xander said, crossing his arms across his chest proudly. He watched as I leapt and somersaulted toward Lex, my dagger aiming for her thigh. She blocked my blow effortlessly, as she always did. She'd clearly been training her entire life.

I bent over, my hands resting on my thighs in between breaths–when Locke came out of the woods. He carried a rabbit, surely our dinner. Cyrus trailed behind him like always, a rabbit dangling from his mouth as well.

Everyday I asked him the same question. When would he take me back? And every day he told me I needed more time. This morning: *you need more time*. But every day I felt a tightening tension around the fact that I needed to free my sister.

Why are you keeping me here? What do you want?

I wiped the sweat off my brow and glowered at him, despite the gift he'd given me. I found it hard to be grateful when I felt my chest tighten and my legs went numb like jelly. When my hands were bloodied and bruised. When every night I fell into bed exhausted beyond measure, hardly able to formulate a thought in my head about what my next steps were.

I spent day after day training, and before I knew it almost two weeks passed. I spent my evenings making small talk with Xander, trying to earn his trust so that I might ask him to use his power to help me find my sister.

A swipe to my legs took me out of my thoughts and I was down in the dirt again, the breath knocked out of me. Lex stood above me with a wide grin on her beautiful face. "Distractions are dangerous," she told me. "Eyes in the ring. It only takes a second for your opponent to get the advantage and kill you."

***

That night my dreams plagued me again.

Sitting in a tiny room on the floor, our backs to the bed.

In front of me is a rug made of the most beautiful feathers I've ever seen. They are green and gold and blue, shimmering in the light of the afternoon sun.

The walls are painted with snow capped mountains, a black dragon perched on top, and then willowy trees. A unicorn hides out among the trees, its spiraling horn catching my eye. Fire birds soar across the sky, flames erupting from their beaks. A castle made of ice stretches up toward the sky, its towers glimmering like crystal. And then I see an expanse of sea and a small island filled with huts and even more fire birds of all different colors, just like the ones in the rug. Rain clouds hover over the huts putting the village in a perpetual state of wetness. It looks like the painting was made by the hands of a child.

A woman is beside me and she holds a hand over her arm. I realize she is hurt and trying to stop the bleeding. She clenches her teeth. Sweat is trickling down her brow. She has long chestnut colored hair with small braids at the front of her hair, bright brown eyes.

"Just do what they tell you to and everything will be ok," she says but there is fear in her *eyes. She knows it will not be ok, but she's trying to be strong for me.*

There is another body on the other side of me. A little girl. She looks back at me with bright brown eyes.

Two soldiers come in, flashes of shiny armor with a red insignia, and pull us out.

I hear shots.

I see blood.

Rain drops hit my face in an unrelenting pattern. The rain tries to wash away the blood.

It will not be ok.

I fight back.

The soldier is already touching my arm. It makes it all too easy for me. A moment later he is frozen, blood trickling out from his eyes, nose, and mouth, and then he's down on the ground. Dead.

I wait for them to shoot me, stab me, anything, but a man's voice rings out, "Don't kill her!"

The man kneels in front of me. He's wearing a red blood suit, his blonde hair is combed back meticulously, and his bright blue eyes study me intently. I count the rain drops falling on his face. "This one is different. Special."

I can hear the continued shouts around me, guns firing, and see the brightness of flames as soldiers began torching the small homes around me. I watch as the flames lick at the thatched roofs, orange and angry, fighting against the rain.

A few of the beautiful, magnificent birds fight back against the soldiers, bursts of flame emitting from them, and I watch as multiple soldiers come up from behind and fell one. I watch as it's beautiful form crumples to the ground in a heart rending screech and I feel tears slipping down my small face.

"What's your name love?"

I turn my eyes to meet his, flames dancing in them that the rain will never douse. "Cora."

I awoke with a jolt as if coming up from underwater. My breathing heavy, ragged, and sweat clinging to my skin. Moments passed before I felt steady.

I forced the strange dream to the back of my mind when I realized Cyrus laid beside me, his body flush against my legs and his head resting on my thigh. He lifted his head to look at me, his eyes deep pools of intelligence sensing my unease, and wanting to comfort me. He nuzzled my hand with his snout affectionately.

"You're a good boy aren't you?" I reached out a hand and hesitantly laid it upon his head. He leaned into my touch and I felt my breathing normalize.

I laid back down and stared at the ceiling. Visions danced behind my eyes of a far off village filled with Firebirds who displayed their fiery feathers with the same pride as peacocks. A village where it always rained, the ground ripe and lush with vegetation, trees, and flowers. A village where the emperor killed everyone and took a little girl from her family–a little girl–that looked like *me*.

I clenched my eyes shut, but the visions remained, and the first trickle of hot tears fell down my face.

8

I dodged a punch that came dangerously close to my face. I was better at dodging versus landing an actual hit and my knuckles were already bruising and bloody from days of practice despite the gloves I wore. It took getting hit in the face once to realize I didn't want to do it again.

Locke watched us carefully from beside the fire as he roasted our meal.

We worked with daggers next. I felt more dialed in today, anticipating Lex's every move. I blocked more blows than normal and Xander let out a howl when I managed to land a kick that knocked her off balance for a moment.

"I never thought I'd see the day a human would get a hit in on you," Xander was never going to let her live it down. "Maybe we should talk to your father. Ask her to join the team."

Lex shot him a look indicating he needed to shut up and then she stared into my eyes, her breathing coming quickly. I could sense her heart pounding in her chest. Mine did too. Perhaps she wondered how I'd improved so fast.

Because this isn't the first time you've fought or used a weapon.

I ignored the little voice in my head as much as I tried to ignore the visions.

"Not bad Cate," she said with a nod. "You've got a bit of a fighter's spirit in you."

I wondered at Xander's comment. Who was Lex's father? He said they both came from important families.

Locke stood beside Xander now, his dark green eyes studying me. I was too focused on the fight to hear him approach. He appeared deep in thought, his brown curls distractingly falling into his eyes in a way that made my heart beat faster.

"Are you going to stand there and stare or are you going to get in the ring?" I challenged him with a smirk. I knew I looked a mess, sweat and dirt coating my hair, but I wanted him to know my strength. That I would be strong enough to make it back to the human realm without him if I needed to.

"You're not ready to fight me," his green eyes flashed and I felt a strange heat in my stomach. "It wouldn't be a fair fight."

I didn't let it go. My pride wouldn't let me. And I knew exactly how to push his buttons. "You won't know unless you let me fight you."

"I know that I would knock you on your ass in two seconds," he said as if it were fact. "Because you fight with your feelings."

Why would he say that to me? What did he expect from me?

My fists curled at my sides and I stood straighter. "While I appreciate the lessons, *respectfully*, I don't have time for this anymore," I narrowed my eyes. "When are you taking me back?"

We stared each other down, tension rippling between us, his green eyes darkening, before Lex interjected. "Shall we call it a day?"

I pulled my leather gloves off my hands and threw them down in the ring pointedly before storming off toward the lake. My face felt hot. My knuckles hurt. My legs ached.

As I removed my boots I heard Lex say quietly, "What are we doing Locke? She's only a human." There was clear disdain in her voice despite her earlier compliment.

This only fed into my theory Locke was keeping me around for other reasons. Why didn't he want me to leave?

I stripped down to my undergarments, too angry to care about modesty, and waded into the lake to rinse off the sweat and grime. The water felt cool and refreshing and I sank into it, holding my breath for as long as I could.

I thought of my sister. I'd imagined scenario after scenario of what might have happened to her after I left, every one worse than the last, but I held onto the hope she would survive. She was strong. And she would be waiting for me.

I would liberate her and we would run away together.

I couldn't waste anymore time here.

***

That night the dreams came again. So real. So vivid. As if I were living it all over again.

I was back in Hawthorne's house, the blow hitting the side of my head, and then all the rage of the last few years came pouring out of me as I touched him and watched him fall to the ground.

Then running barefoot through the forest, the cold wind whipping at my nightgown, the tears and dirt streaking my hopeless face.

And then I saw Emperor Arias again...

But this time it was different.

"All will be as it should again..." he said, placing the gold circlet on my head. "You belong to me."

And then I felt nothing.

Everything was black. Muted.

Someone else came into the room.

A boy, slightly older than me, with wavy golden hair and bright eyes.

I stared at him brokenly, not computing.

There was something in his eyes. I didn't understand what he was trying to convey. He couldn't reach me.

All I knew was to listen to the emperor. His words were in my head.

"Touch him," the emperor said.

I reached my fingers toward the boy and he didn't flinch or back away. He kept staring into my eyes.

"It's ok Cora," he said quietly. "You won't hurt me."

But as I reached closer I didn't care about not hurting anyone. I didn't care about him. All I knew was to obey. And so his words meant nothing.

Even as he grimaced and a small trickle of blood made its way out of his nose.

***

I opened my eyes, my hand going to my chest. Moonlight filtered into the room, cutting through the darkness. My breathing was calm but my mind was a mess. Dreams? Memories? I could no longer tell.

The blue eyed boy with the emperor was also the boy in the garden, but older. Who was this strange boy that haunted my dreams? He lingered in my mind like soft tendrils of smoke. Something about his eyes–the way he looked at me–made small butterflies dance in my chest and my skin tingle with warmth.

I threw the covers off me and swung my feet over the side of the bed until my toes touched the cold wooden floor, my head resting in my hands as I took deep breaths.

I couldn't stay here any longer. I decided at the lake earlier. While grateful to Locke for giving me the time and space to train, I felt the need to leave just as strongly as the first night I tried. This time, I trusted I could fend for myself. This time I would find my way out of Wisteria.

I got up and changed into pants and a black tunic quickly - so that I would blend in with the night. I put my hair up into a bun and stared at my reflection determinedly.

You don't need to feel guilty for leaving, I told myself. There was no reason for me to stay. I owed these people nothing. They owed me nothing. *You simply need to survive.*

I pulled the cloak over my head and slipped on the gloves Lock had given me, but my mind nagged at me. He had helped me. I thought of the moment he brought me the salve for my feet, how he saved my life from the Cursed, how they trained and taught me.

Emotions I didn't understand or feel comfortable with welled within me. This was the problem with letting people in; letting them help you. You did begin to feel indebted to them. You did feel guilt for taking and giving nothing in return.

I have nothing to give them.

I grabbed a small pack to put a dagger and some food into and headed into the sitting room. I quietly grabbed a loaf of bread and some cheese from the kitchen and placed them in my pouch.

I turned and reached the front door, my hand on the handle when I heard his voice low in the night. "I don't know why you insist on putting yourself in the most dangerous situations possible."

I felt the hairs on my neck stand up. He must have been sitting in the dark and I missed him. I wondered if I walked out the door, if he would let me go, or would try and stop me.

"I don't know why you care so much if I do."

I had barely spoken when I felt him behind me. I turned and his hands pressed on either side of me on the door. I faintly traced the shape of him in the dark, the curls of his head, the green of his eyes, the sharp cut of his jaw.

"I believe you and I agreed to a challenge. And I don't lose or forfeit easily." His voice came out low and earthy in the quiet of the room. He smelled of the earth too, cedar and patchouli. "I care about *that*."

"And I'm tired of playing games. Let me go."

His eyes burned a trail down my face, settling on my lips, and then back up to my eyes again. So close, I felt the heaviness of the energy settle between us like an aching pulse. Slow and steady. Continuous. Cautious.

I couldn't follow where that energy might lead.

Intimacy is dangerous.

"I've only kept you here to keep you safe. You're not a prisoner." I thought I imagined the softness in his voice, especially when it hardened again and he added, "If you're so keen to get yourself killed, be my guest." He lowered his arms and took a step back. "Knock yourself out. Then I'll know for sure you can't possibly be who I think you are."

Who? Or what?

He knows what you are.

My breath shuddered and I grabbed for the door handle again, turning it and stepping out into the night air. I needed to leave. I needed to be free. But my curiosity was piqued at his words. If he thought I was a Silencer I needed to hear it from him.

"And who exactly do you think I am?" I turned on my heel to face him, holding his gaze steady despite the fact my heart beat like a wild rabbit in my chest.

Locke crossed his arms over his chest and leaned against the doorframe. His green eyes narrowed, darkening. "Tell me why you can't touch anyone."

I stiffened. "Maybe I just don't like to be touched."

"Or maybe you have a power that you don't yet understand."

I stepped back again, farther away from him, farther away from the truth.

He knows.

He tried again. "I want to help you. But I can't help you if you won't trust me."

Again he asked for something I didn't know how to give.

Trust him?

How did trust begin? Was it born from one small act, from a series of small acts? Was it born over time? How could one measure the amount of trust between two people? Was it infinite like a mother's love for her child, or did it have limits?

As I pondered this and bit my lip I realized Locke looked at me a little too intently.

I knew that look.

I caught glimpses of it before–even if I tried to hide the fact it was there–staring us both in the face. I caught it in the way he watched me when he didn't think I was looking. In the way his eyes would catch mine across the fire when we ate in the morning. It confused me because it didn't make sense. He didn't know me. But I knew desire when I saw it.

"Please stop doing that," his words were low as his gaze swept from my eyes back to my lips again. "You do that often when you are deep in thought and it's highly distracting."

I stopped, feeling a slight blush stain my cheeks. I could feel the heat of his body, the shallow rise and fall of his chest, and as my eyes rose to meet his I mustered up the last amount of retaliation I had left before they could suck me in and steal my resolve. "Sorry to *distract* you. Who knew a human could do such a thing?"

He leaned in even closer and I sucked in a breath. "You just can't help yourself can you? Always the smart ass." But teasing filled his words; a fondness.

And then I couldn't help it - I thought about his lips, my eyes languidly falling to his own.

And that was a very bad idea because kissing would require touching.

And I would never.

"Cate," he said, my fake name jolting me out of my dazed thoughts. "Tell me what you were running from," His eyes didn't leave my face watching my every expression.

I did my best to keep my face screwed into stone. "No."

He took a step back from me and I breathed a sigh of relief. "It must have been something terrible for you to leave your sister behind."

I stiffened at his words, at the reminder that I left her.

"You and I share something in common," he said to my surprise. "We both have others counting on us." He paused and my thoughts flashed to the people of Loom, how they all showed him such respect. "It's not easy to carry such responsibility. Is that what you dream of every night? Your sister?"

71

I was taken aback by the rugged concern in his eyes. Or was it confusion? I was simply a puzzle he was trying to put together. An amusement. I couldn't speak. I opened my mouth but nothing came out.

What did he know of my dreams? And why was he asking me so many questions? None of it would matter once I went back to the human realm anyway. He would never need to see or speak to me ever again. Whatever arrangement this was between us; it was temporary.

He took a small step forward closer to me again. "Every night I hear you. Every night you cry out. Every night." He said the words and I felt how badly the truth hurt. My lip quivered for a moment and I knew he caught it. There was no hiding it.

"Tell me - what are you running from?" His eyes were so unusually imploring, seeing through my carefully crafted barrier; the walls I'd built around my heart.

But somehow a crack began to splinter up the wall like spider webs. I couldn't stop it from happening.

"Everything," I whispered. And a moment later I felt hot tears forming in my eyes betraying me. I turned my head away from him and stared at the ground, not wanting him to see, but knowing he'd already seen too much. Weakness. I angrily blinked them away, refusing to let them fall. I wouldn't cry.

Put your walls back up.

But instead of the mocking I expected he stepped forward and I felt his fingers dangerously close to my face, brushing a strand of hair away. I sucked in a breath and felt my pulse quicken. His fingers found my chin and right when I started to panic that he was touching me, I realized he was wearing gloves. He lifted my face so that he could see my eyes.

I stared back at him, blinking back the tears still threatening to fall. I wouldn't cry in front of him. I wouldn't give him the satisfaction.

"You don't always need to be the strong one."

I lifted my chin. "Yes I do."

For a moment I allowed myself to picture sinking into the warmth of his chest, letting him envelope his arms around me. It sounded selfish, dangerous. His eyes burned green and gold and I wondered again if I was just a curiosity for him, an amusement, or something more.

I let my gaze fall to his lips again.

But then a memory flashed in my mind, playing before my eyes like a projector. A blue eyed man holding my face tenderly in his hands, his lips on my own. But it was I who wrapped my fingers in his blonde hair pulling him closer, my lips more demanding and hungry than his own.

As soon as it appeared, the memory was gone.

I pushed Locke away, my breath heightening, my cheeks flushed. What was happening to me? Where were all these visions coming from?

Locke watched me carefully like I would break if he made one wrong move. "If you're going to leave please wait until I say it's safe to do so. That's all I ask," his voice was quiet, measured. "I will make sure you get back to your sister. When the time is right and the soldiers lighten their patrols. Tell me you agree to this." His eyes implored me again.

I fought against my nature to be stubborn, swayed by the concern in his voice. "Only because you asked so nicely." I walked past him and back through the door, not wanting to meet his eyes and see what might lie there, but as I walked by I felt him grab my arm gently, and my blood stirred, pounding in my chest. Even with the gloves on, his touch stirred parts of me to life, but my mind flashed back to the blue eyed boy.

"It's a beautiful night." A pause. "Would you care to join me outside?"

I should say no. I should go back in the room and shut the door. I feared another vision overtaking me, clouding my judgment and my grip on reality, but instead I nodded and followed him outside. He headed to the lake and sat on the ground beside the water. I sat beside him.

The moon hovered over the rows of trees in the distance past the lake. It reminded me of an old painting I'd seen long ago. A flicker of a memory came back of standing in a large ornate hall with red and gold carpets. Staring up at a large painting of a starry night shrouded by trees and mountains. There was something ethereal about the painting that made it impossible to look away.

That's exactly how this night looked and felt.

My mind flickered back to when I awoke outside Sageburn. I'd remembered being in a castle then; someone ushering me to safety, telling me to flee. Something told me the painting and the castle were connected.

But when have I ever been in a castle?

I felt hyper aware sitting next to Locke in the darkness alone. Just the two of us. I was aware of every subtle movement he made, the rise and fall of his chest, the way his eyes swept over the horizon, and then finally back to my face. He stretched out his long legs in front of him.

"Loom is my hometown," he said at last. I let the words hang between us. "I grew up there with my father, my mother, and my two sisters." His eyes left my face again and settled somewhere far away across the lake, lost in a memory. I remembered him telling me about his sisters before.

"Five years ago the empire attacked Loom. They rounded up those with power they deemed valuable and slaughtered the rest. I was away at the time." His eyes dimmed and a muscle in his cheek twitched. "I came back to find my town in shambles. My family dead. And all I could think was...if only I had been there that night."

I knew what one was supposed to say during these conversations.

It's not your fault.

You couldn't have known.

But instead I listened.

Let him speak.

"The fountain in Loom with the statue...it's of my father. It serves as a painful reminder of what the empire took from me. I decided the night my family died that I would do everything in my power to fight back against the evil of the empire. To drive them out of Wisteria. That is why I hate humans. The empire. And now...I do everything I can to protect Loom and its people. They've been able to rebuild over time...but it will never be the same. They will always live in fear. Until the empire is no longer a threat."

I felt like I understood him a little better. And in sharing, he showed me that he also understood me. Protecting those we loved was all we had to hold onto; for him the memory of a family he lost.

The empire did not pick and choose who it hurt or destroyed; the damage went both ways, and now I understood the empire painted Wisteria as the enemy to further control its people.

"The Resistance," he said hesitantly, "Doesn't like to share resources to protect small 'insignificant' towns like Loom. They'd rather focus their sights on bigger cities like Coriander - the capitol. Places with bigger populations. Places that would be more 'detrimental' if they fell to the empire."

I noted the resentment in his voice.

"But I protect my hometown the best I can. And fortunately Lex and Xander have been willing to help temporarily, but smaller towns like Loom are most at risk of being attacked by the empire."

"For what it's worth," I said quietly speaking into the darkness, "I'm sorry." I picked up a rock and held it between my fingers, giving myself something other to focus on, to ground me. "And I agree with you...the empire is evil. I've spent my life dreaming of escaping it. And I've tried not to let it consume me and claim me. I think it's noble that you protect your home."

He looked at me curiously. "You really don't have a home?"

I shook my head. "Not anymore. In fact," I drew my knees up to my chest and sighed. "I'm not sure I ever truly did." He waited and letting out another sigh I chose to give him a small piece, one small bit of information. Perhaps to test the waters of trust. "I lived in a conscription lodge with my sister the last few years of my life." It settled quietly between us like the stillness after a storm.

His brows drew together. "Your parents died?"

I shook my head. "I never knew my mother. She died. But my father...he..." I swallowed feeling stupid for getting so emotional over something long past, something I told myself didn't matter anymore. "My father sold my sister and I to the empire when I was sixteen. Two years ago." The words tasted like lead. "So many in the empire are simply trying to survive. Harsh decisions have to be made."

He studied my face, another piece of the puzzle clicking into place for him. "And after you go back for your sister, where will the two of you go?"

"Away from the empire. Somewhere we can make our own home."

He looked deep in thought. "Perhaps a home is not a solid, stationary place." His eyes found mine. "But somewhere your heart can be safe. A place where you don't have to pretend to be something you're not. A place that won't seek to claim you."

There was something in his eyes, like he was trying to coax me further out of my shell, to trust him, to tell him more. I was grateful for the dark of night so he couldn't see my cheeks burning. What would be the price I'd pay for my revelations? If life taught me anything it was that every bit of yourself you revealed could be used against you.

"Thank you," I said quickly, "for sharing your story with me."

He nodded. "Thank you for staying when you want to run." I turned to look at him more fully. I felt like he was stripping me bare with his words, seeing past my carefully constructed armor. "I know you have all the reason in the world to run. To not trust me. But I hope soon you will trust me enough to share *all* of your story with me."

Why was he so damn perceptive?

We sat in silence for what felt like forever before he finally said, "There comes a point where you get tired of running. Eventually you have to start living Cate."

I nodded and went inside, his words haunting me.

9

The next morning when I awoke, the first rays of morning light filtering through the window and onto my face - I felt different. Hopeful. But also sad.

As much as I yearned to go back to my sister, a part of me was beginning to feel comfortable here. Part of me hoped I could find meaning the more Locke opened up to me and I understood what his life entailed, what mattered to him.

His hatred for the empire and humans was clear, but I wondered if, over time, he could come to trust me, to think of me as something more than just a 'human'. That perhaps we could become friends.

I could find a place to call home where I could stop pretending. Stop simply surviving and start living. Stop running.

I scolded myself for my ridiculous thoughts. Clearly opening up to Locke last night unlocked doors that shouldn't be opened. It was turning me into a vulnerable idiot.

After caring for my needs, braiding my hair and putting on a pair of leggings and a tunic I stepped out into the main room. The cabin was quiet. I peered outside and frowned. I'd become so used to seeing Locke sitting by the fire in the mornings carving his wooden figures, or Lex and Xander sparring in the ring.

I went outside and the chill of the morning air made me shiver. I heard a splash and turned to see Xander in the lake, swimming.

"Morning," I said, making my way to the edge of the gleaming lake.

He beamed at me and then rose up out of the water, his dark skin wet and glistening. He hesitated.

"Hand me a towel? Unless you want to see me naked."

I kept my hands over my eyes as I stumbled toward the glimpse of a towel on the shore. "Gods Xander. That would be like seeing my brother naked if I had one."

He laughed heartily. "It wounds me you're not attracted to me, Cate." But there was nothing but teasing in his words.

I handed him the towel and when he wrapped it around himself I lowered my hands from my still flushed face.

"I'm assuming you've seen a naked man before."

"Of course! That doesn't mean I want to!"

He chuckled again.

I turned to face the woods while he changed behind me.

"Where are Locke and Lex?" I scanned the perimeter of the woods, still silent. Not even Cyrus was around.

"They had some business to take care of."

I learned this was code for information I wasn't privy to. I still suspected they were part of the Resistance or perhaps another faction of a rebel group. When they would leave and come back tired or wounded without telling me why I could only read between the lines.

I still harbored a small hope the Resistance might help me save my sister.

"Xander?" I figured now was my opportunity and as good a time as any. "Can you find someone you've never met before?"

He stood beside me now wearing black pants and a dark green shirt. "I've been wondering how long it would take you to ask."

My eyes widened. "Can you find her?"

He smiled and hope filled my heart like a balloon. "I can try."

***

"Tell me about her," Xander said, laying a hand on my sleeve. "It might help. This would work better if I could touch your skin, you know."

We sat on the settee, the fire crackling next to us. "This will have to do," I told him.

And this better work.

He closed his eyes, waiting for me to speak, and I hesitated. What if he saw something terrible? What if she was hurt? I steadied my breath and drew on all the strength I could muster. I needed to know.

"Her name is Danielle." I pictured her in my mind, big brown eyes, the dimples in her cheeks when she smiled. "She has dimples. Her eyes are darker than mine. Her hair is darker too. But she's my twin. She loves to sing and play guitar. She can't stand vegetables, but loves fruit. Especially strawberries." A distant memory of making her a strawberry cake entered my mind. "She's afraid of snakes. She loves the color yellow." I breathed out heavily. "She's so smart. But not only book smart. She has this way of knowing exactly the right questions to ask or the right things to say. The last time I saw her she was in the lodge. I need to know if she's still there. Is she...alive?"

Xander opened his eyes and removed his hand from my arm. He bit the inside of his cheek before his eyes met mine. "I see her. She's alive. I catch glimpses of her in a castle...but also in Wisteria. Does that mean anything to you?"

My eyes widened. "She and I - we were merchant mules and sometimes we delivered goods to the castle, but we never went inside. Perhaps she's making a delivery?" I tucked my legs up beneath me, deep in thought. "But what do you mean you see her in Wisteria?"

He smiled weakly. "It's not an exact science my Gift. Perhaps I'm seeing you and not her; you two look awfully alike."

"But she could be here?" My voice trailed off.

Why would she be here?

If she were here it would be a mistake for me to go back to Sageburn. But I needed to know for sure. How could I find her?

Before Xander could respond the door burst open and I turned to see Lex enter, her arm wrapped around Locke. He staggered and fell to the ground in a heap. Lex winced and she clutched a wound at her side.

Cyrus bounded in behind them, a low whine in his throat. His green eyes found mine as if imploring me to help Locke, his tail swishing in agitation.

"We were attacked," Lex gritted through her teeth. "Empirian soldiers. Locke was stabbed. I suspect poison."

Xander and I were at Locke's side in moments. His skin appeared clammy; feverish. A wound in his side festered and bled. He could barely keep his eyes open and he groaned.

I'd suspected every time they left and came back with injuries that they were doing something dangerous; they were a part of something bigger. But I'd never seen Locke with such a wound.

"What were you two doing?" I dared to ask. Lex only glared at me in response, her eyes shutting me down.

Lex and Xander picked Locke up, wrapping his arms around their shoulders, and helped him to a room in the back of the cabin. I followed hesitantly, unsure of how I could help. I'd never been to the back of the cabin, never seen his room.

It was tidy with a small desk, green curtains, and more of his wooden carvings. They laid him on the bed and Lex promptly removed his boots while Xander lifted his shirt to get a better look at his wound. Cyrus leapt up onto the bed and curled down by his feet, resting his head on them protectively.

I'd never seen Locke so vulnerable, so human. His curls clung to his sweaty forehead and for a moment his green eyes met mine and I could only hold them remembering our conversation from the night before.

This was why intimacy was dangerous. It made you start to care. It slipped in slowly, sometimes undetected, and before you knew it, it dictated your emotions, your choices, and it made you vulnerable.

I could feel its tendrils coaxing me now as I stared at Locke.

"He needs an antidote," Xander said, his face contorting at the sight of the wound. Green ooze spread from it and black whorls of infection began to snake their way up his side.

Lex wrapped a piece of fabric around her own wound. "I'll go."

Xander's hand went to her chest. "You're injured. You're not going. I am. Stay with Locke. Healing herbs for this and make sure he stays hydrated."

When she didn't object Xander left the room. I cast one last look at Locke, his form so weak and still, and the tendrils coaxed me again, squeezing my heart and driving my legs down the hall after Xander.

"Cate. No." Xander grabbed a cloak and a small pack of supplies before I could say anything.

"Take me with you. I can help. I'm useless here."

"Stay with Locke. He values your company. That will be more of a comfort to him than anything right now." Xander's eyes bore into my own, but I could already see an inkling of his resolve fading.

"Lex is here. I want to help. I'm going." I placed my hands on my hips and there must have been a fire in my eyes because finally Xander relented.

I followed him outside, grabbing a dagger and sheathing it in my boot.

"You must really care about him," Xander said as we headed off into the forest. It began to rain, a slow drizzle, the clouds in the sky ominous.

"He's my friend," I said, testing the words. "And he helped me when I needed someone. It's only fitting I return the favor."

"Hmmm," he purred. "Simply a return of goodwill."

I ignored his lingering stare, the truth of what he said, because I wasn't willing to admit it to myself just yet. Locke *was* my friend. Locke *did* help me. And I couldn't sit back and let him suffer, not if I could help.

We walked for nearly an hour, the rain pouring faster, making the ground slippery and muddy. Lightning bolts danced across the sky in silver zig zags. My clothes were soaked, water dripping into my eyes, and pieces of my hair clinging to my face.

"Let's stop here until the storm dies down," Xander said, leading us into the mouth of a small cave. "Hopefully this weather keeps soldiers off the road and we don't run into any. We're not far. The antidote should be located in the Water Caverns."

"Water Caverns?" I peered up at him from where I leaned against a cool, but ragged cave wall, relieved to be free of the pelting rain.

He rubbed his hands together. His clothes were also wet and clinging to his tall, muscular frame. "There's a lake to the north with caverns and inside them grows a plant called White Thistle. That's the antidote."

"Sounds easy enough."

Another bolt of lightning flashed across the sky.

He laughed. "As long as we don't run into any Belvens. They stick close to the caves, and they favor White Thistle. Keep your eye out and keep your hand close to your dagger."

I removed it from my boot, feeling the cold steel in my hands. I remembered the shaggy wolf-like creature Locke dispatched. Was that a Belven? And was I strong enough now to fight one?

"Just think fast and act swiftly. We'll move out as soon as the storm settles."

I laid my head against the wall of the cave and waited for the sound of the rain to let up, but all I could think of was getting the antidote and getting back to Locke. And my curiosity piqued again at what he and Lex were doing; why were they so secretive?

I turned my eyes to Xander who sat across from me now, against the wall of the cave. "You're part of the Resistance aren't you?"

His eyes met mine, dark and wide, and a small smile played on his lips. He didn't say anything, but he didn't need to–his response was all the answer I needed.

***

I thought of the farm while we waited, the rainy mornings when I awoke before the sun rose up over the mountains, only utter darkness and stillness besides the sound of my sister snoring and the rain against the roof.

She's alive. The thought fueled me.

"The storm is settled," Xander said, taking my arm and snapping me out of my reverie. "Let's head north to the Water Caverns."

I wasn't sure how long we trudged in the mud, each step feeling heavy and no closer to where we needed to be, despite the calm in the storm. The cold bit into my skin, the wind still whipping at my face, my eyes. My fingers felt frozen despite the gloves I wore and my feet frozen in my boots. But I kept walking, kept following Xander's hurried steps...until finally he stopped.

"Here," he said, pointing through the mist. "There's the lake. And the caverns."

The lake shimmered; crystal blue. Large pine trees littered the expanse around it, rain dripping off the needles. On the other side of the lake lay a dark cavern beckoning to us. That was where we would find the antidote.

"Follow me, let's make this fast and then we can get the hell out of here," Xander said as we made our way to the cavern. We didn't speak of the Resistance again, but once again I wondered if there was a chance they would help me save my sister.

The cavern was dark, eerie, no light to pave our path.

Xander continued on in the cavern, his steps painfully slow, the echo clinking off the cavern walls. I followed, my hand ready to grab my dagger.

We weren't very far into the cave when a pile of bones caught my eyes. White angled masses of them.

"Belvens," Xander muttered with disgust. "This must be their den. Keep your eyes peeled."

A little farther into the cave and no sight of bones, but we discovered a beautiful hanging plant, growing in the walls of the cave. It was white, like its name implied, and green flowers grew on it in small patches.

"The antidote," I breathed with satisfaction.

We each took our daggers and cut at the plant. I put a generous portion into the pockets of my pants. Xander did the same.

"We did it," I said with a smile.

He nodded. "Mission accomplished...almost. Let's go save our friend."

Friend.

I liked the sound of it, the word causing my heart to shift and grow bigger in my chest.

We headed out of the cave and our joy was cut short. Standing at the entrance of the cave were two beast-like creatures. They had thick manes of straw colored fur, large dark eyes, and snouts with sharp fangs. These were Belvens.

A sharp intake of breath and I steadied my dagger.

"Remember your training," Xander whispered as he readied his stance. "Wait for them to strike. Aim for the belly, throat, or eye."

I nodded, my eyes still on the creatures who were now pacing, preparing to make us their next meal. We were in their territory, in their cave. They snarled, snapping as the drool flung off their fangs.

A moment later they were rushing us, their snarls echoing off the walls of the cave. I maneuvered around the Belven as it lunged for me, swiping and knicking its hind leg with the dagger. It cried out, but turned and came for me again with a snarl.

Xander somersaulted away from the other Belven and rose up as it came for him again, his knife ready to slash at its belly.

The Belven's sights were on me as it came again. I dodged it again, but this time its claw swiped at my leg as I evaded and I felt a searing pain in my upper thigh. I cried out, but steadied myself.

Xander glanced over at the sound of my cry, but continued to fight the other Belven.

This time when the Belven came for me and it jumped I was ready. Its sharp fangs were aiming for my chest, but I slid underneath in one fell swoop, my dagger coming up to slice underneath its belly. I felt its guts spilling out as I skidded to a stop and realized it lay unmoving, slain by my hand.

I breathed out a sigh of relief, a laugh of pride, as I watched Xander drive his dagger through the eye of the other Belven, his other hand on its throat. It let out a mottled cry and slowly sank to the ground.

"Not bad Cate," he said with a grin. "I think even Lex would be impressed."

***

By the time we made it back to the camp it was dark, the ground still muddy from the storm, the trees still dripping water on us as we walked. My thigh hurt and bled, but I powered through thinking only of Locke.

Lex ran out to greet us the instant we reached the camp, eagerly taking the White Thistle from Xander.

"How is he?" Xander asked as we entered the cabin.

"He's weak, but with this he will be fine." She turned to me, slight approval in her eyes. Her eyes trailed down to my thigh. "This is what I used for Locke's wound," she said, handing me a bowl with green paste. "It will help yours as well."

I took the bowl from her. "Thank you," I said.

I went into my little room and peeled the wet clothing from my skin, wincing as my pants came down over my thighs. I took a warm bath and then carefully wiped the green sludge on my wound, tying it off with a bandage when it was done. I put on a clean pair of clothing, braided my hair and laid down in the bed, trying to sleep.

But I couldn't.

I needed to see Locke.

I crept up from my bed, my footsteps light on the floor and grabbed my gloves. The main room was dark, except for the fire still blazing. I tiptoed down the hall and opened the door to his room. I could make him out in bed, rays of moonlight spilling across the floor, the blankets pulled up over him, Cyrus resting at his feet.

He appeared peaceful, his breathing steadier than earlier. His face held a healthy glow, no longer flushed and feverish. I gently brushed the curls from his forehead with my gloved hand, wondering what his skin would feel like beneath my finger tips. It was funny how I took something like touch for granted until I could no longer do so.

His eyes opened, blinking rapidly as he took in my face. "Cate?"

I pulled my hand back. "I'm sorry. I didn't mean to wake you."

His hand caught mine. A question lingered in his eyes. "Stay."

It was one word. One simple word. But it was funny how much meaning a word could hold when spoken between two people who had slowly, but surely been gravitating toward one another.

"Are you sure it's safe?" I hesitated. "I don't want to hurt you."

"Bring me my gloves there," he said, his eyes drifting to his desk. "And lay your head on my chest. You're wearing long sleeves and gloves. There's a blanket between us. You won't hurt me." He sounded so certain.

I nodded and grabbed his gloves, watching as he pulled them over his hands. My heart pounding, I climbed onto the bed beside him and lowered my head to his chest, hearing the beating of his own heart, feeling his warmth even through the blanket.

We lay together, still and silent, only our steady breaths and thumping hearts in the darkness. And I knew at that moment, my heart was no longer mine. Maybe it never had been.

It broke into little pieces that I gave to those around me. Little moments of daring to care. Little moments of allowing trust to build. Little moments of allowing myself the luxury of friendship.

My sister had my heart. But so did Xander. And Cyrus. Even Lex wiggled her way in despite her attitude. But Locke...

He had my heart in a different way.

His gloved fingers went to my head, gently caressing the strands of my hair. It felt intimate. Soothing. I closed my eyes. It reminded me of when I would hold my sister and do the same to her.

I let us have this moment.

Let myself have something good.

Intimate.

And I stayed.

10

I opened my eyes slowly. Warm sun hit my face and birds chirped outside. I blinked, my recognition foggy as I took in the room around me. Then I remembered. I stayed in Locke's room. I stayed because he asked me too, but also because I wanted to. I sat up, awkwardly rubbing the sleep out of my eyes.

I laid my hand on the empty space beside me; still warm and smelling like him. I couldn't help the smile that broke across my face. I'd slept peacefully; the first night the dreams didn't plague me.

I made my way out to the main room of the cabin, feeling sheepish although I had nothing to be ashamed of. I found it funny how something like simply sleeping in the same bed together could be so intimate.

Locke and Lex sat at the table, steaming cups of tea between them. They were laughing at something Xander said as he refilled their cups. I felt a twinge at the way they interacted so easily with one another, like they each belonged to this place, but felt relief that Locke appeared healed; a healthy glow on his cheeks.

My attention turned to Cyrus who sat on the floor beside Locke, clearly asking for scraps of food. His long tail swished on the ground as his eyes followed Locke's every movement, his ears alert.

"Let me get you some breakfast Cate," Xander said, noticing me first. He quickly went about pouring me a cup of tea and piling a plate full of meat and fruit. I didn't miss the sheepish look in his eyes.

Locke's eyes met mine from behind his cup as I slid into a seat at the table. Xander placed the plate of food and cup in front of me. Lex gave me a small curt nod in a way of greeting, but I didn't miss how her hands tightened around her cup.

"Thank you," I said, taking my first sip of the tea. I could still feel Locke's watchful eyes lingering on my every movement, but I waited to meet them. "This is unexpected. No training today?"

I still wouldn't acknowledge Locke as I picked at my food. I could feel the tension filling the small space. Could feel his eyes probing mine, willing me to look at him. I worried if I looked at him the intensity from the night before would overwhelm me. I worried what would be revealed in my own eyes. Too much tenderness?

You went too far.

I did my best to ignore the chiding voice in my head, reminding me again that intimacy was dangerous and I'd already stepped off the edge of a precipice.

"Good morning," Locke said quietly, a small smile on his lips.

"Good morning," I responded. "I take it you're feeling better?"

"Thanks to you." I met his eyes at last, warm pools of green. "And Xander," he tacked on.

"She took down a Belven." Xander couldn't contain his grin. "She spilled its guts everywhere."

"There goes my appetite," Lex rolled her eyes and pushed her plate away, but I caught the teasing smile she gave Xander.

"Did you?" Locke's green eyes sparkled with appreciation. "I would have liked to see that."

Cyrus whined from beside me, his piercing green eyes focused on the meat on my plate. I held out a small piece of meat for the beast. He took it eagerly, more gentle than I would have thought. He nuzzled his snout into my hand after with thanks. I ruffled the fur of his head, a smile finally breaking on my face.

Locke continued to watch me, but it wasn't in the clinical way he often did like I was a puzzle he wanted to decipher. He pushed back his chair. "Let's go outside. There's something I want to show you."

I realized then that the table had gone quiet and Lex and Xander were both watching and listening to us intently. Their eyes averted my own with the realization and they both feigned interest in their breakfast. Lex pursed her lips together disapprovingly but Xander tried to hide a smile.

Locke's invitation was meant for me alone.

I pushed my chair back and accompanied him outside, curiosity fueling me. Cyrus followed happily behind us.

The day was gorgeous as always, the sun high in the sky filtering through the trees. The sound of birds met my ears singing sweetly. For a moment I could close my eyes and pretend that this was my home. Could buy into the lie of safety, permanence, normalcy.

Locke paused, putting his hands in his pockets and staring up at the sky in thought. "I wanted to thank you." As soon as the words were out of his mouth I felt uncomfortable, vulnerable. "What you did for me. You didn't have to go with Xander."

"You've helped me. I wanted to help you."

His eyes met mine, a quiet knowing in them.

"Humans don't often help our kind."

"But friends do," I countered. I felt almost silly, stupid, saying the words. Would he laugh in my face? Would he tell me I wasn't his friend? But he did neither of those things.

He looked down at Cyrus who sat patiently by his side, his green eyes assessing the two of us as if he were listening to our conversation.

"Cyrus told me the day I met you...that we would become friends. I suppose I should listen to him more often."

"He told you?"

"He did." He continued walking and I followed. "He's my familiar. We can communicate with one another."

I watched Cyrus curiously. "And how long has he been your familiar?"

"Since I was a child. He found me when I was a boy shortly after my magic manifested. I was hunting in the forest at the time. I remember aiming my bow at him...and then hesitating. There was something in his eyes that stopped me. He chose me."

"And what does a familiar do exactly?"

We kept walking, past the fire pit, past the sparring ring, and into the confines of the trees. I watched him walk, wondering where he was leading me.

"They offer companionship. But they also strengthen your magic - your tether to source. They can help you in battle if you're fortunate. But there are certain creatures it's more rare to have as a familiar. Firebirds for example. They reside on the island of Lumeria. And even rarer I've heard to have a dragon."

My eyes were wide. "Dragon?"

He laughed and little creases showed by his eyes. "I keep forgetting...you're human. You didn't grow up here. This is all new for you. Yes...there are many dragons near Frostblight. But they don't often bond with us. Ask Xander about them."

I was beginning to think that he might *like* the fact it was all new for me. That he enjoyed having someone to share his history with – even if I was a human.

Although he now clearly suspected my reasons for not touching him were due to my power. What would he say if I told him? If I told him that I was terrified and I didn't even understand what was happening to me? If I told him that I was the very thing he hated?

Silencer.

I watched the two of them curiously, Locke and Cyrus as I warred with myself. I wondered what it would be like to have such a loyal companion, if I indeed possessed power, if a familiar would be available to me as well.

My mind flashed to my recent dreams of Firebirds. I saw the great beautiful beasts blasting balls of fire at the soldiers, as the emperor knelt in front of me and said that I was 'special'. Saw the flames dancing in the background as screams filled the smoky air, and I felt a sinking feeling in the pit of my stomach.

What did it all mean?

What was my connection to it?

We stopped in front of a much larger tree.

Its trunk was thick and wide with peeling brown slabs of bark running up. Towering branches full of thick green leaves hung over our heads, and hanging from the branches were ripe looking purple and blue fruits.

"What kind of tree is this?" I asked, unable to hide my awe. I reached up my gloved hand and trailed my fingers along the branches and down back the trunk, my woes momentarily forgotten. "I've never seen anything like it."

His eyes lit up in response, soft approval in them of my interest. "We call it the Tree of Life. It's rare. It's only the second one I've ever seen in Wisteria."

"Why Tree of Life?" I leaned back against the strong trunk.

"This tree has many benefits. We can eat the fruit, the leaves, the bark. We can use the seeds and bark for medicinal herbs. To us Wisterians it represents tenacity. Life itself."

His eyes lowered. "We Wisterians value life more than anything. Our life. The lives of our animals. Our familiars. The earth itself."

He turned his focus to me. "What do you value Cate?" He stood right in front of me now and reached up to grab a piece of ripe purple fruit from the tree. It made a small snap and he held it in front of me as an offering. I was hyper aware of the shape and strength of his body in front of me. The broadness of his shoulders. The muscular planes of his chest leading down to his chiseled abdomen and strong legs.

I took the fruit from him and twisted it in my hand.

This moment felt intimate. The fruit. The tree. The way he was looking at me. The question.

"I value my family," I said, staring at the skin of the fruit and thinking of our conversation from a few nights ago. "I care about getting my sister to safety, to a place where she is free to make her own choices. Where she won't be controlled or have everything decided for her. Where she can find an actual home. Away from all of this. I value freedom."

His eyes softened. "And is that what you wish for yourself too?"

I thought a moment. What did I want? The thought didn't occur to me too often outside the realm of saving my sister and getting her to safety. To get away from the empire. To not simply survive, but live.

"There were a lot of things I used to want. But I stopped letting myself."

He met my eyes. "Why?"

"You know why," I said, biting my lip, the truth hovering over us like the branches of the Life Tree.

The truth was any time I let myself want something or even have it–it was taken away from me. What I loved, what I cared about...gone. Even fleetingly.

My home, my father, my sister, even Dean.

You're meant to be alone.

The space between us felt infinite and yet I knew in a moment he could close it if he wanted too. He could take one step toward me and draw me into his arms. Touch me. Kiss me. Anything. All things he most definitely should not do. Things I wanted him to do.

"Because we can't always have what we want." He finished the words for me. "It hurts less to hope. But sometimes hope is the only thing that keeps us going."

Possibilities. Dreams. Hope. I thought I abandoned all of those long ago, but now they broke through the surface as if treading ocean waves.

"What do you hope for Locke?" I continued to feel the leathery fruit with my thumb as if it were a tether keeping me grounded, keeping me out of the clouds and away from my delusional longings.

"The same thing as you. To be free of the empire. To free my people. To no longer live in fear." He cleared his throat. "One way or another this war will end. And there's no way in hell my people will ever stop fighting the emperor or bend to his demands."

"And what about...when this war ends?"

Another dangerous question.

He stared at me stoically looking much like a fae warrior I might have imagined at one point in my childhood against the backdrop of the willowy trees. Lethal. Beautiful. Every inch of him built to protect this land, his people.

"I suppose I haven't let myself think that far ahead," he admitted, his eyes darkening. "I'm not sure this is a world I would feel safe bringing a family into. I can scarcely protect my people as it is."

His words had my wheels spinning. I wondered about having a family. Having children. I'd never truly let myself consider the possibility. But if I met someone that I could trust–that I could love–perhaps it wouldn't be such a far fetched notion. I'd never been in love. It seemed a luxury not afforded to me or anyone else trying to survive in the empire.

"I can scarcely manage to feed myself," I countered. "I doubt I could keep a child alive."

"And that's why you have me to cook for you."

I tried to ignore the way his eyebrow rose, the grin that spread across his face revealing those all too alluring dimples and I cleared my throat, "I'm not sure eating rabbits every day is the luxury you think it is."

"What about spending every day with me?" He took a step closer.

Alarm bells went off in my head. Where was this conversation going?

"Sounds torturous." I met his eyes, but he seemed to be able to see through me, pieces of him slipping in and twining with my last remnants of resistance, slowly unraveling the chains of my heart.

"Torturous?" His lips curved in a smile and before I knew what was happening vines and roots slowly, almost tenderly, sprung up from the ground beneath me, wrapping around my wrists and my waist. I felt myself pulled back against the tree. I knew I could fight them, I could release myself if I wanted to; but I resisted the urge to flee; my eyes locked on his own. My wrists were held tightly above my head.

He simply stared at me for a moment admiring his handy work.

My breath came faster as he took a slow, but purposeful step closer to me. My chest rose and fell, my cheeks were heated. Adrenaline coursed through my veins, but I stayed still.

Was this what it meant to trust someone? To let your instincts go? To be vulnerable?

He stood close. I felt his breath at my ear. I inhaled his scent - rich like the earth. "Do you trust me?" He whispered the words aloud although he'd been asking silently all along.

I met his dark green eyes and nodded.

He slowly lifted his hands up to where my wrists were bound and a moment later they came down, and my hands with it, my wrists free of the vines. He ran his hand over the vines still over my fingers and little blue and yellow flowers began to spring up all over them, one by one, covering my gloves.

A vision of a blue orchid clouded my mind and I willed it away.

"I want you to trust me, Cate. I know it's hard for you. That you've been hurt. But I hope with time–you can."

I lifted my eyes to his face again and he was staring back at me, drinking in my expression. The look he gave me rivaled anything felt or seen in my eighteen years. Had anyone ever looked at me like this?

I imagined it inspired the greatest poems of all time, the longing strings of a violin, the moment in between the end of a performance and thunderous applause. A pining. A desperation. I wanted to bottle that look up and take it with me forever.

"Locke?" I tasted his name on my lips.

His eyes roamed mine.

Our freckled noses practically touched.

If either of us moved our faces closer our lips would meet.

Tension rippled between us.

His next words broke me, a whisper I could practically touch and taste.

"I really want to break your no touching rule."

I felt my breath hitch and a blush crept up my neck and to my cheeks. Everything felt hot. My knees were weak. My throat was so dry with words I wanted to say but wouldn't.

"I want to," he continued, his eyes landing on my lips. "But I won't." His eyes flicked to my face, holding my gaze. "I won't touch you unless you want me too. Until you trust me."

My breath caught in my throat. His gloved hands rested on mine gently. The touch alone felt entirely too intimate, too dangerous.

"I thought you said I was a pain in the ass." It was the only argument I could muster up. The first thing that popped into my addled brain. It sounded ridiculous. The way he looked at me, the way he spoke to me, managed to turn me into a simpering mess.

"You are definitely a pain in the ass." He grinned now, a dimple showing in his cheek. "But you're a pain in the ass I've grown fond of."

My eyes clouded as I avoided his gaze and stared at the ground. "I don't want to hurt you." All I could see was Hawthorne, the blood pouring from his eyes and nose after I touched him. All I could see was death.

"I imagine it would be an enjoyable sort of pain if it came from you." He exhaled and took a step back, his gloved hand still in mine. And then on a more serious note, "We should get back to the camp before I change my mind." But it was said in jest. I knew he wouldn't change his mind. He meant what he said; he wouldn't touch me unless I wanted him too.

We made our way back quietly, not speaking a word, and before we went in the door I felt his hand at the small of my back, a delicate touch over my clothing. That alone, enough to set my skin on fire.

He removed his hand and left me alone in the main room. I didn't miss the way Lex and Xander exchanged glances. I curled up on the settee by the light of the fire and read a book, determined to get my mind off Locke. Off the impossible. Away from hoping.

Curling up with a book felt foreign after years of not reading. It took a moment for my eyes to drink in the words, for my mind to find the rhythm again of getting lost in a made up world. But I found that I still could. That part of me was not dead like I thought.

And over the coming days I found that other parts of me were not faded either. They were still deep inside clawing to find their way out. And perhaps the moment at the tree of Life was the catalyst.

I saw it in the way I was eager to learn as Lex taught me how to mix different herbs and plants in a mortar and pestle to make healing remedies. In the way I felt eager to put quill to parchment again in the quiet of the evening. In the way the woods of the encampment became a sanctuary, as long as I stayed within the boundaries outlined for me.

And in the way I became all too familiar with Locke's patterns. The way he sat quietly in the morning roasting meat over the fire, always having a plate ready for me. In the nods of approval he gave me when I sparred in the ring and successfully dodged a punch. How he would put all his focus into whittling down wood into something beautiful, but save enough to feel his eyes landing on me in a curious glance.

And then there were all those unspoken stolen looks. Over morning tea. Over the fire. When I would look up from the words of my book or from scratching the spot behind Cyrus's ears. When I took a dip in the lake and rose from the water to see him far off - but his eyes always on me. Careful. Curious.

And when I would meet those eyes they would linger. And then I would feel that familiar sensation of foreboding - like falling down a deep, black hole with no end in sight just waiting to hit the bottom.

And I was afraid of what would happen when I did.

11

Locke decided it was time for me to learn how to hunt and how to survive in the woods. We spent the next set of days going deeper into the woods. He taught me how to fashion ropes from what I could find, how to start a fire, what berries were safe to eat from what weren't, how to fashion weapons like spears I could use to defend myself and hunt fish.

These were skills that would be useful to my sister and I–once we were on our own and settled down in our own home. I found myself trying to justify the ever increasing time I spent here–with Locke–but I knew I couldn't stay forever. I needed to find my sister. And soon.

I sat cross legged on the ground in front of the tiny fire I'd finally managed to start, pride swelling in my chest. I'd tried for days and finally, today, I saw a spark ignite and the kindling came to life with a small orange glow.

I held my dagger and whittled down a thick stick into a sharp spear, just like Locke taught me. I cut the wood with careful strokes and felt his eyes on me.

"You're learning," he said quietly.

I peered up at him. There was something like pride in his eyes.

"You're a good teacher," I told him.

The small, fragile unspoken thing settled between us again.

When I finished fashioning my spear I got out my sketchbook and a piece of charcoal. Locke gifted me the book, encouraging me to write, draw, whatever came to mind. It felt exciting everytime my finger held the charcoal in my hand. In the empire I would be doing something highly illegal. Here I was free to do as I pleased.

My sketches were remnants of my memories and visions.

An orchid.

A circlet.

A firebird.

And then a man, not much older than me. Looking at the sketch no one would know the color of his eyes, the color of sea glass. No one would know how golden his hair was, falling in soft waves just past his ears. No one would know that I knew what it was to feel his lips on my own.

Locke was watching me in his quiet way and I instinctively closed my sketchbook. Shame came over me in waves. My secrets seemed to grow by the day. My grip on reality slipped too.

I could feel and see the change of the season coming the further I spiraled into madness. The warmth of the sun was replaced with cooler days, the mist of the air settling over my skin like soft dew. The leaves of the trees were rapidly changing color and falling from the trees preparing for the winter season.

He smiled and I could already see the mischief forming in his gaze. "We've still got to work on those combat skills. Don't think I won't kick your ass, even if you can take down a Belven."

I stood up and wiped my hands on my black pants. Slowly put my gloves on. And gave him an alluring smile. "Why don't we test that theory?"

"I won't go easy on you," he warned as we already began to circle one another in the small clearing.

"I don't want you too," I replied, my stance ready.

We stared each other down, mere inches from one another.

"No weapons." He put on his own pair of gloves.

I nodded.

"Ready?" But even as he spoke I was already closing the space between us, my fists ready. I aimed for the more vulnerable position near his ribs, just like Lex taught me, but he was too quick. He blocked my blow.

I tried again, aiming for his face this time, careful to keep my other hand in front of my face, protecting myself. He blocked me again.

He was smiling now, an irresistible grin on his face as he blocked blow after blow. "I would have beat you so many times already Cate," he said with amusement. "You're too careless. Too emotional with your punches. You're wide open."

He *was* going easy on me.

He watched me as I readied my stance again. I took note of his own stance, his knees bent slightly, his core straight, his feet feather light and ready to strike. I wondered how many years I would need to train before I could best him. How many years it took for him to become the warrior who stood in front of me.

I swung a punch again and to demonstrate his point he swept my feet out from under me with his legs in one quick motion and I fell flat on my butt with a thud.

"Your stance needs work," he said simply turning away, but I caught his lips curve into a grin as he did so.

I got up and took a running leap for his back. I hung onto him like a monkey, my arms around his chest as he fell to the ground. But when he fell it was only to go down on one knee, my weight not enough to knock him over, and he promptly flipped me off him and onto my back on the ground.

He straddled me, his knees on either side of me pinning me to the ground. He held my forearms down by the sides of my head with his hands.

My breath came in steady heaves. My chest rose and fell as I stared into his eyes. He hovered over me, his curls falling gently as his green eyes roamed my face.

I could feel heat building from where our bodies joined. A familiar aching. My cheeks grew hot in response. Everything felt so damn hot. Resisting him, resisting whatever this was between us, was fast becoming torture, especially when I knew he desired me.

It made it all the worse when I felt him harden on top of me. Whatever this was, he was feeling it too. I'd never wanted to be desired by a man before; never felt safe enough to. With Dean it was all about control; a distraction. It never held deeper meaning. This...felt different.

"You said you weren't going to go easy on me," I told him. My voice sounded strained even to my own ears. I knew he could see the heat in my cheeks, feel it in my body.

"The alternative was to seriously injure you or kill you," he whispered, his eyes falling to my lips. "And I've decided...I prefer you in one piece. Beneath me like this even." He gave me a seductive smile and I felt my cheeks grow redder.

"I don't think that's an appropriate thing to say to a *friend*," I whispered back.

He leaned closer, his breath warm against my ear and I fought the urge to move my hips against his own, a delicious heat continuing to build. "We're not just *friends*, are we Cate?"

Before I could respond the sound of pounding hooves met our ears and we both froze. The playful banter and expression from a moment ago disappeared from Locke's face. He helped me to my feet quickly, motioning for me to be quiet.

He quickly put out my tiny makeshift fire I'd worked so hard to create and then beckoned me to hide behind a tree with him as we waited.

The sound of hooves came closer, but now I could hear and see they were heading a distance away from us in the trees north of us along the path. Soldiers. Flashes of red and black in the afternoon sun. There were about five of them riding brown colored horses.

They pulled a palette behind them and laying on it was a black horse.

I watched Locke's shoulders stiffen and his eyes narrowed as he saw it.

"What is it?" I whispered.

"It's not a horse," he said quietly. "It's a Unicorn."

I looked closer as they continued past. The magnificent beast indeed had a flowing mane of gorgeous fur and a spiraling white horn.

"What do they want with it?"

"It's the empire," he said hotly. "You tell me." He sighed. "They might want to train it, to make it fight for them. Unicorns have powerful lightning magic. Some healing powers. It would be useful to the empire."

"I thought you said your familiar has to choose you."

"Yes," he said, standing up straighter as the horses and soldiers were now out of sight. We could only hear the far off clip clop of hooves. "But animals get lonely too. I wouldn't put it past a beast to bond with the enemy, not as a familiar, but as a creature seeking companionship."

"Sometimes you don't have a choice," I murmured thinking about all the times in my life I'd simply needed to survive and choice was a luxury.

He thought for a moment, resolve forming over his face. "There were only five of them."

"Meaning?"

He smiled and his hand went to rest on his dagger. "I can take them." And then, "You want a chance to prove your worth to the Resistance?"

My eyes lit up.

"Let's go save a Unicorn."

***

We skirted along the trees, following the path, and following the soldiers. Thankfully they trotted along at a mediocre pace, giving us time to keep up with them by foot.

"There's an Empirian base near here," Locke told me quietly as we walked, careful to stay low. "That must be where they are taking her."

Sure enough a camp came into view. It appeared small, tents set up surrounded by a low brick wall. I could see smoke from a few campfires rising up and hear the soft chatter of soldiers.

We watched as the soldiers dismounted their horses, tying them up in a small stable away from the front of the camp, far enough for us to be out of sight when we rescued the unicorn. Four of them removed the Unicorn from the palette somewhat roughly and into a pile of hay. She lay there unmoving, but I could see the small rise and fall of her chest.

"General Arias is on his way," one of them said. "Checking in on us like we're a bunch of children."

"Get used to it," another one said. "He's been making his rounds since the uproar in Sageburn last month. No one's seen the Red Reaper since. And with the Resistance growing bolder...think it's a coincidence?"

The soldiers all went into the camp, disappearing into various tents.

There was that name again. *Red Reaper.*

"What were they talking about?" I asked Locke. "Who's General Arias? Do they mean the emperor?"

His eyes moved to my face carefully. "General Arias is the emperor's son."

I felt the breath leave my lungs.

The Heartless Prince.

The stories came flooding back to me.

"So he didn't run away with his love or join the Resistance," I said quietly. Disappointedly.

Locke didn't seem to know what to make of my disappointment. He crouched low to the ground as we peered through the trees. His eyebrows arched. I could see the wheels turning in his head. "Well now that we know the General is coming...we need to work quickly. There's a poison dagger in the Unicorn's side. Do you see it?"

I looked closer and sure enough I could see the weapon. I nodded.

"It's how they immobilized her. She was unable to use her magic and fight back due to the poison." His throat bobbed. "Unicorns are very trusting creatures. They make it way too easy for the empire to get their hands on them unfortunately. If we can get close enough to pull the dagger out," he went on, "it will give her time to heal and then she can defend herself. She can even get away without them noticing."

We formed a plan. I would sneak across the path to the stables and remove the dagger from the Unicorn. Locke would hang back in case any soldiers saw me or came after me. He would act as my offense.

"It's now or never," he told me as the sun began to set. "Ready?"

I met his eyes and nodded.

"After you remove the dagger, run into the woods. I will come after you and find you as soon as the coast is clear. Understand?"

I checked both sides of the path again. It was clear and silent aside from the distant sounds of soldiers on the other side of the camp. They were clearly getting inebriated and settling down for the evening. I could hear the quiet sounds of a fiddle and guitar being played and boisterous laughter. I felt a twinge of resentment that the soldiers were allowed to play and enjoy music so freely while the rest of us in Sageburn were killed for it.

Shaking the thought from my head I ran, bolting across the path in seconds.

I knelt in the hay beside the Unicorn. It turned out *she* was actually a *he*. I gently laid my hands on him feeling his strong but slow breaths. I could feel power emanating from him. I stroked his long mane and stared into his jewel blue eyes. Up close I could see just how beautiful, how magnificent he truly was.

I placed my hand on the dagger. "This will hurt for a moment," I told him. "But know that I'm trying to help you."

I pulled it out and he let out a small whinny. I tossed the dagger to the side. I watched as the wound in his side slowly, but surely began to close up and heal and I wondered again at what magic he must possess. I stroked his face gently.

"You must run away from here as soon as you are able," I told him. He looked into my eyes as if he heard me, understood me. He rolled once and then he was up standing tall and strong.

He turned and faced me, his hooves clopping gently in the hay, and his long spiraling horn pointed at my face. His eyes were level with mine. He held a sentience far beyond the intelligence of an average horse or animal. We stood for a moment, our eyes taking in one another and I felt like we understood each other. We knew what it felt like to be taken and used by others. Craved the same taste of freedom. Both possessed the same wild spirit.

Thank you brave one, the Unicorn spoke into my mind. *My name is Arthur.*

I blinked. He talked. He talked right into my mind.

I reached a hand up and touched his horn tentatively, mesmerized by the way the light reflected off it. *You're welcome*, I said back. *My name is Cora.*

I will repay your debt if you are ever in need, he spoke again. *I have a feeling we will meet again soon.*

I heard the sounds of voices and footsteps and my spine stiffened.

My eyes darted down the path where the voices were coming from.

Three soldiers emerged from the camp and in front of them stood a man not wearing a typical soldier's uniform. My eyes trailed up to see black boots, black cargo pants, and a red button up shirt underneath a black jacket, the red insignia of a fire bird on it.

He pushed the blonde hair that fell into his face away as he listened attentively to something the soldier said to him.

This must be General Arias.

When I saw his face the world stopped spinning and I felt sick to my stomach. Smooth skin, high cheekbones, strong jaw, straight nose. His hair was longer than I remembered and it stopped just before his shoulders in waves. But his eyes drew my attention. So blue, but on the verge of green.

Eyes that were slowly turning and looking at me now.

Shit.

His eyes widened and then narrowed. "Cora?" A level of disbelief entered his voice and then relief that I couldn't take the time to register because I was now urging the Unicorn to run and then taking off after him as he bolted for the woods.

My legs and lungs felt on fire, fueled by adrenaline, fueled by disbelief.

I could hear the clang of swords from behind me and knew Locke must have stepped into the fray to slow them down and help me.

The Unicorn surged forward, his black frame disappearing from my sight, and I breathed a sigh of relief knowing he'd made his escape deep into the forest.

But I was not so lucky.

I could hear him behind me, this strange soldier who knew my name.

This man that I drew in my sketchbook and that haunted my visions.

His legs were longer than mine. He gained on me.

"Cora!" He called.

Urgency filled his voice. A desperation I didn't understand.

I dared a glance behind me. He carried a gun.

Was he going to *shoot* me?

I tripped on a large branch I must have missed when I glanced back at him, lost my balance and went sprawling forward, my hands and knees scraping against the ground.

I rolled over to face him, my hands behind me as I tried to crawl away, my hands crunching against the fallen leaves - as I tried to get back up and run. But it felt like my body was broken at the sight of him towering over me now pointing a gun in my face.

I stared down the barrel, black and sleek, and then my eyes swept past it to his face - met his eyes.

I could barely breathe.

It felt like everything happened in slow motion. Everything else fell away except for the two of us.

Him.

Me.

The gun.

He didn't move, except for the steady rise and fall of his chest.

His grip on the gun controlled; intent.

I swallowed the lump in my throat and waited.

Who are you?

I saw my hands tangled in his hair and his lips on my own.

I saw him holding out a blue orchid to me.

I saw myself touching him and him telling me not to be afraid.

Why didn't he shoot? He just stood there looking at me with those eyes that were entirely too piercing. Eyes that danced between green and blue. Eyes that reached inside me like tendrils drawing out all my secrets. Did he know who I was? How did he know my name?

There are few moments where time seems to stop. Few moments where you feel the weight of every shift in the air, every subtle movement, every trace of a gaze. But this was one of them.

I thought he might stand there forever aiming his gun at me, staring into my face like he was facing the biggest existential battle of his life...

When suddenly I felt hands grab me, yank me off the ground, to the side, and then beside a tree before he could even realize what occurred.

Lex stood firm and still against the tree looking like a lethal assassin in her leathers, her long hair wild around her. She held a finger up to her mouth telling me to be quiet. She kept a hand on my arm, over my clothes. She stayed incredibly still and I did the same as we peered at General Arias.

He did a double take, turning once to look behind him, and then in front of him again, encircling the space with his gun still aiming as if he expected me to suddenly appear behind him.

He passed by us, turned, looked around, even looking in our direction. But he didn't see us.

I noted Lex's hand firm on my arm.

He was looking right at us.

Right at me.

But he couldn't see me.

I was incredibly grateful for Lex's gift in that moment.

I watched as Arias ran a hand through his blonde hair again and his mouth fell in confusion. He was trying to figure out how I'd outrun him. How I'd disappeared so fast. His brows furrowed, his eyes were glassy, his lips set in a sad line.

He looked like something out of a poem standing there, alone in the woods in the setting sun. A sad soldier. A broken man. His firearm hanging limply at his side. But then the voices of other soldiers filled the space calling for him and his countenance changed instantly. His stature straightened, his eyes hardened, and he became the picture of composure.

"The other one got away," I heard the soldiers saying. "Any luck General?"

He shook his head and walked away.

I let out the breath I'd been holding in slowly and Lex tightened her hold on my arm. "We stay connected," she said. "So they can't see us."

We headed deeper into the woods, farther away from the Empirian base.

"Thank you," I said to her quietly after a few minutes passed and it felt safe to do so. "I thought he was going to shoot me."

"Don't thank me," she replied coldly with a flip of her dark hair. "You shouldn't have been out here. Locke should have never involved you. He's not thinking straight."

I tore my eyes away from her angry face and walked on, the sounds of our steps crunching on the forest floor gently. I wondered what it would take for me to get in her good graces? For her to trust me?

"The Unicorn got away," I said quietly. And then I smiled at the realization. We'd managed to free the Unicorn and while we'd been spotted momentarily, it sounded like Locke had escaped.

"I'm sure you're pleased with yourself," she said as we found the path again that would lead back to Locke's camp. "Still...what you two did today was far too dangerous."

"Is Locke safe? Did he get away? The soldiers sounded like-"

"Yes," she said. "I saw him fighting them and I used my gift to help him and told him I would find you. Xander had a vision. He saw the two of you in trouble."

I wondered how often Xander had visions and what triggered them–making a note to ask him later.

We were just about to reach the camp when I turned to her. "I mean it. Thank you. If you weren't there..."

She released her hold on my arm. "The General seemed *very* interested in you," she noted, her eyes sweeping over me inquisitively. "He called you 'Cora'. Do you know why?"

"No. I don't." Another lie.

She was hard to read. "Hmph."

Suddenly Locke and Xander were descending on us, relief on their faces.

"Thank the Gods you're ok," Xander said, wrapping Lex in his arms. "What about you kid? You in one piece?"

I nodded, giving him a smile.

Locke stared at me.

A beat passed.

And then his arms wrapped me in a hug, my face pressed against the shirt on his chest. I relished in the closeness, the warmth of him, the relief that flooded my bones at being held by him, his earthy scent.

"She got away," he whispered quietly, only for me to hear. I smiled into his chest.

"He," I corrected him. "He got away."

12

That night I dreamed of General Arias.

The emperor's son.

I saw him standing in the woods again, trying to find me, but never seeing me. He called my name out again and again.

I reached my hands out to him, trying to help him see.

I stood in front of him and lifted my chin to look at his face.

"I'm right here," I said to him. "I'm here."

I couldn't understand the pain on his face, in his eyes. Why was he so sad? Why was he so desperate to find me? How did he know my name?

I reached for him, but as I did he vanished, and then I woke up in a cold sweat and I wondered why I was reaching for him in the first place.

***

"We need to talk about my sister." I brought up the subject from where we sat in our sacred oasis in the woods. "It's been weeks and the soldiers have not lightened their patrols. I'm worried about her."

Locke laid on his back, his arms behind his head as he soaked in the afternoon sun. He lazily opened his eyes at my words, and slowly they drifted to me.

"You can't help your sister if you are captured by the empire."

I plucked a berry off a bush. "I know that. But the more time that passes...the more it feels like I'm running out of time. She needs me."

"What if she's stronger than you give her credit for?"

I paused, contemplating his words.

"Give me a little more time Cate."

There it was again. More time. More time for what?

I nodded, shoving down the frustration that welled in my chest.

I would trust Locke. If he thought it best I wait...then I would wait, as much as it killed me to do so.

"Let's spar," Locke said, getting up from the ground. "It will help release some of that frustration I can see on your face and get your mind off your sister."

He gave me a knowing smile when my eyes flicked up to meet his.

"I thought you didn't want me to fight with my feelings?"

"I'll give you a pass this time. Just get it all out." His eyes darkened and I swallowed down the lump in my throat, readying my stance and my fists.

He blocked every punch and kick as I threw my weight into fighting him. I didn't feel anything at first, almost numb, but slowly punch after punch, the feeling of anger and frustration grew, swirling into an unstoppable cyclone in my chest. I let it out until my limbs ached and my hair stuck to my face in a sweaty sticky mess.

Locke swiped my legs out from under me and I stayed on the ground, too tired to get up, staring up at the branches of trees overhead. It felt good to stare at the sunlight filtering through them, to give in to the way the sun burned my gaze.

He settled on the ground beside me, his elbow propped on the ground and his hand holding his head up. "Feel better now?"

Before I could think better of it I climbed on top of him, my legs straddling him and I pressed his arms down at his sides. My breath came fast, hot, my chest rising and falling as his eyes trailed my frame, his lips curving up slightly in anticipation.

I felt him harden beneath me and instinctively I rocked my hips, pushing deeper and harder against him, a delicious feeling building in between my legs. I did it again and a low moan left my lips.

His eyes widened and then grew hazy.

I moved to climb off him, a flood of embarrassment washing over me.

He placed his hands on my hips and stopped me, holding me in place.

"What's wrong?"

I didn't want to meet his eyes.

"I'm not going to use you."

When he didn't respond right away I met his eyes.

He cocked an eyebrow. "Who says you're using me?"

"When I was in Sageburn...there was someone I used to meet in the stables to...fool around with. I didn't really care about him. I used him. As a distraction and a way to feel something...even temporary...and then he died and I didn't...I didn't care and I should have..."

Locke held my eyes with his own. "And so now you're afraid to let yourself have a distraction. You think it means you don't care about me?"

"I'm not going to use you," I repeated. My hands went to his, where he held my hips. Four hands, two pairs of gloves.

"Then don't," he whispered. "Let me give something to you."

Before I knew it he'd flipped me over onto my back and he now straddled me, his hands holding my own above my head. One of his hands held my wrists and the other hand began to trail down my arm and then my side, coming to rest beneath the hem of my shirt. His fingers teased and pushed the shirt up and then they skirted down my hips, angling for the band of my pants.

"Is this ok?" His eyes watched me, drinking in every facet of my face. He gave a pleased grin when I nodded and then his eyes fell to my lips and his eyes clouded with the same want and need as my own.

We were playing a dangerous game.

"I want to touch you Cate." His words whispered against my face.

I prepared myself to pull back, fighting the increasing desire to give in. To touch him. To feel him. To take a chance.

"Do you want me to distract you Cate?"

He moved beside me on his knees and his hand continued to tease, skimming the delicate skin of my stomach. Even with a glove on his touch felt electric, sending a fire raging to my core.

His other hand left my wrists and trailed down my chest, his fingers slipping under my shirt and under my bra, skimming the underside of my breast...

But waiting, lingering.

"Yes," I gasped before I could stop myself.

He wanted to give me a distraction and I needed one.

He grinned and his hand covered my breast, his thumb swiping over my nipple, sending a jolt of yearning through my body, while at the same time his other gloved hand dipped beneath my pants and undergarments to press again the bundle of nerves at my center.

I bucked against him instinctively, my hips arching up as waves of pleasure soared through me. His hand pressed harder against me, his fingers finding where I was most sensitive.

I leaned into the feeling of letting go, of letting him distract me.

His hand left my breast and went around the back of my head, pulling me up and against his chest as he continued to pleasure me, his fingers making rhythmic strokes against my center. I gasped into his chest as he continued, never slowing down.

It was animalistic, primal, the way I arched my hips into his hand, the way he drove me mad with the need for release. I felt all my frustration building up beneath his palm like I was an atomic bomb about to detonate.

I could hear his heart pounding in his chest and his breath increasing in my ear and I wondered what it would be like to feel him without clothes between us, without gloves, skin to skin.

But this...

I would take this. I would take any part of him.

He slipped his fingers inside me, pushing deeper, and his thumb rubbed my delicate nerves, creating sparks of fire within me. I purred into his chest wanting to feel him deeper, harder.

I bit my lip and moaned as I felt myself growing closer, climbing higher and higher, about to jump off the precipice.

"Come for me Cate," he murmured into my ear. "I want to hear my name on your lips."

I was undone.

"Locke!" I cried out against his chest as the orgasm ripped through me, all the little pieces shattering into the universe as I rode wave after wave of intense pleasure, my fingers digging into his back as I held on for dear life.

But as I came my vision clouded and another face entered my mind.

I stared into eyes a mix between blue and green fringed by dark lashes. His golden hair combed back out of his face, falling in soft waves.

General Arias.

You loved me first Cora.

I blinked the image away, slowly coming back to myself. When my breathing slowed down and I no longer trembled, Locke slowly lowered me back to the ground, his hand cupping the back of my head.

He held my eyes. I could still feel the flush on my cheeks. My chest rose and fell slightly. I tried not to let my vision spoil the moment between us, but it lingered like black smoke, filling me with a shame I did not understand.

"I'm not sure you enjoyed that as much as you could have." His tone was teasing and knowing. It was written all over my face how much I'd enjoyed it.

"I don't know," I replied sheepishly, "I may need you to distract me again to be sure."

A devilish glint appeared in his eye. "I will happily distract you again."

***

I picked berries the rest of the afternoon while Locke sat by the small fire I built and carved a piece of wood. I loved watching the way his hands worked, how every stroke of his knife was intentional, careful. The way his eyes could be so focused yet find time to sneak glances at me. It made a blush creep up my neck at the memory of his hand on me.

I'd never wanted a man to look at me before. Never thought I could enjoy the way it made me feel. Not until Locke looked at me.

And when he touched me I wanted it to be more than a distraction. I wanted it to mean something. It made my mind drift to other things I'd like to do with him. Other desires that made my face flush and the heat flare in my core. But those kinds of desires were forbidden to me now. More impossible longings.

"I've been thinking about what you asked," Locke said quietly, snapping me out of my thoughts, his voice trailing off into the wind. "About when this war ends."

I paused, my fingers resting on the berry branch.

"I think I'd like to start a school," he said, setting aside his carving and standing. He took a step closer. I was aware of his every movement. "A school for Gifted children to learn how to defend themselves. Many of them rely too heavily on their magic. If they could learn combat skills, survival skills even - it would give them an advantage against the empire. Or anything else like the empire that might rise up to take its place."

I turned and smiled. "You want to teach children?"

He nodded. "You inspired me, Cate. Watching your progress, the way you've become stronger, more capable...it's encouraging to me. It makes me think things could be different."

I wanted to smile. To feel vindicated by his words, but they only served to remind me of my own lies. That I'd lied to him about my name. Who I was. I was far from a source of inspiration.

"You don't like it?" He asked, taking another step closer. He was beside me now. He lifted a hand gently just beneath my shoulder near the top of my back. His closeness, his touches, they were all drawing out an unmet need from deep within me. A need I'd long shoved down and ignored. A need deeper than a distraction.

I wanted to belong to someone. To share a home with someone.

"I do," I insisted, giving him a smile and meeting his deep green eyes. "I think it's a beautiful ambition."

"And when this war ends...you'll have a place there." I didn't miss how hard it was for him to say the words, to be vulnerable with me. "You would be great with the children. A good teacher. If you want it."

I felt the breath catch in my throat and I tried to swallow the lump there. "Thank you," I told him. "For asking me. For trusting me."

I shoved down the reminder that I couldn't stay. I needed to leave and find my sister. And now...by letting Locke touch me...I'd complicated things further.

He pulled something out of his pocket.

A wooden carving. It looked similar to the one I'd seen that day in Loom when I studied the wooden carvings in the stall. It was a dove.

"I made this for you," he said softly.

I tentatively took the dove from his fingers and held it in my gloved hands like precious cargo. I felt tears brimming my eyes. "It's beautiful," I said.

"You're beautiful," he countered. I looked up from the wooden carving in my hands to his face abruptly. How did he know how to make the ground fall out from beneath me so fast? Why did he say things that made my heart do silly things like think about the future? Why did he make me want to stay?

"Do you say that to every stray human you pick up?" I tried to make light of the moment, but he wouldn't let me. He didn't lessen the intensity at which he stared at me.

"Only the one that has somehow managed to make me reconsider my hatred of humans - and think about the future." He lifted a gloved hand to my face and his fingers gently ran down my cheek, over the curve of my bottom lip, and then to my chin. And then he continued down the slope of my neck and I felt myself shiver. I closed my eyes.

What if I am a Silencer? I wanted to ask. *What if you're right and I have a power I can't control? Will you still want to touch me then? Will you still want to hear your name on my lips?*

He placed both his hands on either side of my face and drew me closer so that our noses were almost touching. Too close. I placed my gloved hands on the planes of his chest where his shirt lay open, feeling the pacing of his breaths increase, feeling the beat of his heart.

His hands went to my waist and slipped underneath the fabric of my shirt, skimming the sides of my stomach. That alone was enough to send me reeling, butterfly wings fluttering against my skin, a heat building low in my core, my head spinning with want again.

But will I see another man's face again?

The snap of a twig pulled me back into reality, and the thought faded, replaced by a very real Locke still in front of me.

I looked around but saw nothing.

"What is it?" His eyes searched my own.

I felt familiar shame wash over me. "Nothing."

I watched the rise and fall of his chest, felt his searing gaze sweep from my eyes, to my lips, and then back up again, seeing the lie. "Sometimes it feels like you are here and then you disappear. Your eyes glaze over and you're gone."

I swallowed. As usual, he was too perceptive. I wanted to tell him he was wrong. I wanted to tell him that I wanted to stay right here in this moment, but something kept pulling me away, kept whispering to me. A ghost chased me. And how could I tell him that?

His hands left my waist and I swallowed down the desire for him to put them right back, to tell me he wanted me, because there was nothing in the world like being desired by Locke, but the thoughts felt hollow suddenly, as if I were trapped in my own web of denial.

***

Lex and I stood in the kitchen as I taught her how to make bread. Cooking was obviously not her forte, but she listened attentively and followed my every direction. She stared at our concoction, her eyes narrowing as we rolled the dough.

I was grateful to have something to do to get my mind off Locke and what happened in the woods earlier. I reflected on the gift he gave me, what it meant. What he'd asked me. I thought about the future. Even more, I thought about my past. The strange visions and dreams becoming stronger as time went on. Was it safe to trust myself? To trust anything I'd felt?

"There's something I've been meaning to say to you," Lex said quietly breaking me free of my reverie.

I could tell from her tone I wouldn't enjoy hearing it. I never missed the way she placated Locke when it came to me, the way she was always on the defense, withdrawn.

And she'd been even more withdrawn since the day Locke and I saved the Unicorn.

I waited for her to continue, but Locke stepped into the kitchen watching me.

He came forward and lifted his gloved hand to my face. His thumb brushed across my cheek and I felt my heart beat faster in my chest, loose and wild like the rabbits he hunted. His eyes slowly met mine, knowing in them. My mind flashed back to the moment we shared in the woods. "You had flour on your face," he said simply, and then he walked away, an unmistakable grin on his lips.

I let out the breath I held in and Lex quickly averted her all too knowing eyes from my face and focused on the bowl of dough on the counter. She was too quiet. Her shoulders too tense. Her lips in a hard line.

I kneaded the dough, very aware of the sudden shift in mood. She followed my lead and then at last she spoke.

"Whatever is going on between you and Locke won't end well."

I scoffed. "Nothing is going on."

"Anyone with eyes and ears can see differently." She turned to face me now, hands on her hips. "I know you don't know me, Cate. You have no reason to trust me. But trust me when I say you getting as far away from here and from the empire as you possibly can is in your best interest." Her eyes flashed. "And in his."

"He asked me to stay," I said quietly, no longer in the mood to bake or play house with these people I realized I truly didn't know. I hated how pathetic I sounded saying the words. And I was reminded again that I did not belong and never would.

"Locke's problem is that he wants to protect everyone. Even you. When he shouldn't." I realized how right I'd read Lex. Her original warm welcome only for show, to placate Locke. "He will have to make a choice between protecting you and thousands more. And I'm telling you now he will *not* choose you."

I took off my apron and put it on the counter. "I know what the empire did to his hometown. He told me everything."

"Everything?" Her tone was condescending, her eyes pointed. "You don't understand duty. You don't understand where his loyalties lie. It's about more than Loom."

"Then what is it about? Tell me." I crossed my arms.

"He will never choose you because of who you are."

Her words hurt me, but I'd heard it before. "Because I'm human?" I took a step back feeling my cheeks heat.

"No. Because of *who* you are."

I stared into her dark eyes feeling my stomach sink, my throat growing dry as tears welled in my eyes. I clenched my hands at my sides, Locke's words coming back to me again.

"Then I'll know for sure you can't possibly be who I think you are."

"I don't know what you mean."

"You're not a human *Cora*." My face paled when she said my name. She knew. "You're a Silencer. And Silencers are not welcome in Wisteria." She took off her apron and left the dough on the counter. "You need to leave. Tonight. If you care about him...you will." Her eyes flashed. "This is your one and only warning. If you don't leave tonight...you won't get the chance again."

***

That night I ate my dinner in complete silence avoiding everyone's eyes. But I could feel them on me. Lex's were like daggers–sharp and deadly. Xander tried to break through the tension with jokes. Locke watched me in the clinical way he always assessed me.

When I went to my room I didn't sleep. I sat up and waited for the house to quiet, for the sure sign that everyone was in their own rooms. And while I waited I sat with my thoughts, replaying words in my head over and over again.

"He will have to make a choice between protecting you and thousands more. And I'm telling you now he will not choose you."

I put on my cloak and boots, grabbed my pack that contained a small amount of food and my sketchbook, and climbed out the window. It felt like deja vu. This time I felt more prepared with a dagger at my hip and knowing how to fight. And if it came down to it...I would protect myself by any means necessary. I put my gloves in my pocket, along with the wooden dove Locke made for me, took a deep breath and headed out into the night.

I didn't make it very far out of the camp before I heard a soft whine and turned to see Cyrus behind me, his bushy tail swinging hesitantly. I crouched and pet his head gently. He leaned into my touch.

"I can't take you with me buddy," I said quietly. "Unfortunately this is goodbye. I have to go. And you need to stay with Locke."

I continued on my path, leaves crunching softly in the moonlight, but Cyrus continued to follow me. I wondered how long before he would give up and go back. And yet he didn't.

"You will find..." a familiar voice said in the darkness. "That he is more stubborn than you."

I didn't want to feel relief at the voice. Tried to stop myself from turning and looking at him, but he was like a magnet and I couldn't resist the pull.

Locke stood behind me, his form strong and steady against the woods.

"I couldn't persuade you to stay...could I?" His eyes were filled with things unsaid.

"How did you know?"

He smiled sadly. "It was *very* obvious at dinner that something was wrong. You were so in your head. And I'd be an idiot if I didn't know by now your default is to run."

"So you've got me all figured out?"

"Getting there," he smirked.

"Why would you want me to stay anyway? I'm just a useless human." I echoed his words back to him, words he'd spoken to me nearly a month earlier. But the way I said it was teasing, and dangerous, for it opened the door to something we both knew was impossible.

"Perhaps that's what I like most about you."

I raised an incredulous eyebrow. "That I'm useless?"

"You're far from useless."

He took a step closer, but suddenly we were not alone.

I could see the red glow of their eyes on all sides of us before they moved. The cursed. Their fangs shone in the light of the moon.

Last time there had only been one, this time I could see at least five, the trees looming ominously behind them. And not only that, but they weren't all men. Two of them were women.

"Cate!" Locke's voice rang out. "Don't hold back!"

I saw him ready twin daggers as the pack of them descended. They were fast, feral. Three were circling Locke and two came at me.

I ducked as one swiped at me with a sword and then side swept his legs, taking him down. The other was at my back, its dagger coming dangerously close to my shoulder as I somersaulted to the side.

I jammed my dagger up, hitting it in its chest as it came at me again. It shrieked, but kept coming, fueled by rage. I dodged the sword again, but they were relentless. I'd never fought two against one, it didn't feel like a fair fight.

Locke fared much better than me with three on him. He dodged their blows effortlessly, moving with the grace of a leopard, dodging and then striking back. Again and again.

I swiped my dagger as they came at me, but too slowly. I felt the tip of the sword slice my flank, searing and hot. I cried out and fell to the ground.

"Hold on Cate!" Locke called as the cursed advanced on me.

Cyrus was suddenly there. He arched his back and a bolt of lightning shot out of his tail and struck down one of the Cursed, but the other still had me in its clutches.

In a last ditch act of desperation to survive, I placed my bare hands on one of them...and nothing happened. I felt its hands wrap around my throat. I couldn't breathe.

Why didn't it react to my skin?

Right when I thought there was no way I could survive this, or that Locke could take on five of them by himself, the ground began to shake. A low vibrating rumble, shaking the ground beneath me.

Suddenly roots were shooting up out of the ground and latching around the legs of the Cursed. I watched as the unforgiving roots wound their way up, wrapping around their bodies tightly. I felt the hands loosen from my throat.

I turned my head and risked a glance at Locke. He kneeled, his hand pressed to the earth. He whispered something quietly under his breath, his eyes closed.

The three Cursed previously attacking him were also wrapped tightly in roots, unable to fight back.

I watched as the ground continued to rumble and began to break open in front of me in jagged cracks. I scurried back and the demons sank into the earth, one by one, their cries echoing as it claimed them. And then the ground closed back up, perfectly sealed, and an eerie silence was all that remained.

My chest was heaving, my breath fast and heavy.

I tried to get up and then felt the shooting pain in my side again and hissed as I fell back, holding myself up only by the weight of my elbows.

Cyrus was at my side first, a low whine in his throat as he licked at my hands. Locke knelt at my side a moment later, one arm on my back and the other on my elbow. "Can you stand?"

I nodded, put my gloves on, and let him help me up.

"How badly are you injured?" He asked. I tried not to read too deeply into the worry etched into his eyes. I let him lift my shirt so that he could see the wound. I only saw clinical assessment there, nothing more.

I tried to ignore how close he was to my skin as he inspected it. "And all you showed me was the vine trick? You could have said I can open up the ground and let it swallow people whole."

He allowed a smile as he tore a piece of my cloak and carefully wrapped it around my side covering where the blade cut me. "Impressed?"

"Very," I said, wincing as he tied the fabric into a secure knot. "And you didn't bother to tell me Cyrus could shoot lightning out of his tail."

"I did tell you not to underestimate him." He let his gloved hand linger at my side for a beat longer. Even with the glove between him and my skin I felt like I was on fire. "I can heal you if you let me touch you."

"So the earth swallowing isn't all you can do?" I pushed his hand away gently. "You can't touch me."

"What happens when people touch you?" He could ask the question a million times, but he already knew the answer. I could see it in his eyes. He'd been reading between the lines for a long time.

"You already know. They get hurt." I pulled my shirt down gently trying not to be preoccupied with the fact that my touch seemed ineffective against the red eyed Cursed. "And it's not a risk I'm willing to take with you."

"Is that why you keep trying to leave?"

"That and I obviously don't belong here. I almost died again. And I have to get back to my sister."

"I promised you I would keep you alive." He was too close. His words too caring. At some point we'd moved from banter disguised as loathing into something more vulnerable. And this must be why Lex told me to leave.

"And you did. Again. But you said it yourself...I'm a human. There's nothing here for me. I don't belong."

"What if...you're not?"

I blinked. "Not what?"

"Human," he said the words so casually, like he actually believed them. But they were words I needed to hear. A truth I'd been denying for far too long. "That would explain...why you hurt people when you touch them. What if you're a Silencer and your powers manifested late?"

He knows. Just admit it already.

I shook my head vehemently. "I'm not like you. I can't control it. It's not a gift. I'm not Gifted. It's more of a curse than anything."

"What if you could control it somehow?"

"That sounds too good to be true."

I took a step and hissed again, the pain in my side throbbing.

"If you won't let me heal you we'll have to go the traditional route. Healing herbs and stitches. Can you make it to Loom? It's close."

I nodded and I let him lead the way. Without him I would never know the path to make it back to Loom. He seemed to know these woods like the back of his hand, his steps careful and measured. He kept an arm wrapped around my elbow, trying to take the weight off my side as much as he could.

As we walked Lex's words came back to haunt me.

"He will have to make a choice between protecting you and thousands more. And I'm telling you now he will not choose you."

"Locke," I spoke into the darkness. "When you said that you understood...that you had others counting on you too...you were speaking of Loom weren't you?"

He nodded, but I sensed there was more. "And the reason you blind folded me every time we went back to your camp?"

A muscle twitched in his cheek. "It's very hard to hide from the empire."

"You don't want to be found," I concluded. I bit my lip.

"The empire sends soldiers into Wisteria constantly. They round us up. They steal our power. They kill us." His eyes burned. "I told you, the small towns are most at risk. There are those Empirian bases all over Wisteria. Where do you think the Cursed come from?"

"You think the empire is creating them?"

"All I know is that those that are taken away and not just killed...they are never seen again. But what we have seen are those red eyed demons. And some of them...I recognize."

I couldn't fathom the horror. Did taking power from the Gifted turn them into those creatures? Was that what he was telling me?

"How does the emperor remove powers? I don't understand."

He looked at me carefully, cautiously. "He must have some kind of weapon. Perhaps another Gifted that has that ability. The emperor wants power. And he will stop at nothing to get it. We have some theories." He paused. "I'm part of a group that is fighting back, trying to stop it."

I could at last confirm what I'd suspected all along.

"You're part of the Resistance?"

And you didn't tell me this whole time?

For a moment he looked like he regretted sharing that bit of information with me, but he nodded. "As are Lex and Xander. I asked to protect the people of Loom."

I tried to wrap my head around it and my complicated feelings. I understood why he kept it from me, but I also could have used his help to save my sister. He knew how important she was to me.

Lex's words made sense now.

She knew that Locke's first priority would be to protect his people and she didn't want me to get in the way of that. I was a distraction. Dangerous. Because he cared for me. I couldn't fault her for trying to protect us both.

"I understand," I said, laying a hand on his arm gently. "You can trust me. But I wish you would have told me sooner."

He stilled and his eyes closed for a moment before meeting mine again. "I wanted to tell you but-"

His words were cut off by the shout of a small voice echoing in the woods, ping ponging off the trees.

"Locke!" A young girl, about seven, emerged from the trees until she stood in front of us. She wore a green cloak and a pair of brown boots.

Locke went down on one knee and took the child's hands in his. Clearly she ran here, desperate to speak to him. She pushed her hood down and tried to speak, the words catching in her throat.

"Locke," she said in between breaths, "We need you. Soldiers. The village. Fire."

His eyes flashed and he stood. He turned to face me and I could read so much unsaid in his face, but we simply didn't have time.

"Cate," he said. "Stay away from the village."

"I can help," I protested, but he held a gloved finger up to my face gently and traced the line of my jaw. "Let me come with you," I pleaded.

"It's not safe for you. Go back to the camp with Laura," he indicated to the little girl beside me. "She can show you the way. Lex and Xander will help you get back to your sister."

"Why does it sound like you're saying goodbye?"

His hands cupped my face one last time and then he was gone, Cyrus hot on his trail.

13

I tightened the wrap around my wound, gritted my teeth and made Laura take me back to the village. Locke knew one thing about me; I *was* stubborn.

Flames of fire licked at the night sky and danced over the trees ahead. Shouts and screams grew louder as our steps brought us closer to the village. The little green and red buildings appeared in the distance. I saw flashes of swords, heard gunfire ringing out, saw magic zinging in the air, and could already see so many bodies on the ground, more villagers than soldiers.

My dream of a tiny village burning flooded my mind. I stood as a little girl again watching everything around me be destroyed. I could feel the heat. See the angry orange glow of fire. See soldiers killing people without mercy. I shook the memory away.

"You need to stay here," I told the little girl. "Stay safe and hide."

She nodded before I found my way into the village, sneaking my way behind one of the buildings. My only priority was helping Locke and I was fully prepared to use my power to do so. He had protected me so many times and now I was going to return the favor. I wouldn't let the empire have him or destroy his hometown again.

I could only imagine what he must be feeling having to go through this again. But this time he was here. And this time I would help him.

I took my gloves off and took a deep breath as I rounded a corner and headed into the mayhem.

A villager lay on the ground. An older woman. I watched as a soldier kicked her and then raised his sword to kill her. I reacted instinctively, thrusting my dagger into his neck.

A quick and easy kill. Adrenaline coursed through my veins as the realization of what I'd done settled in and he slumped to the ground, blood pooling around him.

"Thank you," the villager said before running off into the night.

I stared at the pool of blood before me in a daze.

I'd killed someone. Again.

I wasted no time to stop and feel sorry for myself as the cries of more villagers met my ears. Some of them were able to fend for themselves, wielding magic in the form of lightning bolts, shards of ice, and poison. It flew around me in sparks of color and light.

And then I realized the soldiers yielded magic as well. Humans, utilizing magic.

Stolen magic.

The soldiers were gaining the upper hand. They not only possessed the ability to use magic, but they were clearly trained in combat. Watching the fight rage on I could surmise that these villagers did not know how to fight.

And now Locke's desire to start a school and teach others how to fight made so much more sense to me.

It was a slaughter.

I could see Locke in the distance. Still fighting two soldiers at a time like it was nothing. I watched as he twisted and turned, exceeding their ability in every way. He dispatched one and then the other.

I didn't mean to distract him, but his eyes met mine for a moment, a flash of disbelief as he spotted me in the crowd. His shirt was torn and bloodied, his face already bruising. He tried to make his way to me, but more soldiers stepped into his path and he was forced to fight again, Cyrus by his side shooting lightning bolts out of his tail.

The screams of villagers in the square diverted my attention. They fought back against the soldiers, but they needed help. I propelled my legs forward to join the fight, but as I went to swipe my dagger a hand roughly grabbed my arm and the weapon knocked out of my grasp. With my weapons gone, all I could rely on were my hands.

The soldier shot a bolt of lightning into my body. I could feel it seizing me for a moment, but suddenly it released from my body and I sent it back in his direction. The action felt natural to me, as if I'd done it a thousand times before. My body knew exactly what to do. He went flying back, but not before I could register the shock on his face.

The other soldiers paid me more attention now. A group of villagers looked on as the two soldiers approached me, blood dripping off their swords, fresh from their kills. How could they so easily claim life? To these soldiers it wouldn't matter if I was a human or Wisterian. They would kill me just the same.

One lunged toward me, his sword falling towards my shoulder and I dodged out of the way. He angled his sword again, ready to cut me down, and in a panic I pressed my bare hands to his face.

Time slowed.

I felt the blood pumping in my chest, the power that surged through my veins.

All I could see and taste were flames and smoke.

He ceased moving. Blood poured out of his eyes, his nose, his ears, his mouth. He made a guttural sound as he fell to the ground. Dead.

The other soldier backed away slowly.

"It's *her*," one of the villagers shouted. "The Red Reaper!"

"She's killing the soldiers!"

Red Reaper.

I wanted to tell them no. They were wrong. I was not the Red Reaper.

I shook and held my hands out in front of me. They were covered in blood. Evidence of my lethal touch.

I lifted my eyes and Locke stood just behind the group of villagers, momentarily paralyzed at the sight of me. His eyes filled with sadness, disappointment, grief. He flinched like it hurt to look at me. And all hope leached from my veins as I tried to understand.

Then the realization hit me - I was exactly who he thought I was and it destroyed him. Someone dangerous. Someone who hurt others. Within all the gaps of my memories the truth settled. And the reason he wanted to hide me.

Why he asked if he could trust me.

Why he didn't want to tell me he was part of the Resistance.

Why he always made me wear a cloak in the village.

Everything suddenly made sense.

Lex's words came back to me with new meaning.

She wasn't trying to protect me. She was trying to warn me.

I'm the enemy.

Not just a Silencer. The Red Reaper.

In the distance Locke wielded his daggers as more soldiers converged on him, and the villagers scattered now; seeing me as another threat.

I stared at the blood on my hands. Numb. Questioning my reality more and more with every inhaled breath, every pulse of my heartbeat, every scream of another villager struck down.

Everything sounded far away, but not far away enough to let me be. To let me pretend it was all a bad dream.

The flames blurred in my vision although I could still feel the heat on my cheeks.

"Tell Arias we have the Red Reaper. We are bringing her back to base." Before I could register the meaning of the words, another group of soldiers surrounded me. Something hard hit me in the back of my head and I blacked out.

***

Tell Arias we have the Red Reaper.

My head bumped against the wall where I sat abruptly. I opened my eyes. My body still ached, my mind was fuzzy. My hands were bound together tightly in front of me. A carriage compartment?

I heard the sounds of the carriage moving along, the sound of a horse trotting. I tried to use my head to pull back the little curtain on the carriage window to make out my surroundings.

All I could see were the outline of trees and the inky night sky, utter darkness against the shroud of mist.

Where am I?

My gaze drifted to the figure across from me, shadows of moonlight falling across his familiar face. Locke sat on the little seat, our legs barely touching in the small space of the carriage. Relief replaced the weight on my shoulders.

He appeared unscathed. I remembered the last way he looked at me, with grief, with pain. I never wanted him to look at me like that again.

"You're ok?" I breathed. "Where are we? What happened?"

"You don't have to pretend with me anymore." He avoided my gaze. I could hear the resignation in his voice. I could see *I give up* in his eyes. "I figured out who you were a long time ago. And I didn't want to believe it at first. But all the key pieces were there. And I thought that if I just had more time-"

"I'm not pretending," I cut him off. My tone was hushed, but direct.

"Even Lex figured it out. She told me you were dangerous. But..." he hesitated. "You were nothing like they said. You were weak. I knew you were running. I wanted to trust you. To help you. I kept telling myself it couldn't be true. You *weren't* the Red Reaper." His eyes were burning and his pain started to make sense. "I suspected you were a Silencer. I suspected you had power you didn't understand. But this-" He gestured to me. *This. Me. Who I was.* "And now all I can wonder is why I kept denying it when I know you have the power to kill me. To use my own power against me." His voice broke. "I was a fool."

"I'm *not* who you think I am." My voice shook. "And I know I have the power to hurt people. But I don't want to. I don't want to hurt anyone. You're right about that. I have been denying my power because I don't understand it." I took a deep breath and met his eyes knowing I should have told him the truth sooner. "My name is Cora. Not Cate. I lived on a farm by the sea with my father until I was sixteen years old."

He shook his head. "Stop. I don't want to hear this."

I continued, "Then I was sold to the empire by my father. I went to live in a conscription lodge just as I told you. A man named Hawthorne Billings was my overseer for two years. And then I killed him trying to defend my sister. I escaped and came here. That's what I was running away from. And that is the *only* time I ever remember touching someone and killing them."

He shook his head again and his hands went to his curls as if trying to hold himself together. "But that can't be true Cora." He lifted his green eyes to meet mine and they were shining with so much sadness. "Because I saw you. I saw what you did. You have always been by the emperor's side. When the empire lays siege, when it comes to capture more of the Gifted, you come with the soldiers. You immobilize the Gifted. That's why he needs you. I always saw you from afar. Never up close. But I've been seeing you for *years.* So what you say...it's not possible."

I felt my cheeks grow hot and tears were stinging my eyes now.

He's wrong. It's impossible.

125

"When I saw you kill that soldier with your bare hands in the village...I knew it was you. I recognized you. I just didn't want to reconcile who I know you *are* with who I wanted you to *be*."

His words cut me deeper than I thought they could.

"You're lying! How dare you tell me who I am or what I've done. I wish to the gods every day that the memories I have were not real. That I didn't spend two years in that house being abused every day and working for an empire that doesn't give two fucks about me! That my father didn't sell me. And you're going to sit here and tell me that none of it ever happened? *What are you saying?*"

My voice seeped with despair and denial, but he only stared at me with pity. I could see in his eyes he'd already made up his mind about me and who I was.

He didn't know me as Cora. Or even Cate.

He knew me as the Red Reaper. A weapon for the emperor to yield.

And suddenly I questioned everything else. Every memory. Every vision. Every truth of who I thought I was. My mouth grew numb and my eyes glazed over as panic began to overtake me.

"Cora..."

"No!" I hit my bound hands into his chest now trying to push him and the truth away from me. Because it couldn't be true. My memories were real. My life was real. He had me confused with someone else. The visions and dreams that plagued me took on new meaning now and each one dug its claws deeper into me willing me to accept them as truth.

He grabbed my arms and instead of pushing me away he pulled me tight against his chest. He held his gloved hands in my hair and held me there. I could feel the pounding of his heart. Tears were streaming down my cheeks, hot and angry.

The empire already took so much from me. My freedom, my dignity, my family, my hope–and now it took something else. My sense of self. My identity.

Who the hell am I?

"I should hate you," he said quietly. "I should hate you but I can't. And all I want to do is touch you–even knowing it will kill me."

I didn't want to lose this, not yet. Being with him was the closest I'd felt to intimacy, to human touch in so long. I hungered for it. I would take whatever crumbs I could get. And beyond that–in him I found someone I wanted to trust. Someone I could see a future with. Someone I wanted to fight for. I couldn't stand the thought of him hating me, thinking me a cold blooded killer.

If I lost him what did I have? Who would love me? Who could I give the broken pieces to?

You loved me first. Blue eyes filled my vision again and I angrily shut it down in my mind. More lies?

"I want to protect you...but I can't. Do you remember what I told you...about others counting on me?" I nodded into his chest. "But there's still a part of me that wants to believe that you're not a monster. That this is real."

I pulled back at last and met his eyes, let my gaze trail over his sun kissed skin, the smattering of freckles below his eyes, and then down to his soft lips.

All I want to do is touch you.

"This is real," I told him. "I'm not who you think I am."

"I want to believe you...that you can't remember," he said sadly. "But the Resistance won't see it that way."

"Then make them see differently! Will they not listen to reason?"

"They will only see you as a threat. An obstacle. You've killed too many of our own."

The truth was evident in his eyes. I now had two enemies and not just one. The empire. And the Resistance. And I was the Red Reaper. A Silencer.

"Is that why you insisted on blindfolding me? Why you tried to hide me in the village?" He nodded. "You were trying to buy time. Until you figured out what you were going to do with me."

Our eyes met across the carriage. So close, yet so distant.

"I meant it when I said you could trust me," I told him. It felt like a plea.

His eyes gave no sign of hope. "It's not me you need to be worried about."

***

I sat in a room fit for a princess. Laying atop a king sized bed with blood red blankets, a book in hand. The room felt too big and I felt small inside of it. But I also knew it was meant to keep me docile. Placated. Caged.

There were shelves with rows and rows of books, painting sets, calligraphy, sewing kits. And on other sides of the room were various instruments, a violin, a flute, a guitar. All items meant to keep me occupied.

But the books were my favorite. They allowed me to lose myself in other worlds, in other possibilities, and I never needed to stop and think about why I was in this room.

A small knock sounded on the door and a boy came in quickly closing the door behind him. He appeared to be about fifteen, caught in that awkward transition between childhood and manhood, but I found myself drawn to his face.

I sat up in the bed and set my book down. "Who are you?" *I asked.*

He came closer, raising his finger to his lips. "I only have a few minutes."

"Do I know you?" *There was something familiar about him.*

He smiled at me, a dimple showing in his right cheek. His hair was wavy and golden, his eyes bright blue. "You know me," *he said assuredly.*

Can you keep a secret Cora? He was in my head now, his thoughts filtering into my mind as he continued to smile at me. He pulled something out of his pocket.

What is it? I thought back to him.

I also wondered if I should be concerned that a Gifted was in my room with me. Something in the back of my mind told me that the Gifted were dangerous. The emperor wanted the Gifted. I remembered now. And that's why I was so special to him.

I touched the top of my head and felt like something was missing. A part of me was not there. I was feeling too much. Thinking too much.

"Cora," *he was speaking aloud again, his voice warm and soft.* "Don't be afraid of me. You never need to be afraid of me."

"You're Gifted," *I said to him.*

"But so are you. Do you remember? Do you remember me?"

There was a pleading in his eyes.

Please remember me, he said into my mind.

I want to, I responded.

He came closer. Reached out his hand, and as he took my fingers in his own I felt a searing warmth. Affection. Tenderness. Longing.

And then the realization that I was not supposed to let anyone touch me. And that I was only supposed to touch those the emperor told me too. But I never wanted to touch anyone, for I didn't want to hurt them.

And that's why...

I reached for the top of my head again. Something was missing.

I turned my eyes back to the boy. "You touched me."

"I can always touch you. You don't hurt me. Not anymore."

He reached for my fingers again. "I have something for you. So that you never forget me. Remember Cora...I will always find you."

***

I opened my eyes. I had fallen asleep. I touched my cheeks and they were wet with fresh tears. What a beautiful confounding dream. Once again I felt like I was losing my mind and the space between reality and fiction, was lost to me. And there was no denying the familiar boy who plagued my visions. A boy who was now a man.

I will always find you.

The carriage jolted to a stop suddenly, commotion sounding outside. I could hear voices yelling. I moved the curtain with my face again but only a sea of dark trees greeted me.

I met Locke's eyes.

"They are taking us to one of the Empirian bases."

I closed my eyes. "I'm sorry Locke. I didn't mean for this to happen."

"They would have taken me anyway. I'm leverage. They said that if I went with them willingly they would spare the rest of the village." His eyes darkened. "But what they don't realize is I will never give up the location of the Resistance headquarters. They will have to kill me."

I opened my eyes and met his. "Don't say that."

It must have been minutes, but it felt like forever before the doors of the carriage opened, arms grabbing me and hauling me out to the ground. Not gently either. And then Locke behind me.

We were inside a heavily walled compound. All stone. Except for the light snow on the ground. The treetops in the distance I could see over the walls of the compound were littered with it. The cold bit into my skin.

I wanted to take my gloves off and feel the snow between my fingers. I'd never felt snow. Tasted it. It didn't snow in Sageburn. Or on the farm where I grew up.

If I grew up there at all.

I didn't know what to believe anymore after Locke's revelation about who I was.

Soldiers filled the compound. They wore red and black, the empire's colors. One of them in front climbed down from his horse and came towards us. My eyes swept up to see black boots, black cargo pants, and a red button up shirt underneath a black jacket. And I recognized him immediately.

General Arias.

When he stopped in front of me I felt a range of emotions. Something inside me knew him, recognized him. But another part of me feared him. Yet another part felt shame as I clutched my bag with my sketchbook closer. The motion did not go unnoticed.

"She reappears like an elusive ghost." His words evaporated into the air like smoke. His wavy golden hair was the only part of him that did not look meticulously put together. His deep set blue eyes held my attention. They were so sharp, so attentive in their assessment of me. Careful. Precise. Revealing nothing.

"It's her," he said, giving me the most fleeting glance possible before turning away. He spoke now to one of the soldiers. "Take them upstairs. Begin interrogating the vermin and I will handle the Reaper."

With that he walked away, his steps crunching in the snow as he headed inside the large looming compound. I stared after him. How could this possibly be the same boy from my visions? The one that gave me blue flowers, that kissed me, that spoke so tenderly to me?

He knew your name.

"You heard General Arias. Move it." One of the soldiers shoved Locke forward and then I felt another soldier pushing my back forward, indicating for me to follow suit. I stumbled forward into the snow.

"Locke-"

He turned his head to look at me and the soldier pushed him again. "Keep your mouths shut and move."

We entered the building.

All I could hear were Locke's words echoing in my mind.

"They will have to kill me."

14

Locke and I were separated.

I sat in a small room with a bed pushed up against the wall and a tiny bathroom. The floors were linoleum and cold. The only bit of color in the room was the red blankets on the bed, the empire's calling card, a blood red reminder.

I wondered if Locke also sat in a cold room. And then my mind jumped to a darker conclusion. What if he was being interrogated now. Hurt. Broken down. Until the only choice was to yield or die.

I kept replaying the way he looked at me in my mind. The grief, the disappointment, the sadness. I kept replaying our conversation over and over again in my head.

My name is Cora Corinthia and my life is not a lie.

I repeated the phrase again and again in my mind, willing it to be true. This was all a wild trick invented by the empire to control me, to get me back in Sageburn, to punish me for thinking I could escape, that I could best them. I thought of all the laws I'd broken in my time here, all the things I would be punished for. Listening to music, reading, writing, sketching. But worst of all - betraying the empire.

But another dark possibility plagued my mind. What if it were true? What if my life was a lie? What if the empire claimed me long ago and all my fighting was futile?

The door opened and when General Arias walked in I sat up straighter, my body responding to his cool, calm presence. He demanded attention. He could hold the attention of an army with his gaze alone. He could also melt me into a quivering pool if my visions were correct. And at the moment, that gaze turned on me.

Once again I was taken aback by how beautiful he was. No one should be allowed to be that attractive. It was disarming. Distracting. There was something about him that dug its hooks into me; perhaps the visions were to blame. It made me trust him even less than I already did. In the last few weeks I spent with Locke I'd lowered my defenses and walls, and now I was in a position where my survival depended on my ability to put them back up.

"Good. You seem to be in one piece." His voice was all business. "You will need to cleanse yourself and change and then we can do a mission debrief."

I narrowed my eyes. "Mission debrief?"

He paused. "The emperor will want to know all you learned while you were held captive by the Resistance. And also...how you came to be held captive. Very curious how that happened."

I opened my mouth to speak and nothing came out.

Another pause from him. He assessed me, his eyes roaming my face curiously. "Did they harm you?"

I shook my head, but his eyes trailed down to my flank where my clothing was torn.

And then a chink in his mask. "Why didn't you fight back?"

"I don't want to hurt anyone."

He blinked. "I'm afraid hurting people is in your job description, General."

General?

First Locke. Now him. What were the chances they both had me confused with someone else?

Before I could say anything else he paused, his eyes falling to my pack. He took it and left the room and I said a prayer to whatever gods might be listening that he wouldn't look too closely at my sketches.

***

I took my time bathing, careful to avoid the slice in my side. It looked more red, enflamed. It needed stitching. But I wasn't about to ask for help from these people. I tore off a piece of my old clothing and covered my side carefully.

I put on a red outfit I found laying at the end of the bed and a pair of black boots. The color made me feel sick.

There was also a pair of leather gloves.

I put them on more for my own peace of mind.

I braided my hair down my back and then did my best to get a birds eye view from the window of my surroundings.

Tall concrete fences lined the perimeter of the property. In the distance I could see birch trees for miles and miles, but nothing else except snow covering the ground.

Soldiers were gathered on the grounds of the compound, some of them sparring, some of them sitting around huddles enjoying food and drink in the light of a fire. A sea of red and black against the backdrop of the snow.

A knock sounded on the door.

He entered again and his eyes dimmed when he saw me. "That's more how I remember you."

The words faded as he indicated for me to leave the room. I wondered at their meaning. It sounded like he was talking about more than just our short introduction in the woods.

He waited for me to walk in front of him and I sensed a hesitancy in him. He didn't want to walk in front of me. The realization confused me as the words of the villager came back to haunt me.

Red Reaper.

Did he fear me?

We made our way down an empty hall, our boots echoing off the floor. The compound reminded me too much of a similar room. 4 concrete walls. A concrete throne. And the emperor standing in front of me.

And it forced me to look at the man behind me in a new light.

This was not just an ordinary soldier or fixture in the empire.

I dared to take a glance back at him and he quickly averted his eyes.

"Go left here," he told me motioning toward a doorway.

I obeyed and opened the door and when I stepped in, again it was a plain and simple room with a metal desk and two metal chairs. The room was dark aside from a few stray rays of the fading sun coming in through a slat window.

I noticed four more soldiers joined us, each looking at me with wary eyes.

"Wait outside the door. If anything happens you know what to do," he said quietly to them. "Not a word is breathed to anyone outside this compound that she is here. Understood?" I couldn't help but notice the way they exchanged knowing looks before he closed the door behind them and turned back to face me. "Sit General."

I sat in one of the metal chairs and watched him.

And he watched me back.

"Are you at liberty to discuss the details of your mission?"

"Mission?" I again couldn't help the confusion in my tone.

His lips parted and he scoffed. "Why are you being coy?"

I shook my head. "I don't understand."

His brows drew together and he took a step toward me. "Did the emperor say the details of your mission were classified?"

"I'm not on any mission," I said with more urgency this time.

"So am I to understand that you were taken captive? Why were you with the Resistance?"

"Where is Locke?" I asked instead, lifting my chin in defiance.

He ran a hand through his blonde waves slowly. To anyone else it might have meant nothing, but I saw it as evidence that my response bothered him.

"I know my father likes to play games. Likes to keep secrets. Were you on a classified mission or were you taken captive?"

I had to ask. "Your father really is the emperor?"

"Why are you being dense?" His hands tightened at his sides despite his carefully measured tone. "Do you not know who I am? Do you not remember me? What you *did* to me?"

I felt my breath quicken at his words. Who was I to him? The Red Reaper? He had called me Cora in the woods. What did he remember about me?

I met his piercing blue eyes begging to find some answer there. "Do I know you?"

He was laughing now, a low earthy chuckle. And even that coming out of his angelic face was too beautiful than it should have been. I knew him. I knew him as General Arias. But my visions said I knew him as something more. What was I to believe?

"Did my father put you up to this? Is this a test?"

He came closer now and before I knew it he pulled a dagger out of his hilt and held it up to my throat. He was so close now. I could feel his warm breath dangerously close to my face. He smelled like sandalwood. He smelled familiar. My body knew his scent, and responded to it.

This is a weird sort of torture.

"You should know that if you dare to touch me I will slice your throat open. I don't care that you are my father's pet. I will kill you if you so much as try to touch me again." His words were cold, his eyes burning and I swallowed the lump in my throat and felt the cold steel at my throat. Clearly he did not remember me the same way I did him. It made me more doubtful of my visions.

"I'm not playing his games. I am going to let him know you are here and by this time tomorrow you won't be my problem." He was talking to himself now. "I don't care why he sent you. You won't stay here."

I stared into his eyes, the dagger at my throat. This man was far different than the sad broken one I'd glimpsed in the woods when he thought no one was watching. But a primal part of me did not fear him. I remembered how he aimed the gun at me in the woods and didn't shoot. He wouldn't shoot. And I knew he wouldn't hurt me now.

He met my eyes, finally seeing me and he took a step back, removing the dagger.

"You're not afraid," he said.

I said yes with my eyes, not wanting to move and offset him.

"Why are you not afraid of me?"

I watched the rise and fall of his chest, the tension in his arms, the searching gaze of his eyes.

"You could have shot me and you didn't." The truth of the words fell between us like a thin veil. "Why didn't you?"

I'd momentarily disarmed him. He took a step back, his eyes flashed.

"You won't hurt me." I decided. "But I need to know...why others fear me. Why I can't remember..." my voice trailed off. "What year is it?" I asked.

A pause. "What?"

"Tell me the year." The realization hit me. The gaps in my memory. The way others feared me. My last memory of being with the emperor.

The father of the man standing in front of me now.

I closed my eyes and braced myself for his answer. When he told me I let out the breath I'd been holding in.

"My last memory is from three years ago...when I was eighteen."

It made sense now. Why when I saw my appearance I looked older, more mature. I was twenty one years old. Not eighteen.

He shook his head, his eyes darkening. "I don't understand."

"I don't know you...but I feel like I should," I admitted at last. I braced myself for his anger, his disbelief, but it didn't come, again he remained level headed. Calm. He simply stared at me.

"My father made me train against you. Do you not remember it?"

My silence was answer enough.

"Do you not know why they call you the Red Reaper?"

Silence again.

"You are a General in my father's empire." I could only blink at him, everything sinking in. "You are a Silencer. And a rare kind at that."

Everything in me was screaming that *no* I was not, even as the truth of it settled around me like the soft snow outside. He only confirmed what I already knew. I was a Silencer. My touch could kill.

And something was *very* wrong with my mind.

My memories.

My sense of reality.

He was pacing now. Back and forth. Back and forth.

"I need to tell my father you're here."

"Please don't make me go back." The words were out before I could stop them, but the last thing I wanted was to forget again. To do things I couldn't remember. To hurt people.

"My duty is to the Arias empire General. As is yours."

"Please," I choked out. "Before you do anything...tell me more. I can't remember anything. The last memory I have..." I trailed off, not even sure I wanted to share it with him.

136

He sat in the metal chair across from me, waiting.

"I don't remember anything I swear. And I don't want to hurt anyone."

"You said that before." His eyes were more curious now, probing again. "Why should I believe you? When I've seen with my own eyes what you can do?"

I closed my eyes and fought tears from falling down. I would not cry in front of him. I breathed deeply. "I know I can hurt people."

"You can do more than that." An unamused smile played across his lips. "You're the Red Reaper."

"I'm more than that. And you are too." His eyes widened at surprise and he lifted his chin. The emotion in my voice was not lost on him. I pictured the young boy in the garden who showed me the beauty of the flowers, the beauty of choice. Was he in there somewhere behind the cold facade of General?

"I'm my father's son. Born and bred for war - to fight in my father's empire." His eyes grew distant. He wouldn't look at me. "That's who I am."

That's not who you are to me.

I held the words back, biting my tongue, but his eyes found mine again, light sparking in them. He took a step closer to me. "It took me a long time to be able to best you. To use my own power against you."

My father made me train against you.

"I don't know what you mean."

He was standing in front of me now and I felt my breath hitch.

"In our sessions...you always initiated contact." He said the words carefully as if lost in a distant memory. "My father wanted to limit contact between us. Because every time we touch...I can see your memories."

I shook my head as he came even closer. "Don't touch me. I don't want to hurt you." And I meant it. But he didn't listen. His eyes found mine again, blue orbs sucking away my resolve. There was something in his eyes. I wanted to trust him.

Before his fingers touched my temples he said quietly, "you won't hurt me."

As his fingers found my face I braced myself for what came next.

I waited for him to begin dying, for the blood to pour from his eyes, his nose, his ears...but nothing happened.

He didn't flinch when he touched my skin. He remained untouched by the strange power within me.

And I hated that part deep within me that wanted to be touched. That longed to feel another human's skin on mine. That leaned into it and responded. It felt like sizzles of electricity awakening every part of my body. A live wire waking me up from a long lonely sleep and with it more feelings, more memories. A lightning storm that danced across my skin.

Moments passed, and I watched as his eyebrows furrowed. His lips parted, and at long last his eyes opened. When they met mine I waited. Eyes so bright–a dance between green and blue. An unspoken exchange passed between us. And I felt the breath catch in my throat as his fingers trailed down my face and met my chin.

"You really can touch me." It came out as a statement.

His lips curled slightly and a dimple showed in his cheek. Still so close to me.

I felt the absence when his hand left my face.

"I can always touch you." The words were said with sadness, not defiance or arrogance. "I'm an Empath. My gift is channeled by emotions–as is yours."

I failed at ignoring the way my skin burned to be touched again.

"What did you see?" I asked.

Instead of answering he left the room.

15

I sat in the concrete room in the metal chair for what felt like hours. I got up eventually and paced the room. Over and over again. The realization that there was someone in this world who *could* touch me reverberated in my mind. Over and over again.

But also the truth of who and what I was.

Silencer.

The truth of what had been stolen from me. My free will, my life, my family.

I finally resigned myself to sitting in the metal chair again and letting my eyes close when I heard the click of the door.

He was back.

He stood beside the door for a long time, his eyes meeting mine and curiously assessing me again. The way he held himself was so careful, so measured. I wondered if he was always on the defense. Always aware of the eyes that watched him.

Finally he took a seat in the metal chair across from me. He sat up straight, betraying no sign of emotion, but I could feel his piercing blue eyes watching me, contemplating.

Finally I broke the silence. "If you're the emperor's son...how do you have a Gift? You said you trained to be able to use your own power against me."

He didn't speak for a long moment, a haunted quality to him. "I'm half. My mother was Wisterian."

This was a revelation. The emperor who detested Wisterians had a child with one? Why?

"That is information that few know. And if it's shared it will be labeled a rumor. You already know what the emperor does to those that spread rumors."

I exhaled the breath I'd been holding. "What did you see? When you touched me?"

Instead of answering he set down a bag he brought in with him and took out my sketchbook. I swallowed the lump in my throat. Of course he'd found it and looked at it.

He flipped open a page. The gold circlet.

"Do you know what this is?" His eyes held mine steady as if reading a secret code only he could see.

I saw flashes of the emperor before me putting the circlet on my head and then everything going black. I saw myself as a young girl staring into the fountain and taking off the circlet, feeling and experiencing every sight and sound as if it were the first time. And then the emperor telling me to never take it off, that it would keep me safe.

I shook my head. "No."

"But you drew it."

I nodded.

He stared at the image for another moment before flipping the page.

The blue orchid.

"And this?" There was something in his eyes, an openness not present before.

I shook my head again not wanting to meet his eyes. "It's just a flower."

"Tell me what this is. Why did you draw it?"

I wouldn't yield. I closed my eyes and fought against the memory of the young boy handing me the flower in the garden. That was private. I didn't know if that boy even existed. The one before me now was a soldier. I absentmindedly twirled the sapphire ring on my finger.

He caught the movement, his eyes landing on the ring in question. Finally, with painstaking slowness he flipped the page and silence fell between us.

"And this one," his voice trailed off. "Why did you draw it?"

I stared at the likeness of General Arias on the page and then allowed my eyes to meet his. The hardness of his face slackened and his lips parted. I saw a bit of the boy in his expression then, a flicker of the past coming to life.

He blinked, realizing his error, and he cleared his throat. "I saw enough to know that you are telling the truth." He sighed and flipped back to the sketch of the gold circlet. "My father has a preferred method of ensuring absolute obedience."

I waited for him to continue.

"You have gaps in your memory for a reason. The moments where you were under his control...you can't remember. And he made sure to make you forget anything else that he deemed a distraction to you."

"Controlled how?"

His eyes fell to the page again, to the gold circlet. "With this on your head...you will do anything he asks you too."

I closed my eyes and saw the emperor putting the crown on my head. I remembered how everything went black when he did so. How I forgot all the in betweens and experienced gaps in my memory. What did he make me do when I wore that crown? How many people did I hurt?

"I don't know how to use my power. It's out of my control."

He shook his head. "It's not. You can learn to master it. Just as I did. But until you accept what you can do and stop fearing it...it will continue to control you and make it easier for *him* to control you. You've never been given a chance to master it."

"Why are you telling me all this?"

His lips parted and he raised his fist to his mouth in thought. "Why didn't I shoot you in the woods?" His eyes met mine, a perpetual question in them. He stood now and put his hands in the pockets of his cargo pants. "My father would say this is exactly why he didn't allow me to touch you. Maybe it's why he sent me here away from you. He always says I lean too soft. He tried to beat it out of me as a child. Harden me. He wanted me to *hate* you."

He wouldn't meet my eyes now.

"Empathy is for weak men. And you will not be weak." He said the words quietly as if reciting something his father said to him from memory. "Turn it off and obey."

I couldn't say I disagreed with the words. From the time I was sixteen I knew that empathy would not find me. Would not free me. And it made my own heart harden and feel hopeless. But hearing him say it felt wrong. I felt a strange desire welling up to comfort him.

And now I found myself questioning everything I thought I knew about my own life. My experiences. My beliefs. How could what I believed, the very core of who I was, how I had survived, be true if my memories were unreliable?

I wanted to tell him he was wrong, but instead I said, "Sometimes it's easier to obey."

He met my eyes again. They were sharp, guarded. I could see pain behind those eyes. Pain that when he wasn't careful he let slip in my presence. I could also feel it coming off him in waves. Confusion. Shame. And something else I couldn't put my finger on.

Why did you draw my portrait?

The thought was not my own.

"I don't know," I whispered.

His eyes narrowed. "You're channeling my power. You said you couldn't control it."

"I can't," I replied. "I don't know what I'm doing." I shook my head in disbelief. "Did I just...hear your thoughts?"

Are you reading my mind right now?

Yes, I said back. But this time not aloud. In my mind.

We simply stared at each other.

"So you can read minds and see memories? That's your power?"

"I told you. I'm an Empath. But my powers are more abundant than typical. I can probe minds. I can read thoughts. I can sense emotions. I can see memories, but that requires touch. It's proven advantageous for my father, especially in the use of interrogation. It's a Gift I'm able to hide well from others. But I try not to utilize it unless absolutely necessary."

He was standing in front of me again.

"Why not?"

He smiled again, it was a mix of mocking and sadness. "Because it's ridiculously exhausting to feel *everything*." He paused and met my eyes. I wondered what he'd already heard and felt from me. Suddenly I felt incredibly vulnerable.

He cleared his throat. "I know you can't remember much of anything...but were you on a mission from my father or were you taken captive? Why are you in Wisteria? And what were you doing with that *thing*?"

By *thing* he meant Locke.

"Why don't you just read my mind and find out." My eyes flashed in a dare. I was still trying to wrap my mind around the truth of who I was and what I did for the empire. How much of my life was I under his control?

"I'd rather stay out of your head. Once was enough." But there was something in his words, the way I saw the tendons in his arm flex, the twitch in his cheek...that made me wonder what exactly he saw when he touched me. "And you should really learn to better shield your mind. Your thoughts are loud."

I would work on being more guarded around him, but my main priority at the moment was Locke. "Is Locke going to be ok?" The thought plagued me. It was my fault after all that he was here. My fault that there needed to be a Resistance in the first place. That his village wasn't safe. If he had reason before to think I was a monster this would only cement the fact.

"Did he know your identity?"

I shook my head. "He didn't. Not at first. I didn't even tell him my real name." My eyes lowered and my voice trailed off, "But now he knows exactly who I am."

He ran a hand through his blonde waves again. Slowly. Deliberately. "I suppose you've done the empire a favor by finding him. He's one of the leading members of the Resistance. We've been looking for him for a long time. Now all that's left is to find their headquarters and eradicate the rest of them. They're like locusts...as soon as you kill one...another appears to take its place."

"You disgust me." I said the words knowing they were a lie, but if he was even thinking about hurting Locke, Lex, or Xander, I would stop him. "And I will never help you find them."

"There she is," he said with that cruel captivating smile, the boy I caught a glimpse of earlier vanishing. "There's a bit of the monster I remember."

"I don't remember anything about you." I bit back the lie. The proof was plain as day in my sketchbook; in my visions. I *knew* him.

He stood now. "The longer that crown is off your head, the more you will start to remember. In pieces. The memories you think you have...may not even be real."

"I don't know what you mean."

"No? No strange dreams lately?" He was close again, staring into my eyes. "You said it's easier to obey. It's also more merciful not to remember...to not wonder what's real from what's not. To not know what parts of your life you've completely imagined. That's my definition of hell. Are you sure you want to join me there?" He handed me the sketchbook open to the picture of him. "It looks like you already have."

***

He took me back to the room from before. Soldiers carefully fell behind me, quiet whispers anticipating my every move. I realized more and more that I was something to be feared. They knew me as someone else. Something else.

When we reached the room he indicated for me to enter and he followed behind me, the soldiers staying in the hallway.

I looked around the cold room again for good measure, the small bed with the red blanket, one tiny window to look outside, before meeting his eyes. "Are you going to send me back to the emperor?"

The question carried the weight of a thousand bricks. The thought of going back, of missing more years of my life that I couldn't even remember, being forced to do horrible things...was that truly more merciful than remembering? Than not knowing who I truly am?

"What other option is there?" he said, his face devoid of emotion. But once again, there was something more in his eyes. A small window into a part of him that I felt compelled to reach, but also scared me. "It will earn me great favor with my father, which is something I'm severely lacking in these days."

"The other soldiers...they know I'm here. How do you know they won't send word to your father before you and claim some of that favor you so desperately crave?"

He took a step closer and his taunting smile sent shivers down my back. And it made me wonder what he would look like when he truly smiled. Did he ever smile? A ghost of a memory of the smiling boy flitted across my mind. A boy not yet hardened by war.

"If you think for one moment that I crave the approval of my father you would be very very wrong. It's more of a hate hate relationship." His eyes scanned my face. "And my soldiers are very loyal to me, seeing as I can easily read them and be two steps ahead. Nothing gets past me."

Nothing? I questioned.

His eyes stayed trained on my own.

144

"Please don't do that."

A knock sounded on the door and he stook a step back from me as if remembering himself. "What is it?"

One of the soldiers opened the door. "General Arias...would you like General Bel to continue interrogating the Reaper? She's available now."

"No." His eyes flashed for a moment, a brief show of displeasure. Anyone else would have missed it if they weren't paying close enough attention, but I found myself unable to stop noticing his little patterns of movement, every brief change in his facial expressions from the way his cheek twitched, to the raising of his brows, or the sweep of his eyes. "The only one that interrogates her is me. My father will expect me to handle her. No one else is to touch her or speak to her unless they want a bullet in their brain. Is that understood?"

The soldier shot me a curious glance. "Yes sir."

"And no one is to speak of her presence. Is that understood?"

"Yes, General."

"Leave us."

The soldier left a moment later and once again I stood alone with General Arias, the quiet of the room settling around us. I studied him, wondering at the flash I saw in his eyes a moment ago.

"Who is General Bel?"

He cleared his throat. "Another Empath. Although her methods are more...unsavory."

"I see."

I felt a pit in my stomach at the realization that she might be the one interrogating Locke.

"What you said...about strange dreams and memories," I felt vulnerable saying the words, "how do you know what's real from what's not?"

His blue eyes settled on my face. There was a wisdom and maturity in them far beyond his years–far beyond what he should carry at his age. "I find that with time, the truth is always revealed. And the more times a truth reveals itself...the more apt I'm to believe it."

I tried to wrap my mind around the meaning of his words.

"You must be tired." The words sounded strange coming out of his mouth. "Rest," he said. "There will be more questions tomorrow. And this time I expect answers or I will need to probe your mind again."

He left the room and all I could think was that the truth that kept revealing itself over and over again–was a boy with blue eyes and golden hair–and I wondered if that boy still resided in the General or if he was gone forever–a ghost that only remained in my memory.

16

S creams rattled through the air.

Fire and smoke loomed into the night sky.

Despite the chaos happening around me I felt calm, steady.

I felt like a lion crouching in the confines of the grass, waiting for the perfect moment to strike when my prey would least suspect it. I was wound up and ready. Waiting for the command.

"Search every room in this hovel," *a voice was saying. I recognized the voice of Emperor Arias. He stood beside me looking regal as ever in black pants and his red cape draped over his shoulders. Despite the chaos happening he looked calm too, mirroring my response.* "The rats will run if you flush them out."

The emperor's enemies were my enemies.

"Keep the ones with promise. Destroy the rest." *The soldiers took off into the night, heeding his orders.* "Reaper," *he spoke to me now.* "Your services are needed."

He led me to a small group of Gifted. They appeared brave despite the fate that awaited them. One of them spat in my direction and I felt nothing.

They looked like ordinary humans, but I knew there was power flowing in their veins.

"These are undesirables," *the emperor was speaking to me again.* "You know what to do with them."

He took a step back and waited as I went to work, heeding my orders.

I started with the broad shouldered man. He tried to fight me. They always did. But the magic he used against me simply absorbed into my skin. There was defeat in his eyes as I lifted my hands to his face and touched him.

He died quickly.

The others watched helplessly, unable to flee as soldiers held them back. There was no use fighting me. They couldn't harm me. Not when I was so unrelenting in my power. In my duty.

I finished another and she fell to a heap on the ground.

The last was a boy. He was younger, perhaps twelve, but the youth meant nothing to me as I approached him. He stared back into my eyes and I lifted my hands to his face, but as I touched him something like defiance crossed his expression even as I was leeching the life from his veins and he lifted his hand to knock the crown off my head.

It fell to the ground in a clatter, as he did.

I was suddenly aware.

Death was all around me.

Fire was raging and hot.

I was taking everything in, but nothing made sense.

Where was I?

What was I doing here?

I sank to my knees, my hands reached for the dead around me. My hands went to the face of a young boy, and then realization hit me, to my own hands, covered in his blood.

I did this?

I was shaking.

Sobs racked my body.

"Go get him now," *a familiar voice hissed from behind me.*

Time ticked by slowly. I was caught up in my own self loathing. My own confusion. Holding my hands out in front of me and staring at them as if I could reverse the damage I caused.

"Make her put it back on. She will listen to you."

A moment later there was a man on his knees in front of me. He wrapped his hands in mine before I could tell him not too. There was a faint echo in my mind that no one should touch me. And yet he did it without fear.

I looked up and his blue eyes met mine. They registered the sadness in my own and I saw a hint of regret, but his eyes held mine steady and I held onto them like he was a raft and I was drawing in the ocean.

"Cora," *he said softly.* "Everything is going to be alright."

"No it's not," *I said back.* "Everything hurts."

"I know it does." *He pulled me close against his chest and held me.* "If you want to stop the pain," *he was saying now,* "Put this on your head. And everything will be alright." *He held out a gold circlet to me in his hands. And although I wanted to believe his words, I could hear in his tone that he didn't quite believe the words himself.*

I took it from his hands and stared at the intricate lines in the design.

I will always find you.

He didn't speak or even think the words, but they suddenly flooded my mind. A memory. A memory of him saying those words at a different time.

"I know you," *I said looking into his eyes again.* "Don't I?"

His eyes dimmed in confusion. "We are both Generals in the empire."

But I knew there was something more. And for some reason...he could not remember. "I will always find you," *I said out loud. I said the words to hear them on my own lips, to taste them, to savor them.*

His eyes dimmed in question. "What?"

I could feel the weight of the emperor behind me.

And felt the urge to protect the man in front of me, the way recognition began to light up his eyes as if he too were reliving a distant memory.

I placed the crown on my head.

***

I woke from the dream and felt a searing pain in my side. My wound bled. It hurt worse than before. I knew I couldn't keep denying medical help for much longer as much as I wanted to refuse them.

I sat up in bed, throwing the red blanket off me. Flashes of my dream came back to me.

"No strange dreams lately?"

General Arias' words came back to haunt me.

"You said it's easier to obey. It's also more merciful not to remember...to not wonder what's real from what's not. To not know what parts of your life you've completely imagined. That's my definition of hell. Are you sure you want to join me there?"

I highly suspected I was in hell now.

And I wondered what he knew of strange dreams and memories—what truths would be revealed. What did he remember of me?

Locke told me in the carriage nothing in my life was real. I'd always been working with the empire. That I was a known, feared, prominent figure in the empire.

It sickened me.

How long had the emperor been controlling me? For how long did I wear a crown that stole my humanity and my free will?

When did the emperor take me?

The only clues I had were the dreams of being a little girl in a far off village with Firebirds and the emperor telling me I was 'special'.

The thought that scared me the most—the one I dared not manifest—was of my sister. If I imagined her, made her up in my head, it would all be too much. Who was I fighting to get back for?

But she must be real. Xander saw her. How could he see her if she wasn't real?

What about my life on the farm?

Being sold to the empire and living in the lodge with Hawthorne?

If all of it was fake and none of it real—then who was I?

Why was I made to experience such awful memories if they weren't true?

The answer was glaring and one I'd always known. To control me. The empire wanted control above all else. And in order to control me the emperor manipulated my mind somehow—and my memories were a swirl of fact and fiction. A life that was a lie in order to control me and keep me small and afraid.

I tried to stand and felt nauseous. The motion pained me and I remembered my wound. I clutched the wall and hissed.

The door opened. General Arias entered the room. As soon as he saw me, leaning against the wall for support, he was at my side. I couldn't conceal the pained expression on my face. His hands automatically went to my stomach and my back trying to steady me and get a look at my wound.

His hands felt warm and I marveled at the sensation of his bare fingers on my skin while simultaneously feeling disgusted with myself. I swatted his hand away from my stomach. "Don't touch me!"

"Why didn't you tell me how badly you were wounded?" His eyes were filled with frustration.

"I don't have to tell you anything," I retorted, gritting my teeth through the pain.

That elicited an eye roll from him. "You're a bit uncivilized today aren't you?"

"Uncivilized?" I balked.

"Let me stitch this up immediately." He ran a hand through his hair, more haphazardly this time than when he was interrogating me. "Unless you'll allow a healer to touch you. I promise you will only hurt them if you let fear control you."

"No," I shook my head. "Why should I believe a word you say? You'd probably love to watch me kill someone."

He scoffed. "As if I haven't seen enough of that from you already. And everyday on the battlefield. I'm a General. Or have you forgotten?"

I winced as he touched my side again. Not in pain, but from the mere fact his skin touched my skin. Nothing in between. I hated the way my body responded to him, as if it knew him. As if I'd felt his touch so many times before.

"How is Locke?"

He stiffened beside me and he withdrew his hand. "Let me stitch you and I will tell you."

"Deal."

He indicated to the bed. "Lie down."

I glared at him before doing so.

I watched as he entered the bathroom and I heard rummaging around for a few seconds before he returned with a first aid kit. "This will hurt a little," he warned.

"I'm no stranger to pain," I told him, staring at the ceiling. I refused to look at his face.

"Are you a stranger to infection? Sepsis?" He didn't hide the condensation in his tone as he applied alcohol to my side. I got the feeling he was used to being right.

I tried to stifle a scream and clenched my fists at my sides. A small whimper came out. I was shaking.

"You don't have to hide your pain from me," he said more gently this time. "I can feel it. Your emotions."

My eyes whipped to his face and I finally looked at him.

He was utterly too good looking for his own good.

Carried himself with *way* too much certainty.

It would have made it easier to hate him if he was unpleasant to look at.

If he came across as insecure or unsure.

But he was neither.

And the memories I carried of how tenderly he touched me did not help, especially when his hands were at my side now, careful, gentle, as if he too could remember touching me like it was second nature.

Gods he can probably hear every thought out of your vapid mind. Shut up.

"Aren't you a little young to be a General?"

His bright blue eyes met mine, studied my face in a way that made me feel like he undressed me slowly. "Age has nothing to do with my ability."

I felt my cheeks growing hot for no reason at all. From the sheer force of his gaze, the way he spoke. It was embarrassing. I felt raw in a way no one should.

"And you should realize that I am only a few years older than you. I'm twenty three. And you are *also* a General." There was a careful lilt to the way he spoke, as if every word he said mattered, deserved to be spoken and heard. I'd never heard someone speak before with such conviction and confidence.

I'd also never *wanted* to listen to someone speak so much.

Again, I was entirely disgusted with myself.

"Ready?" He asked.

I nodded and he began stitching me up. I tried to breathe through the pain, to remember that at the end of this he was going to tell me if Locke was fine. I hoped he was.

"There. Much better." He hesitated a moment. "I'm afraid I cannot allow you much time to rest. It's crucial I interrogate you again. And it's crucial you get back to your training. Father won't tolerate you growing rusty."

He packed everything up and was about to leave when I stopped him.

"What about Locke?"

He turned slowly, his body looked so strong, like stone. Each movement from him was calculated, deliberate. He ran a hand through his hair slowly, and then rested it against the back of his neck in thought.

"You realize he's your enemy? He's an enemy of the empire. And if he refuses to cooperate with us...we will have no use for him and no choice but to kill him."

"You don't mince words do you." I tried to sit up and groaned as my feet swung over the side of the bed. He was at my side instantly.

"Cora-" he cautioned.

I looked up at him. "Glad to know my name isn't a lie too."

He softened and I saw a glimpse of the boy from my memories again. "It's not a lie. Your name is Cora Elaine Corinthia."

The way he said my name sounded like an oath. It disarmed me. I realized I did not know my middle name until he said it. It never became real until he said it. I swallowed the lump in my throat and turned the subject back to Locke.

"Let me see him."

I watched the light deflate from his eyes and his shoulders tensed. "You love him?" His eyes were searching my own as if he were trying to read a part of me I wouldn't say out loud. "Do you have feelings for him?"

I shook my head in protest, my hair falling over my shoulders. I felt if I didn't say something - anything - he would just keep throwing guesses out until I confirmed one. "I just need to know that he's ok." Would he use this against me?

His words were mocking. "No one that comes here as a prisoner is 'ok'. What fantasy land are you living in Cora?" His voice was steady, factual. "This is the *empire*. There is no *mercy*."

"This is Wisteria actually," I corrected him. I lifted my chin to look at him, right in the eyes. "You don't belong here. Even if you are a *halfling*."

His eyes blinked. "Thanks again for that cutting reminder." He cleared his throat, pretended not to care. "They really brainwashed you, didn't they? My advice...don't let anyone else hear you talking like that or it won't be me doing the interrogating."

I laughed mockingly. "Is that supposed to scare me?" And then disappointment. "I guess I should have known the stories about The Heartless Prince weren't true."

He paused, recognition waking in his eyes. "What stories?"

"It's nothing."

He grabbed my arm and I felt that strange familiarity again in his touch. "Tell me."

"Stop. Touching. Me."

He removed his hand from me.

"He's alive. But if you see him—you can't reveal your feelings for him in front of anyone else. Is that clear?"

I nodded, understanding.

"And it won't be pleasant. Our interrogation methods never are."

I nodded again.

"I will see if it can be arranged," he said. "Until then you must rest. You must do as I tell you. And please don't get your hopes up." His eyes dimmed. "There are no happy endings around here Cora. Don't expect one."

17

Another day passed left to my own devices in the cold concrete room. A soldier brought a tray with soup and bread twice a day, shoving it into a slat in the door. My side still hurt, but with the stitches it would heal nicely–thanks to General Arias.

Thoughts of him plagued my mind as much as I tried to deflect them. And more memories were resurfacing as a result of our brief touch. I caught glimpses of him growing up in the castle, from a playful youth sneaking into the kitchens to steal cake, to his first days training with a sword, to the first time he killed a man on the battlefield. It felt like violating all the private, intimate moments of his life. Once again I wondered what he'd seen when he touched me.

A knock sounded and I drew back against the wall as General Arias entered. He wore armor today, metal and gleaming, and a broadsword strapped to his back. His eyes roamed over me once, careful, curious as always, and he tilted his head indicating for me to follow him.

I left the room eagerly.

"Where are we going?"

"Training."

My hope deflated. I longed to see Locke.

"What kind of training?"

We passed rows of soldiers lining both walls of the hall with each stomp of his boots. Were all these soldiers here to guard me and make sure I didn't escape?

We went down two flights of metal stairs before we ended up outside the building, still within the walled compound. Fresh snow covered the ground and flashes of red and black filled my vision as soldiers yielded their broadswords against one another in deafening clangs and clashes. I watched as two men chuckled, one helping the other up from where he knocked him on the ground with the hilt of his sword. As I watched them it became clear these were just men. They may be Empirian soldiers, but they too belonged to the empire. They too had little choice in their destiny.

"I prefer daggers," I said as we stood awkwardly amongst a small alcove away from the soldiers. He grabbed a small luminescent orb from his pocket, it gleamed red. My eyes followed the orb, there was something familiar about it.

"No weapons for you today. Your wound is still healing." He stood about ten feet away from me. "I am going to use magic against you and I want you to channel it back at me. Think you can do that?"

I nodded, thinking of the time I absorbed the lightning magic and shot it back at the soldier in Loom. If I did it once, I would do it again.

He adjusted his stance and unsheathed the broadsword from his back. He placed the gleaming red orb back in his pocket and gripped the sword, his blue eyes as piercing as the blade. "Are you ready Cora?"

I didn't know what to expect. I clenched my gloved hands at my sides and waited.

A moment later he extended his hand and a red blade of fire came soaring at me. I panicked and dodged out of the way, the flame narrowly missing me and shooting past until it dissolved into the compound wall. I landed in a heap in the snow.

A moment later his black boots appeared in front of my face. I peered up at him. "Get up," he said. "You have no reason to fear magic."

I didn't miss the snickering and stares from the rest of the soldiers in the compound. They must think me pathetic. I also didn't miss the way Arias's spine stiffened as his gaze leveled them all like a laser. An uncomfortable silence fell around the compound.

He extended a hand to me. I took it and he lifted me from the snow, pulling me to his chest so that I had no choice but to stare into his turquoise eyes. He blinked once, his dark lashes fanning against his face. My chest rose and fell as small tufts of steam filtered the icy breaths between us, mingling and meeting like smoke.

"They should fear you and respect you," he said softly. "Show them that they should not laugh at you again."

I nodded and once again he created distance between us. He stood ten feet away again, his sword ready. I readied my stance and took a deep breath.

They should fear you.

Those words would normally send me into a spiral. I didn't want to be the Red Reaper. I didn't want to be feared. But when Arias said them it awakened a deep knowing inside me. Power did not have to be corrupt. Fear I could mold and bend to something of my own making. If others feared me, I stood a chance of surviving.

Once again he flung his hand forward and fire surged toward me. This time I did not hide. I did not fight it. I absorbed the flame, feeling it sear my skin for a moment, but it wasn't painful, it sizzled and danced with recognition as my body threw the power back toward him. He held out the blade of his broadsword in front of him and it dissolved again, falling into the snow.

A smile lit my lips, broad and beaming. Was it wrong to find pride in my ability? To enjoy the feel of power brewing in my skin?

Arias smiled too, dimples showing in his snow bitten cheeks, and I felt my reservations melt beneath me, carried away on the soft waves of a river. I clung to them desperately, feeling as if I would drown without them to keep me afloat.

"Would you like to try again?"

We volleyed back and forth, the motion of absorbing the magic and throwing it back at him becoming as simple as spelling my name. It felt natural, effortless, like I was born to wield magic.

By late afternoon when the chill became hard to bear, the soldiers lit up the fire pits and began roasting the nights meal. I expected Arias to take me back to the cold concrete room where I would be served my usual soup and bread, but instead he said, "Join me for dinner tonight. There is something I'd like to show you. Unless you'd prefer soup."

"Fine," I said simply as his eyebrows rose in response. "I suppose something other than soup would be nice."

Another part of me felt guilt at my willingness to dine with him. What about Locke? What was he eating? Where were they keeping him?

We settled around a fire and Arias sent away the rest of the soldiers sitting there with a sweep of his eyes and a tilt of his head. Suddenly only the two of us sat amongst the fire. We dined on roast chicken and root vegetables. My belly felt full and warm for the first time in days.

"Tell me how the red orb works," I spoke at last watching as the flames of the fire danced in his eyes. He leaned forward, holding his hands out to the fire. "You're not an Elemental. So how can you wield fire magic?"

"It's absorbed magic from the Gifted. It allows humans to utilize magic. And those like me, can utilize powers not naturally gifted to them." he paused. "It's a small sliver of what you can naturally do. You can absorb and use the powers of anyone you wish."

I thought of all the soldiers I saw in Loom using magic. "How do you absorb magic from the Gifted?"

His eyes dimmed. "That's a conversation for another time. Come," he said standing, "there's someone else who needs their dinner. I promised her some roast chicken."

"Her?"

He lifted a brow. "Jealous Cora?"

I rolled my eyes and followed him to the back of the compound, the light on the horizon a dim shade of orange and red now covered by misty falling snow. We passed the stables lined with horses who whinnied at us as we walked past. Arias stopped to greet his horse. I watched the soothing way his hand caressed her snout.

"Surely the chicken is not for the horse?"

He gave me a crooked smile as he led me to the back wall of the compound. He unlocked a door and swung it open. This room looked like a greenhouse with glass panes surrounding the tops and sides. Dense greenery and trees surrounded the room, along with what looked like a man made water source.

I realized it was an enclosure for some kind of animal.

He locked the door behind us.

A piercing screech rang out and my eyes found nearly camouflaged by the greenery of the trees, a bird that stood eight feet tall, huge talon like claws for feet, two stretched out wings, and gleaming golden eyes rimmed with green. As she stepped out of the trees her feathers glimmered and turned a fiery red with streaks of gold running through. She opened her sharp beak and screeched again.

"You have a firebird?" I couldn't hide the shock coloring my voice. I recalled my conversation with Locke about Lumeria and Firebirds. How rare they were. How selective they were about who they served. How was it possible?

"Did you take her against her will?" My eyes flashed now.

Arias's eyes dimmed at my accusation as she came closer, each taloned step digging into the dirt. "She chose me. She's my familiar."

He held out the chicken to her and she plucked it from him in one quick movement. She turned her head up as she swallowed the food eagerly. She let out a small screech in what sounded like approval. "I promised, didn't I?"

I looked between the two of them. "She speaks to you?"

"Yes. Perhaps if you get on her good side she will deign to speak to you too."

I thought of Arthur, the Unicorn who spoke into my mind. Not even Cyrus ever spoke to me.

"You created this enclosure for her?"

"It's not like her home I imagine. None of the trees or greenery we have here is native to Lumeria, but it was the best I could do for her. I'm the only one who has access or authority to come back here. She doesn't like the soldiers. Or anyone else for that matter."

"What's her name?"

She stared at me with her gleaming eyes. I noticed her talons digging into the dirt as if my presence irritated her. She turned her head and plucked at a feather and I watched as it lazily fell to the ground.

"Faelin." He said the syllables of her name lovingly, his eyes lighting up when he looked at her. He stroked his hand down the column of her throat and she let out a chortle in response.

"I don't think she likes me," I said, catching her eye again. I worried if Arias weren't here she would try and pluck out my eyeballs.

"She says she knows you Cora...from before. She also senses more than we can fathom. Firebirds are incredibly intuitive creatures, especially with those they serve. She is protective of me. She senses you...unnerve me."

I considered his word choice. "I unnerve you?" I raised an eyebrow. "How did you acquire a Firebird?"

"She's been mine since I was a young boy. I can't remember her not being with me." His eyebrows furrowed like dark caterpillars and I got the feeling his words carried more weight than the two of us wanted to admit - he wasn't talking only about Faelin. The words settled between us, more secrets, more history I couldn't even begin to decipher.

We said goodbye to Faelin and he locked the enclosure behind us.

"Doesn't she hate being locked in there?"

We walked past the stables and once again he stopped to see his horse giving her a soft pat as he bid her goodnight.

"She is free to fly and go where she chooses. There is an opening in the ceiling of her enclosure. She chooses to stay close to me. I don't believe in keeping creatures captive."

"But you will keep me captive?" I lifted my chin and he paused in the approaching light of the moon. A muscle in his cheek twitched and his throat bobbed.

He didn't answer my question, but asked his own. "Why did you draw that portrait of me?"

His seafoam eyes held mine and I felt a familiar tug and pull of recognition. I felt a chill as the wind whipped across our faces, but my stomach felt warm and my body gravitated toward him like he was my only compass.

"What did you see when you touched me?"

He smiled coyly and raised his eyebrows. "Would you like me to touch you again?"

I took a step back. "Of course not. You shouldn't have touched me to begin with."

His eyes softened and his smile faded. "Perhaps you're right."

He took me back to the cold concrete room without another word.

18

A few days passed before Arias took me to see Locke. My meals of soup and bread resumed. He didn't come back to train with me again. When he finally appeared to take me from the room again, he didn't speak. Obediently, I followed him down the hall.

He walked beside me this time, not behind. I was hyper aware of the closeness of his body, the way the sleeves of his arm brushed across mine as we walked, the *click clop* of his boots on the linoleum floor, the way his eyes scanned the perimeter meticulously as if he would throw himself in front of me at a moments notice. I noticed as we walked that he carried a gun on him, covered by his jacket.

As we walked soldiers lined the walls of the hall standing at attention. They stood so still, giving a brief nod as we passed. I noticed most of them held a firearm.

We entered a room with a metal door and when General Arias turned on a switch, light flooded the room revealing Locke on the cement floor. He was sitting against the wall, his legs stretched out in front of him. His hands were shackled, chains connected to the wall so he could barely move.

The room was freezing. He had no food or water. His clothes were dirty.

Without thinking I ran to him and knelt on the ground. I reached out a hand to touch him and then drew it back, realizing I wasn't wearing my gloves. I'd forgotten them in the room.

"Locke," I said quietly. "It's me. Cora."

His head hung low. Slowly, every so slowly he lifted it, brown curls falling lazily over his green eyes as they met mine. He looked relieved to see me...and then sad. A bruise bloomed on his cheek and one under his eye. He turned his eyes away.

"Are you hurt?"

He shook his head. "I'm fine. Cora..." he said at last, "you didn't tell them anything did you?"

"Of course not. I would never."

"Good," he gave me a weak smile. "I told you...they will have to kill me."

"Stop saying that," I hissed at him. "Have you had any food? Water? Have you been in here the whole time-"

"While this is all very touching I'm afraid we are going to have to continue our interrogation," General Arias's voice rang out. "Cora if you would come with me." He seemed eager to get me out of the room.

I turned to look at him. He stood by the door still. He watched us with a calculated coldness but I could see behind it. I could see the curiosity of our exchange. I could see him trying to decipher the gravity of mine and Locke's relationship. Could see him realizing that if he hurt Locke I would be the one to break.

"He needs food and water. And a bed." My eyes burned as Locke leaned his head against the wall and closed his eyes, clearly exhausted. In pain. He lied to me when he said he was fine. What had they done to him? "Why was I given a bed but not him?"

Arias shook his head. "I honestly don't know what to make of this display. You are not my enemy Cora. You are part of the empire. Why would we not give you a bed? But he..." he took a step closer and nodded in Locke's direction. "Is not your friend. He is our prisoner. A prisoner of war. Why would we treat him differently?"

"What have they done to him?" I turned my attention back to Locke. He appeared asleep, his breathing shallow and pained. "Why is he unable to use magic and save himself?"

Again that calculated coldness. "I told you General Bel's methods of interrogation are nothing like mine. She can not only feel the emotions of others...but she can inflict an excruciating amount of pain to get what she needs."

My eyes were blinking so fast now. My cheeks hot. I clenched my fists. How much pain had Locke already endured? And how long would they wait before simply killing him?

"Why are you so angry Cora-"

"Get out of my head!"

He seemed taken aback by my outburst. His careful facade broke for a moment as if it pained him that I would yell at him. That my anger was directed at him. He took a moment to compose himself, shifting his shoulders, breathing in and out slowly.

"He can't use magic right now Cora. He can't save himself. He's too weak and tired." He cleared his throat. "The best course of action for both of you is to simply tell us what we need to know. This can all be over. It's up to you."

Arias must have someone on base that could neutralize Locke's magic—it was the only explanation. Why else would he not be able to use his powers?

"So you're saying...if I tell you what you want to know...you will stop hurting him? Will you let him go?"

A muscle in his jaw ticked. "I'm afraid letting him go is not an option *dove.*"

I tried to ignore the nickname. It made something in my chest stir to life, a remembrance of all the times he'd called me 'dove' before. It was not the first time. Once again my body knew.

"And what exactly do you want to know?" I asked quietly.

The decision was not yet made of what I would reveal, if anything. I knew Locke asked me not too. I knew some things were far too important to reveal information that could sway the war. But Locke meant more to me than everything else. I realized that now. Believed that. Saving him mattered more than anything.

I thought back to his words, our conversation—how a home was the place where you no longer needed to pretend. I didn't want to pretend anymore with Locke. I didn't want to hide.

"You would reveal the location of his camp? And the location of the Resistance Headquarters? To save him?" His eyebrows arched in question. There was something else in his expression, a kind of yearning, an amount of disbelief, a bit of judgment.

"Cora," Locke spoke up again warily, his green eyes finding mine, pleading. "Don't tell him anything at all. Don't worry about me. I'll be fine."

I felt the breath leave my lungs. I didn't know the answers to either of those questions. And if that was what they wanted from me—I would be no help.

Arias looked at me like he could read me like a book. He could see that *yes* I would save Locke. He could see that *no* I did not know the answers to those questions.

"You don't know...do you?" He asked, his eyes dimming. His voice showed disappointment, especially as the door swung open and in walked a woman wearing a red bodysuit.

She was tall and exuded an uncanny amount of confidence bordering on arrogance. She also wore a silver chest plate, the familiar red insignia on it of a Firebird. She wore black boots and black gloves. Gloves which she now gleefully took off as she swept the room and her cool green eyes landed on me.

Her eyes were like parasites digging deep into the recesses of my mind. I could feel her probing along my skin trying to get a read on me. It felt different than when Arias read my thoughts, more invasive, cold.

Her hair long and red, cascaded down her back in waves. She was eerily beautiful and from what Arias said, equally capable of inflicting damage if she was who I thought.

"She might not know," she said, her voice deeper and huskier than I thought it would be. The kind of voice that didn't need to be loud to demand attention. When she spoke, you listened. And she seemed to know this. "But *he* does. And perhaps we should test if the feelings in this relationship go both ways." Her eyes met Arias's and he showed nothing. Zero emotion.

Clearly this bitch can sense your emotions.

"Welcome back Reaper," she said to me now with a nod. "Are you willing to make yourself useful? Does this vermin care for you?"

I felt myself go still at her words. She addressed me as if she knew me.

"She seems to have lost a great deal of her memories, Bel. You wouldn't know anything about that would you?" A definite tone of accusation saturated his voice.

This must be General Bel.

"My work is not always your business, Arias," she replied back curtly. "I answer to your father. Not you. Perhaps you should ask him. I assume he knows she's *here*."

Silence.

"Perhaps we should enlighten him then."

He didn't say anything but I could see the slight flinch of his fists at his sides, the way his body tensed, but just as quickly as I caught it he recovered with a haughty smile and said, "I plan to inform him within the week. I will handle it. I know you are so busy with your *work*."

Her green eyes flashed in response.

"Back to my question. Reaper." Her words were clipped. Business like. "Does this vermin care for you?"

I shook my head. "I...I...I don't know."

"There's only one way to find out." She handed her gloves to Arias. "You might want to leave for this General."

His eyes narrowed. "I will stay."

"Suit yourself then." She rolled her eyes and took a step toward me. And then another. And another. She was cornering me back into a chair against the wall. Like I was her prey.

I could make out Locke's eyes watching me from where he sat on the floor, his body heavy and weak. And then Arias, still standing in the same place, as still as a statue, his face a blank slate...

Except his eyes.

His eyes said everything.

He was afraid.

He knew what was coming and he was afraid for me.

I didn't want his pity.

I looked at General Bel, met her green serpent-like eyes and glared. "Do your best."

She smiled back at me. "I always do."

She reached out her hand, her fingers creeping closer to my skin like a spider. And then she touched me.

Searing hot pain that began to spread from where she touched my shoulder down my arm and into my fingertips. The pain spread like a fire over my collarbone, my neck, and then down my other arm, my torso, and into my legs.

It was everywhere, all at once. A wave of pinpricks, each laced with fire.

I fought against her instinctively and then she placed both hands on my shoulders, holding me down, and shooting more fire into my veins.

I arched my back and screamed.

It couldn't be helped. I'd never felt anything like it, like I was burning from the inside out.

She paused, drawing her hands away from me.

"Are you ready to talk now?"

I fought to catch my breath.

Locke shook his head at me. He wanted my silence. I wondered how long it would take for him to break. If he would ever break.

"What about you vermin?" She peered over her shoulder at Locke.

Silence.

Arias moved a step closer, a miniscule detail, but I noticed. His chest rose and fell slightly as he watched me. He was waiting to see what I would do. What Locke would do.

Fight back Cora. He spoke into my mind.

Before I could respond her hands were on me again. This time on my face. She was in my head. I could feel her probing like a spider weaving a web in my mind. She was filtering through trying to take what she could. And then she was pressing deeper, that same familiar fire burning in my head this time.

I tried to send the magic back her way, to fight back, but she was strong and the pain too great.

I unleashed an agonizing scream.

Was this what it felt like when I touched someone?

Did they feel this same kind of excruciating pain?

The kind of pain that made you black out.

And then die.

My vision spotted, purple and black dots swimming before my eyes.

My arms went limp at my sides, heavy and weak.

"STOP!"

I knew who said the words, but I didn't want to admit it.

But they were enough for Bel to take a pause and draw back her hands.

My vision began to return, but barely.

My body felt heavy, exhausted.

I tried to speak and couldn't.

"I think that's more than enough for today," Arias was saying as he came closer. "She can't even speak. There will be more time after she's recovered her wits."

Bel nodded. "I got something small, but helpful. The camp is close to Loom. I will continue with this one." She turned her attention to Locke.

I felt my eyes close again, wondering how she'd managed to pry the information from my mind, and didn't protest when I felt arms sweep me up and off the chair. I knew Arias carried me. I knew it and I hated the relief I felt that I was being taken out of this room, away from General Bel's fiery touch. And I hated that I left Locke behind. That he would suffer again and again.

As much as I hated it I rested my head against his chest and let myself drift further into sleep, unable to fight it.

19

I awoke in a new room on a large king sized bed with black blankets and multiple pillows. The floors were wooden and shiny, impeccably clean, not the cold linoleum of the rest of the compound. A wooden desk and chair sat to the left of the room and large bookcases spanned the walls behind it. There was a balcony with a private view of the compound.

It took me a moment to remember what happened. I saw flashes of General Bel's hands and shuddered at the memory of her in my head setting my skin ablaze. I saw Locke shaking his head at me, urging me not to say anything that would hurt the Resistance. And then I saw the calculated, deliberate show of coldness from Arias...but that deep down he hated what Bel was doing to me. He didn't like it. It bothered him. I could see. And he couldn't hide it from me.

And Arias shouted *STOP*. I heard it. I didn't imagine it.

But why was it him? And not Locke?

The door opened and Arias entered a moment later. He wore a white button up shirt and a black jacket over it. His blonde hair was a mess of waves and there was a subtle difference to his usually bright blue eyes. Dark circles. Like he didn't sleep well.

He carried a tray with a plate of food on it. He closed the door and set the tray on the desk, an awkward silence falling between us.

He ran his hand through his blonde hair slowly and looked at me. There was a carefulness to his eyes, like he thought I was glass that might break under his gaze.

"I would ask how you are feeling...but I already know."

"Then don't. Save us the pleasantries." I knew I shouldn't sound so bitter. I should be kind. But I was afraid I didn't have any kindness left. Especially after seeing Locke yesterday and knowing he was suffering.

"Cora-" he leaned against the desk and moved to approach me.

"Don't." I held up a hand. "Say my name. Please."

He blinked in confusion. "Is there something else you'd prefer I call you?"

"Don't talk to me at all. I would prefer that. You're not my friend. You are my enemy Arias. Locke is my friend. You and I are not on the same team. I don't know how to make that more apparent. I will not dine with you or train with you again. You might think you know who I am or what I've done. But I'm no longer that person. I will no longer allow your father to control me."

He smiled, actually smiled, and it felt like a rare gift for me alone.

It disarmed me.

I saw the boy from my memories, from my past.

"You and I *are* friends. You just don't remember." His voice was so soft. So knowing. I didn't want to believe him. "Or maybe you do and you just don't want to admit it to yourself. I'm only just beginning to remember myself. When I touched you the first time...so many memories came flooding back." His voice filled with sadness. "I'd forgotten you. Forgotten everything."

I could feel my breath coming faster now. What he was saying–could it be true? Were my visions of him true?

"What do you mean?"

He smiled again and it wasn't fair how it lit up his eyes, making him appear more innocent. Like he was someone who I could call a friend. I felt my cheeks heat and I grasped for the anger I felt a moment ago.

"We grew up together. I can only take the pieces I have and try to assemble them with your own...but," he paused and stared at me strangely and I realized it was because my hands were clutching the sheets tightly, I was barely breathing, my mind scrambling to put the pieces together. What he was saying. "We've been a part of each other's lives for a very long time. Since we were children. My father raised you. He used you. But you grew up in the Castle. With *me*."

It's those last words. *With me.* The way he said them.

I felt my anger boiling over.

Denial thrashed in my veins.

"I don't know what you're talking about," I replied coldly. "I grew up on a farm by the sea with my father and my sister. And then I lived in a conscription lodge and worked for the empire." I said the words even though I knew they were a lie now. I knew it and I was so willing to stay in denial and not let him have the satisfaction of being right, of knowing me better than I knew myself, that I would rather lie.

The other side of the coin–the one I was refusing to acknowledge–was that my very reason, my entire purpose, for getting back to Sageburn was evaporating before my eyes. But my sister was real. She had to be. I refused to believe otherwise.

My memories, my past life, my relationship with my sister... They all still felt *so real* to me.

How was I just supposed to accept it and move on?

"Cora-" he paused, remembering my request for him not to say my name. He waited for my anger, but it was currently replaced by the numbness of my feelings. "General?" He tried again. His eyes were tugging at me as if trying to draw water up from a well, to elicit some kind of response from me. "I know it's hard. I know you have so many questions. So do I. I'm going through the exact same thing-"

"No you're not." My words were so sharp I practically whipped him with them. "You have no idea what it's like to be me. What I'm going through. You've never had your freedom of choice taken from you. Wondered who you are. What is real and what is not."

"You're wrong," he said, drawing in a breath and coming slightly closer to the bed. "I have. I do. These last few days have been...*difficult*." He swallowed and once again I noticed the bags under his eyes. "You don't know how torn I am. How much it *hurt* to watch what Bel did to you. How *betrayed* I feel by my own father. By my country. By my own *mind*."

He stepped even closer until his body was standing next to the bed, one of his hands trailing along the blankets. "I meant it literally when I said it was hell to not know what is fact from fiction." His hand was coming closer. "To not trust your own mind. Your memories. And I'm so...so sorry that you have to join me there."

I looked up at him. My eyes were watering, angry tears threatening to fall. I couldn't help it. I could feel it all daring to slip up and over. My heart shattered in my chest. How could I possibly contain all this information? All this feeling? All these lies? Truths?

He met my eyes with equal feeling. He was no longer trying to hide behind the cold, calculated facade of General. Something had changed. Whether it was his memories coming back, along with mine, I couldn't be sure. Or perhaps it was seeing Bel torture me.

But he softened before me, much like that day in the woods.

And it terrified me.

This connection between us terrified me.

The way I wanted to reach for him. The way his eyes could melt my anger away in one fell swoop. The way he could touch me.

"You don't even have to tell me...how you're feeling. I can touch you...and I will know everything. I can understand." His hand on the blanket came closer, slowly, uncertainty causing him to shudder.

He was asking me for permission.

He wouldn't touch me without permission.

I felt the heaviness in my chest.

His eyes were on me. So, so blue.

"Cora...I'm asking you to trust me."

Trust me.

Everyone wanted my trust. Everyone expected it so easily, so willingly. I would not be that girl anymore, despite the raging thought, the ever present possibility, that if I were to trust anyone, it should be the boy before me. My body knew him. My mind knew him.

I looked up at him again and knew I needed to break him.

I had too.

Because whatever was happening between us felt right.

And it scared the shit out of me.

And I owed Locke so much more.

"I'd rather die than let you touch me again."

He drew his hand back, slowly at first, and then the realization seemed to hit him at once of what I'd said. What I meant. My words were venom. His face fell. I could see the hurt in his eyes, the way they darkened. Disappointment. Then shame.

I could feel it all.

But his shame was not for trying...it was because he didn't want to stop trying. He wanted to keep trying to break through to me. He wasn't even touching me and yet I could feel his emotions pouring into me as if had loosened his hold on his power.

As if I'd undone him in an instant.

The hurt was like a fifty pound weight dragging him down into the depths of a cruel, unforgiving ocean.

He blinked and then realizing his error reigned it back in and the feelings subsided. I felt my breath steady again and I stared at the bed, not wanting to meet his eyes.

Because now I was the one who felt ashamed.

How could I feel love for Locke yet feel on fire for the man in front of me?

Did I even know what love was?

Maybe it was better this way.

I was meant to be alone. Without a family. Without a story. Without a purpose.

"You're not," he said gently despite the fact that I'd just rejected him. "You're not alone. You had a family. You have a story...one that you can still write however you choose. And you are *not* without a purpose. Not to me."

"So if you can't touch me you're just going to invade my mind...is that it?"

His eyes dimmed. "I apologize. I don't intend to. I told you before...you're not very good at guarding your mind...or your emotions. You let everything slip through. With practice," he added, "You could better guard your mind. I could teach you."

"First you kidnap me. Now you want to teach me? Which is it Arias? You run hot and then cold. I don't know what to think of you." I sighed. "I told you...I'm not going to let your father control me anymore. I'm not going to go willingly. Or cooperate. Especially...if you plan on killing Locke. I will never forgive you."

"You don't owe him anything," he said quietly. "I know you feel some kind of undying loyalty to him...and that makes you think you can't feel anything for me...but you're wrong. You don't owe anyone. The empire. The Resistance. Him. Me. What do you want?"

I blinked at him. "What?"

"What do you want? Do you even know?"

"I want Locke." I said point blankly. "I want to be with him. Help him. I will join the Resistance."

"So you're happy being a pawn for a different army. That's what you're telling me?"

I scowled.

"It will never happen. Not the way you think." He stood straighter and the shield slowly returned to his form. He held himself a little more carefully, his eyes were guarded. "You are of more value to them dead. They will never take the time to properly train you. They fear you. They will never understand you."

"Locke will. He does."

Arias laughed, but this time it didn't light up his face. It revealed the cruel, hardened lines of who he was brought up to be. Who he was trained to be.

"Do you forget that I've been in his head? I can read his mind? Sense his emotions? I know exactly-" He stopped himself and my eyes widened. He brought a fist to his mouth and steadied himself. He turned away from me.

"You know what?"

"Nothing...Cora. Forget I said anything."

"What were you going to say?"

He turned to face me again and his eyes flashed. "Nothing that you won't discover yourself in time. I suppose I can't protect you from everything."

My mouth parted angrily. "I hate you."

The words hung between us. The feeling danced between us.

"Do you?" He countered. He tilted his head and his eyes took in the flush of my face, the rise and fall of my chest, and I knew in that instant he saw right through me. "Then you will hate me even more when I tell you that Locke escaped days ago." He barely waited for the words to register before he was talking again. "You've been asleep for two days. While you were asleep Resistance members snuck into the compound. They must have had help from inside...which means not only do I have to deal with my prisoner escaping...but I have a traitor in my midst that I need to find. And all of this," he continued exasperated. "Has made it impossible *not* to notify my father of what has occurred. And he will be here in a few days."

I felt numb, like I was caught in a bad dream.

"You're lying."

"I wish I weren't dove. But I don't lie. Goes against my moral compass."

"You don't have one."

"Think what you want of me." His blue eyes were icy, filled with a fire that set my skin on edge. "Hate me. But I'm telling you the truth. Locke escaped. And yes...he left you behind. I'm sorry. The only thing I can account for that is you are currently in my own quarters. Quarters that no one has access to except for me. And security must have been too tight for them to get to you."

"Why am I in your quarters?" I demanded to know.

"I brought you here. After..." he trailed off and clenched his fists. "After General Bel interrogated you. I thought it would be safer." His voice faltered. "And if I didn't...you would probably be gone right now."

I couldn't grasp the level of raw fear that flashed in his eyes. Just for a moment. But I saw it and felt it all the same. Was he that terrified of losing me to the Resistance?

I tried to wrap my mind around his words. Locke was gone. And he left me behind. Was he coming back for me? Surely he must be. Now that he knew the truth of who I was...Cora...not the Red Reaper...surely he would come back for me.

Wouldn't he?

I was replaying the few but intimate moments we shared.

The way he'd always showed up to save me.

The way he looked at me.

The words he spoke to me.

There was something there.

It wasn't all in my head.

"Cora..."

"He's really gone?" I looked up at him and he sighed. He clearly did not want to have this conversation. Maybe he wouldn't have even told me if I didn't provoke him by telling him I hated him.

"Yes. He's really gone. I wouldn't lie to you. Ever."

I shuddered and stifled the sobs threatening to rip from my lungs. I would not fall apart in front of Arias. Never.

I held my hand over my mouth and focused on breathing. In and out. In and out.

"Cora...what do you want me to do?"

"I want you to leave. Get out. Please. I want to be alone right now."

A moment later he turned to leave the room. I watched as he took each step, slowly, carefully, giving me time to change my mind. To call him back. To ask for something else besides his absence.

And I almost did.

THE HEARTLESS PRINCE

The door closed and I collapsed onto the bed.

And fell apart, unable to trust my own mind or my own desires.

20

"Hurry Cora!" *I am running down a lavishly carpeted large hallway. The carpets are blood red and gold. Intricate sconces and paintings of people I don't recognize align the walls as I run.*

My eyes are captured by one that is of a starry night, mountains and a lake glimmering. I want to stop and stare at it, but there's no time. I feel a tug.

I'm holding someone's hand. He looks to be about seventeen. He's leading me down the hallway and someone is chasing us and yelling at us to "stop".

We giggle and keep running, turning a corner. He looks back at me to grin and it's the most beautiful thing I've ever seen in the world.

"Through here," he says and he's hit a switch and opened up a secret passage in the wall. I go through quickly and then he follows me in, sure to hit the switch again. We wait a moment and hear whoever was chasing us pass by the hallway. We've evaded them for now.

He's holding my hands in the dark and staring into my eyes. So, so blue. I feel like I can't breathe. Like I've forgotten my name. And then I realize I have until he said it to me.

"Let's keep going," he says and he pulls me down the dark passageway until we end up outside. We are in a familiar place. I remember it somehow. It's a courtyard with a garden. Flowers are blooming everywhere. There's a fountain in the middle of the garden.

"Your favorite place right?"

I nod. It feels right.

"Why are we here?" *I look more closely at the boy. He's tall and well muscled for his age like he spends all his free time training. And then I remember that he does. He trains against me. Despite the soldier's uniform he wears, he's so young.*

He has a dashing smile, dimples, and the brightest blue eyes. The wildest waves of golden hair. And he's smiling at me like I'm the greatest thing he's ever seen.

"I know you, don't I?"

He nods. "We have this conversation all the time. It's because they make you wear that crown. It makes you do things you don't want to do. And they make you forget. They make you forget me."

I reach up to touch my head tentatively. There's nothing there.

"I hid it," *he says proudly.* "I'm going to figure out how to destroy it so he can't hurt you anymore. The older you get...the more he makes you wear it...it seems the harder it is for him to keep your memories from coming back. I hope...someday that you will always remember me. Us."

"Us?"

The moon is lighting up the garden with white light. I feel like the flowers are watching and listening to our conversation intently.

"We're friends Cora. We always have been. We're...more than friends really. You see that sapphire ring on your finger? I gave it to you. Do you remember?"

I shake my head, but I'm staring at my hand and sure enough there is a sapphire ring on it. It's beautiful and glowing in the moonlight.

"It's a promise," *he says.* "To always protect you. To always find you even when you can't find yourself. When you forget...I will help you remember. And someday...I will help free you so you never have to forget again."

I realize there are tears on my cheeks. His words are so beautiful, so feeling. For being so young, he feels so much. How can I mean so much to someone like him?

"Please don't wonder things like that," *he says as if he can read my thoughts.* "If anyone is unworthy...it's me of you. I could never deserve you. And every time you forget I worry that you will come back to hate me. That you won't feel the same way about me as I do you."

"And how do you feel about me?" *I ask even though I already know.*

Our love is not only due to the naivety of youth.

He's loved me his entire life.

My entire life.

He loves me with a fierceness few ever know or experience.

"Can I show you?" He asks softly.

I nod.

His hands come up to cup my face and then trace their way to the back of my neck and he holds me tenderly as his lips meet my own. And suddenly I'm overtaken by the sheer feeling of his lips on mine. The softness. And then the utter desire for more. A hunger I've never known.

My hands go to the back of his neck too and it's like we are unable to get close enough. Unable to feel enough. To say enough with our lips.

I want to say I love you.

I want to say I'm yours.

I want to say never forget me and I will never forget you.

I've never felt such unbridled fire.

He presses our bodies closer and I gasp.

Suddenly I remember more about him. I see flashes of us as children. I see him touching me, unafraid, because his father wants him too. I see him sneaking to my room to see me and tell me stories. I see him holding a beautiful blue orchid out to me in the light of this very garden.

"Jordan?" I say remembering his name. "Jordan."

He is beaming at me. "I love the way you say my name." He brings me close to him again, wrapping his arms around me. "I'm going to keep you for as long as I can. We will run and hide until they find us."

I look at him and smile. There is nothing more I want than to run away with him and never be found.

Unless he is the one finding me.

***

I knew Arias's first name.

I didn't want to admit it to myself.

But the more memories that came back, the more dreams that plagued me...I couldn't deny that I did know him.

He was most definitely the golden haired, blue eyed youth from my memories. I'd known it from the first time I saw him. I'd known when I sketched my portrait of him. I'd known the first time he touched my skin.

He was telling the truth when he said we were friends, that we grew up together.

I was still putting all the pieces together, and with every piece came more questions, questions I was determined to find the answers too away from the clutches of the empire.

I wondered what he knew, what he could remember.

But again...I wasn't about to open that door with him and go down that road. I wouldn't extend an invitation to let him in.

Because despite what he said and felt now...

Despite the fact he might have been made to forget too...

He was still the emperor's son.

My enemy.

And I loved Locke.

And I would join the Resistance.

***

"I have to visit one of the other bases today." Arias stood beside the bed staring at me. I didn't want to look at him. Didn't want to see him standing in his usual black cargo pants, button up shirt, and jacket, looking meticulously put together–unnecessarily good looking–while I laid in his bed looking like a broken mess of a human being.

I could feel his pity now. Feel his eyes looking at me like he gazed upon a sad pathetic creature.

"It's not pity," he said, revealing nothing in his eyes as he set yet another tray of food on the desk for me. "And you need to eat something. Get out of bed. I didn't realize your sole function for living revolved around a man."

I wanted to hit him. Throw something at him. But I laid there instead.

He put on a pair of leather gloves. He snapped them on his wrist and the sound jolted me like a gunshot. "You are coming with me. It's not safe for you to be here alone and now that my father knows you're here there's no point in trying to hide you."

I didn't want to go anywhere with him. I would have said that, protested, but I thought about getting out of the compound. I thought about the possibility that I could get away. It was tempting.

His blue eyes were unamused on my face. If he knew what I was thinking–he didn't say. He simply threw a handful of clothes at me. "You'll be needing these. It's cold."

He went outside the room and I quickly changed into the warmer clothing and then put on a jacket, boots, and gloves. I let my gaze linger on my appearance in the bathroom mirror for a moment. My skin looked paler than normal, my eyes were void, tired, dark circles underneath them from all the crying and feeling sorry for myself.

My eyes trailed down to the sapphire ring still on my middle finger. I realized I never knew its origins, but I always wore it. I'd even thought about selling it–not realizing the promise behind it.

But now I looked at it differently and wondered...

I sighed deeply and tried to shake it from my mind.

I would use today to look for an opportunity to escape.

When I went outside the room Arias waited for me. He looked me over once, gave an approving nod and then indicated for me to follow him downstairs and out of the compound.

I tried to ignore the soldiers as we walked, the way their gazes lingered on me.

Once outside he paused in front of his horse. A saddle rested on her brown back. A few other soldiers were already mounted and ready to accompany us. He turned to me and I stiffened in anticipation. We stood as two rivals, or two equals I couldn't be sure. Opposite sides of the same coin. Two people that had been used, controlled, and left to pick up the pieces. How many times were we made to forget? How many times did we remember one another?

My words came back to haunt me.

I hate you.

I didn't hate him.

Maybe I hated the way he made me feel.

Maybe I hated the way those feelings made me question everything I experienced with Locke.

I stared at him, nearly impossible not to do with him standing directly in front of me. I studied the planes of his face, the depth of his blue eyes. His face hardened into stone, all business when his eyes met my own. He'd clearly learned his lesson the first time he tried to let me in and he wouldn't make the same mistake again.

"Let's go, General," he said, helping me mount his horse. He lifted me with ease, careful of my still healing flank. And then climbed on behind me.

"Move out!" He spoke to his men and they headed out the compound, us following behind.

I heard the unmistakable shriek of Faelin as she soared in the air above us and disappeared into the trees, a dash of red and gold. She would be coming along too.

A thick mist surrounded us, making it hard to see. Snow fell heavily, coating the ground and the tops of the trees. Tiny bits clung to my face as it fell. Despite the cold I could feel the warmth of Arias' body against my own. I shuddered and felt his arms tighten around me.

I tried to ignore it, the way my back felt pressing into the planes of his chest, the strength of his thighs against me and the horse. How I could feel his breath behind me, hear him breathing slow and steady. Smell the sandalwood scent that I knew was his. Feel his arms brushing mine from where he held the reins.

There was simply no way to avoid touching him, feeling him.

His silence made it worse.

You hate me, remember. His voice spoke into my mind.

I felt my cheeks grow hot and I tightened my hold on the saddle.

I could hear his unspoken words, what he wanted to say, but wouldn't. If I hated him so much, why was it so hard for me to be this close to him? Why was I fixated on his subtle movements, the way he breathed, the way he smelled. Why did my body react to him? Why did I feel like I was losing my damn mind?

Did he face the same battle?

As the horse trotted I focused on counting the trees that passed, heavy with snow. Anything I could to take my mind off him, his presence. I felt like I drowned in it.

Before long we stopped at the entrance to a small base camp. He climbed off his horse and then helped me down, tying her to a small stable outside the base. He gave me one fleeting glance before addressing his soldiers.

"Stay with her," he told them, eyeing them all individually. "If anything happens to her, I *will* shoot you." He paused for a moment as if second guessing leaving me out here with them. "This will be quick. Minutes," he added perhaps more for my benefit as he gave me a warning glance. "Don't do anything stupid."

I watched him walk into the camp and disappear. I felt a strange sense of relief but also like a part of me was missing when he walked away.

The three soldiers stood beside me awkwardly, silent. They were afraid to even look at me, I realized. They were afraid of me.

The fog became thicker and the air colder. I wrapped my arms around my middle and bounced on the points of my toes, trying to keep warm as the snow continued to fall faster.

Arias eventually emerged from the fog and I breathed a sigh of relief. "We're staying until the snow lets up." He indicated for the soldiers to make their way into camp. He took my arm and led me inside the base. "We'll leave in the morning when the fog clears."

"We're staying the night? Here?" I couldn't hide the way my voice rose an octave. "Where will I sleep?"

His blue eyes shifted to mine, zero apology in them. "With me."

I swallowed the lump in my throat. My cheeks were ice cold and numb.

He led me into a larger tent at the back of the base. Inside I saw a cot with thick blankets, a small dining table with steaming cups of tea atop it, a small vase with blue flowers, and in the middle of the tent orange flames dancing within a fire pit. The warmth flooded my face at once, relieving the chill of the snow.

"You don't like the cold?" Arias removed his gloves and warmed his hands by the fire as he watched me.

"It doesn't snow in Sageburn. I'm simply not used to it." I thought for a moment. What if that was another false memory? "It *doesn't* snow in Sageburn...right?"

"It does not." He paused and secured the flaps of the tent closed. My eyes lingered on the broadness of his shoulders, dipping down to his waist, and then his legs. I tore my eyes away, my cheeks flushing. "It's hard not to doubt your own mind isn't it? I told you it was hell."

My eyes trailed back to the flower vase on the table. Orchids.

Arias turned away from the entrance of the tent and his eyes followed my own.

"Shall I tell you something true?"

I nodded.

He took a step toward the table, his hand taking one of the flowers out delicately by the stem. He held it out to me, a question in the gesture. "You like orchids."

I stiffened. "How do you know?"

"The same way you do." His eyes said more than his words did. They caressed my face in a way that felt entirely too intimate, like he'd memorize every inch of my skin if he could.

He remembered?

I took it hesitantly, twirling the flower in my fingers, a kaleidoscope of blues bleeding into one another. "I only like the blue ones."

His eyes danced, blue as ocean waves. "Your turn. Tell me something true?"

I stared into his face feeling my self control begin to unravel. How could he undo me with one look? As he stared into my eyes I knew a truth, a truth about him so raw it terrified me.

You love me.

I didn't know if he heard it, if he felt it. Not at first.

I didn't even want him to confirm it.

But then he smiled and a dimple showed in his cheek.

When he smiled like that it made my knees grow weak. And then I felt guilt.

"What's wrong?"

I wouldn't meet his eyes. "This is all very confusing. I'm still trying to sort out my memories. To come to terms with…everything."

"I know." He removed his jacket and threw it on the cot so that he only wore a red button up shirt now, the top button precariously opened, catching my gaze. "And I don't want you to feel guilty. You never need to feel guilty for wanting me."

I balked at him, setting the flower down on the table. "I don't *want* you."

"You do and you hate it."

I could only gape at him, whatever retort I planned to use eluding my mind. The way his eyes held mine unnerved me. He saw through every lie, felt every flicker of emotion in my heart. It wasn't fair how he could read me like a book.

"I told you I hate *you*."

"Love can often feel like hate when it consumes you wholly."

"Stop." I took a step back from him, my first instinct to run out of the tent and into the snow. To disappear into the fog like a ghost. To disappear from this conversation, from the way his eyes drank me in and broke down my every defense.

"Why?"

"Because I don't love you. I don't even like you. I'm in love with Locke."

His eyes flashed in defiance. "How do you know?"

"How do I know what?"

"That you love him?"

I hesitated. "Because I trust him. He...he saved me. He took me in and he fed me and he taught me how to fight. And he loves me too." My voice sputtered and as a coy smile met his lips I doubted myself even more.

"He fed you?" I felt my cheeks heat at the implication of his words. "You should raise your standards dove."

"Oh and you know so much about love?" Why did I have to give him more ammunition to work with? Why did I play these games with him?

"Yes." The words were an oath as he spoke them. I felt the heat emanating from his body. In the heat of our argument he'd taken a step closer and his face was entirely too close to mine. I stared into his eyes feeling myself swept downstream, getting lost in a game that I wanted no part in. My eyes fell to his lips and I remembered the way they felt on my own in my visions. Soft, yet demanding. I hated myself for it. How I wanted to kiss him now.

Primal need filled his eyes as I realized my mistake. He knew exactly what I wanted and although I spun on my heel to exit the tent, his hand grabbed my own and he yanked me back against his chest.

A small whimper left my throat as his hands tangled in my hair, unraveling my braid, and he kissed me. He kissed me with wild abandon, every touch and taste not deep enough or fast enough, and every thought evaporated from my mind. Every protest. Every reason why we shouldn't do this.

My hands wrapped around his back and I pulled him closer.

Gods I wanted this. I wanted him.

He unzipped my coat and his hands were now under my shirt, riding up over my hips and then to my back, pulling me nearer. I could barely breathe as sensations overtook me, each one more heightened than the last. My body felt on fire from his touch, my lips blazing from his lips.

My hands went to the planes of his chest, hastily unbuttoning his shirt, unable to see enough of him quick enough. A tattoo of a red firebird met my fingertips at the left side of his chest, whorls of red and black ink. My hands trailed down the contours of his abs and then wrapped around his back, pulling him closer.

"Tell me again that you hate me and don't want me," he whispered. Before I could respond his mouth trailed kisses down my chin and then down my throat. I could only hold on, my knees weakening with every kiss.

I'd craved to be touched like this for so long. To feel my skin on fire. To know that I wasn't alone in this world with my strange power. That I could touch someone and it wouldn't harm them. With Arias there were no reservations, no need to hold back, to fear touch. Every part of my body awakened and reacted to his touch, craving it.

"Do you remember me now?" His mouth claimed mine again, possessively as if he'd done it a million times before. And my body responded easily, effortlessly, knowing this intimate dance with him. "You know me Cora. You loved me first."

My head spun. If I remembered him, did that mean forgetting Locke? Forgetting everything we felt? Everything we said we wanted? How could I be so fickle? Did I even know what love was? Was I so starved for touch I would take it anywhere I could get it?

I pushed him away, my breathing coming hard and fast, my body still hot and aching. I fought the desire to pull him right back to me, but I couldn't. Not like this. Not when there was so much unresolved between Locke and I. "This isn't what I want."

He stiffened, his breathing steadying. I tore my gaze away from where he stood, his shirt still unbuttoned and enticing.

I thought we were telling the truth from now on.

"I am."

He shook his head and his eyes dimmed. "When you're ready to stop living in denial, let me know." And with that he walked out of the tent leaving me alone with the sting of betrayal. But did I betray him, Locke, or my own heart?

***

I tossed and turned on the cot, barely able to sleep, the cold seeping in, not only from the snow, but from the chill brought on by the silence between Arias and I. We didn't speak about our kiss again. He covered me with an extra blanket at one point in the night, the only time he dared get close to me again.

Morning came and the soldiers prepared the horses to leave, the fog clearing out and the snow falling lighter than the day before. I caught sight of a berry bush at the edge of the woods. I went toward it and the soldiers watched me carefully. I knew they were waiting for me to try and run off or test their patience.

I picked the last few remaining berries and hovered near the bush pretending to be enamored with it, if only so I wouldn't have to look Arias in the eye and prolong the moment he'd put me on the horse and settle in behind me.

I couldn't get our kiss out of my mind. I kept feeling his fingers on my skin, the ghost of a memory. I wondered how far we'd ever gone together–if my body knew him completely. I could taste his lips on my own and instinctively I raised a finger to my mouth.

It was wrong. I was confused.

I thought of Locke. His wise green eyes, the way the curls of his hair fell lazily into his eyes. How we shared the same desires to overthrow the empire and lead a peaceful life. I wanted him to be the one I kissed. I wanted him to set my skin on fire.

The sound of thundering hooves interrupted my thoughts and I turned to see a group of at least ten soldiers on their horses, a clash of red and black. My eyes were drawn to the front of the line to the man that haunted my dreams, now painfully brought to life before me.

Emperor Arias.

He was every bit as regal and handsome as in my strange dreams. He stood up straight on his horse, a red cape falling from his shoulders. His blonde hair meticulously combed back and his blue eyes piercing. He looked every bit like his son if only Arias were older with specks of gray in his hair and held more hardened lines in his face. A sign of cruelty and age.

When his eyes fell on me they settled with what only could be described as relief. He had been looking for me and now he'd found me. His prize. His possession. My stomach twisted in response.

He smiled, his lips curling at an unnerving angle. "Cora my dear," he said, his voice low and vibrant like music. "I've been searching for you for the better part of a month."

He climbed off his horse. I could once again see his son in his calculated, deliberate movements. He carried himself with such self awareness, aware of every eye on him, of our exchange.

"I'm so happy to see you safe and sound." His hand came up to run a finger over the side of my face and brush back my hair. He wore gloves. Already prepared. "I trust you have been treated well?"

My mouth wouldn't speak. I simply stared back at him, into his piercing eyes that held mine like a leash. Who was this man to me? A captor? A type of father? An emperor?

The emperor's eyes flashed to something behind me. Not something. *Someone.* I could feel him as soon as he was behind me, feel the tendrils of his power reaching out to me to connect.

Cora, he spoke into my mind.

I pushed him away with as much mental strength as I could muster. I couldn't handle him in my head right now and didn't trust his intentions where his father was involved. He might want to kiss me, it didn't mean he wanted to save me.

"General Arias," the emperor spoke his eyes dimming. There was displeasure in his eyes. "My son." He rubbed it in like salt in a wound. He looked at his son and saw failure in his handling of me. He saw a potential problem.

And as he looked between the two of us, not separate, but together, it registered for me that it was another sign, another arrow pointing in the direction, that yes, the truths that revealed themselves time and time again were the most likely to be true.

The emperor did not like seeing me and his son together.

He did not trust us.

"I wasn't expecting you for a few more days father," Arias said, coming up to stand beside me. I tried to ignore his closeness, once again tried to push away the emotions he was trying to share with me. He was afraid, cycling through every scenario possible in his head to get out of this. He was trying to keep us connected, tethered.

I can't focus with you in my head, I sent his way.

If he puts that crown back on your head you need a lifeline to come back to yourself, he replied. *I won't let you lose yourself again.*

I stilled beside him, letting the weight of his words land. He didn't want his father to have me. To control me. He wanted to help me.

Emperor Arias stared between the two of us suspiciously. "Let's take this reunion somewhere more private. Out of the open." He looked around as if he felt the eyes of the forest on him. It made him nervous being here, even with his troop of soldiers. I could see it in his eyes.

General Arias helped me onto his horse and then climbed on behind me. I wondered at first if he would chance taking off, if we could be fast enough to get away from the soldiers and horses. But I knew there were far too many, we wouldn't make it far.

What are we going to do?

I'm thinking, he responded.

My eyes swept the quiet forest, so still, blanketed in a veil of snow. I thought I caught the flash of movement in the trees, but then it was gone.

Why does he want me so badly? Why can't he get another Silencer?

Arias waited a moment before sharing his thoughts with me. *You are the only Silencer he has that can absorb the powers of the Gifted and use them. And he needs you to extract their powers.*

Extract?

My hands tightened and he placed his own on mine, trying to calm me.

Understanding sank deep in my core. I recalled the gleaming red orb Arias used to utilize fire magic. Was it my fault that the Cursed existed? My fault that humans could use magic? What had I done?

We stopped at what looked like an abandoned base. Low wooden walls surrounded a small metal building. Yesterday's snow began to melt, dripping off the metal roof. There were no soldiers in sight except for the ones that accompanied the emperor.

A crow sat perched on a tree branch that angled in front of the building. It watched us with piercing black eyes.

The emperor climbed off his horse. "Cora. Jordan." He angled his head at us along with two soldiers and indicated for us to follow him into the building. I couldn't avoid Arias's gaze as he helped me off the horse. I saw his blue eyes in a different way now. The boy from my memories. A truth that revealed itself more than once. His name. Who he was. It all came crashing down on me and now—would it mean nothing? Would he give me over to his father to be controlled again by the empire?

"Everyone else patrol out here," the emperor said as we went inside. "The Resistance has eyes and ears everywhere."

Nothing but darkness and a metallic smell met us as we walked inside. The soldiers opened the slats of the windows and daylight flooded in, painting shadows on the floors and walls, highlighting the dark stains on the cement floor that could only be blood. I wondered how many had come here and gone to their grave? Perhaps it was a place where the Gifted were tortured, their powers taken from them, and then they were killed. How many were I responsible for?

"Let's do this quickly and quietly." The emperor's words reverberated in the metal building. He stood in front of us, his hands reaching into his flowing cape to remove something from the pocket.

A small, gold circlet. Unassuming and ordinary to anyone else.

But it held the power to undo everything that made me. To control me.

He held it in between his hands and then his eyes met mine. His soldiers looked on expectantly from either side of him, but they were too at ease. They expected me to comply. Perhaps in the past I did. They expected me to be weak.

"Who would like to do the honor?" Emperor Arias's eyes flitted between me and Jordan. "Haven't you had enough of this cruel, dangerous world Cora? Wouldn't you like to go back home?"

Home.

The word felt like a dagger in my heart.

I shook my head. "A cage is not a home."

His eyebrows lifted in surprise. "A cage? Quite the opposite my dear. I've offered you nothing but protection your entire life. I've given you everything you could possibly want. A purpose."

"You took me away from my real home and my family." I held his eyes, feeling my chest tighten with the words. "You took away my freedom. My choice. I've been nothing but a puppet for you to play with. That is not protection. That is not purpose." My fists clenched at my sides. My body shook.

His eyes found Jordan's now and they darkened. "Who has been poisoning her against us? That rebel group of rats?"

189

Jordan gave nothing away in his face or his voice. "She remembers everything father."

"Then we must make her forget. It is a mercy. After she puts on the crown we will take her back to General Bel and then we will go home to Sageburn. Where she belongs."

Jordan's silence filled the room. The emperor did not miss it.

"Have you too forgotten where you belong son? What your purpose is?"

Jordan's eyes flashed. "I have not."

"Good." The emperor held out the crown to him. "Then put this back where it belongs." His words were a challenge. Show me where your loyalty truly lies.

Turn it off and obey. I could remember the words Jordan shared with me, the words his father spoke to him.

I watched as he took the crown from his father and held it in his hands. And then he turned so that he was facing me. He met my eyes. I held my breath.

He held my future in his hands. His choice would determine if I went back to my cage or flew free. My touch would not harm him. I wasn't a skilled enough fighter to best him. But I would not go down without a fight. I would die trying before I let the empire have me again.

I stared into his blue eyes and knew he could see my truth.

I was done being a caged bird.

I saw resolve in his eyes. A flash of the boy that haunted my memories.

And I knew he would burn the world for me.

In an instant he turned, the gun from his jacket pocket in his hands, and he shot once, shot twice, the soldiers at the emperor's sides dropped dead one after the other. And now he was holding the gun out at the emperor. His father.

He didn't hesitate. His eyes narrowed.

Emperor Arias' hands went up protectively, but he smiled coyly. "Jordan. *Really*?" His words were demeaning as if he were talking to a child having a tantrum. "Have you thought any of this through? You know killing me won't bring peace or end this war. There's always someone waiting to take up the mantle."

"It might not," Jordan replied. A wave of blonde hair fell into his face, but he was too focused, too intent to move it out of the way. "But she will be free of you."

The emperor laughed. It was full and hearty, cruel in its resonance. "Is *that* what this is about? Your stupid obsession with that girl?" His eyes blazed as they fixed on his son.

"It is your fault she escaped in the first place. You are weak Jordan. You may be a strong soldier, the best I have. But your heart is weak. And that will be your downfall."

I remembered waking up outside of Sageburn, not knowing how I got there. The pieces were falling into place. Jordan helped me escape. And then the emperor made him forget me again.

"Then I will fall willingly."

The emperor was not laughing now. "Then do it. Kill me. Kill your own father and watch your country fall into chaos. Watch those rats rise up and attack us while we are vulnerable. Do it all for a girl that will betray you the second you turn your back."

Jordan cocked his gun.

He was going to do it. He would kill his father. Kill the emperor.

But he didn't get the chance.

Because a second later the world exploded.

21

I lay on the ground, my face pressed to the cold cement. I heard ringing in my ears and my vision spotted. I could see and hear movement around me, faint and far away.

Slowly things came into focus. Everything became louder.

The metal building was destroyed, still standing, but a wall of it gone as if blasted by a bomb. I could faintly remember the sound of an explosion. Fire.

I could make out some of the voices around me. See faces I recognized. But they were not friendly. I realized this was an attack and Jordan and I were in danger.

The Resistance.

What remained of the emperor's soldiers were now dead around us, perhaps killed by the explosion.

I recognized Lex standing a distance away, talking to a few people I did not know. They all wore black leathers and held weapons at their sides. Other Resistance members.

Jordan.

My eyes found him on his knees. His hands were bound behind him with not rope, but what looked like ice, sharp and cold, digging into the flesh of his wrists.

He met my eyes as I sat up from my spot on the ground. His face was bruised and bloody, already beginning to sport a black eye. His gun had been removed from him and was held by one of the Resistance members who stood beside him, carefully monitoring his movements.

"The Reaper's up," someone said, but my gaze wandered again to what lay a few feet in the distance, bent at a crude angle, a broadsword directly through his back.

The emperor's piercing eyes were open, now void and empty. His mouth open in a state of perpetual shock. Blood pooled beneath him and into the ground, a warning of what was to come.

He's dead.

The emperor may be dead, but it would not bring peace. I could see it now.

"Let's kill them now and be done with it." A burly man with brown facial hair stood beside Jordan. He held Jordan's gun, but he also played with a shard of ice that appeared in his hand.

Elemental. Ice.

And judging from the earlier explosion there was a fire elemental among them as well.

"We wait for my father." Lex spoke now. She looked much smaller next to the burly man but her energy matched his. She was clearly in charge of this little operation. "He wants to meet her." Her eyes fell on mine at last and I searched for some sign of help in them.

She stopped in front of me and grabbed my arm to hoist me up off the ground. Her almond eyes were dark and swept mine curiously. "Don't forget that I can kick your ass. Don't try anything funny."

"Who is your father?" I asked her.

"You're about to find out. Perhaps you'll be a little more forthcoming about who you are now *Cora*." Her eyes went to Jordan. "I knew there was something going on between you two that day in the woods. You almost had me fooled."

"He's not your enemy and neither am I."

She punched me in the face.

I fell back to the ground and tasted blood in my mouth.

"Lex. Stop."

My head shot up. I recognized his voice and relief flooded my veins.

Locke.

I could make out his profile a few feet away from me. His deep green eyes, the curls around his head, the slope of his nose, the cupid's bow of his lips, the broadness of his shoulders.

I couldn't stop the hope that filled me.

Lex glared at him before walking back to the other Resistance members.

Locke approached me slowly, apprehensively.

Then he was there, kneeling in front of me.

"I was happy when I heard you escaped," I told him. The words seemed to pain him, his mouth tensed in response. If they felt like heaping coals on his head it wasn't my intent. Seeing him here, now, reminded me of everything possible once this war ended. Of what we could be.

But reality settled in around me.

"Lex got me out. With the help of a few others."

Of course. Her ability to turn invisible was crucial in escaping a compound full of soldiers and security.

"Were you going to come back for me?" I looked around us, at the destruction, the dead soldiers, the emperor's corpse ten feet away from me, at Jordan on his knees, at the Resistance members that regarded me hatefully. "Or just wait for the opportunity to capture me."

A new cage.

"Lex's father is almost here. You once said that perhaps the Resistance would listen to reason." He paused. "I hope they will. And that you will too."

When he looked at me I could feel that fragile gentle thing between us again. The whisperings of hope, a future, what could be. Was it all gone now? Was it wrong of me to hope?

He will never choose you. Lex's words came back to haunt me. I could see now they were true, but that didn't stop my heart from beating for him.

Locke left me, joining Lex and the others. One of them, a girl with fiery red hair, glared at me as she bounced a fireball in between her palms, a stark reminder that I did not belong. That they would not accept me. But still I clung to hope. To reason. I would join the Resistance if they would let me. I would fight for a different future free from the empire's rule. And I still clung to hope that my sister existed.

I returned my attention to Jordan, still on his knees. His eyes were on mine watching me silently. Now that his father was dead would he be next in line to rule? Did that make him emperor?

My heart stilled. That would give the Resistance all the more reason to kill him. Because of *who* he was, not because of what was in his heart. I knew *exactly* what that was like.

"So this is the infamous Red Reaper." I looked up at the tall man that stood before me. His hair was graying and his eyes were a bright green. He wore black with a gold colored jacket. He looked down on me with a mix of contempt and curiosity. "Just a girl."

I peered up at him.

He held out his hand to me and I took it, again feeling that spark of hope. *He will listen to reason*, I told myself. *They will see that I am not a monster.*

"Do you always wear gloves?" He looked at my hands curiously.

I nodded. "I don't touch anyone. I don't want to hurt anyone."

His eyes dimmed. "So I've been told." Lex, Locke, and the others stood behind him, watching our exchange curiously, guns and daggers ready. It was then that I noticed Xander was missing. "Is it true you were under the empire's control? That your actions were not your own?"

I nodded again, still trying to get a read on this man who now stood directly in front of me. I could see Lex reflected in his mannerisms, the inquisitiveness of his eyes.

"As you may have already guessed I am West Lacey. The leader of the Resistance. And that makes us enemies. You've been playing on the wrong side of this war Cora."

"Then let me join you." I could feel everyone watching us, see the light that sparked in Locke's eyes, but it was Jordan's flinch from where he was still on the ground that drew my attention. He didn't like this. Or he sensed something I didn't.

What is it? I asked him, careful not to let my gaze obviously fall on him. I needed West to trust me. I needed to tread carefully.

It won't work out the way you think it will Cora. But it will be your choice.

"You have killed so many of our people. Resistance members. Wisterians. And yet you expect me to forgive it all and let the wolf into the chicken coop?" He paced, slow steps back and forth as he spoke.

"I am not a wolf." My voice was low and steady. Certain. "The emperor is dead. I am no longer under his control."

"He is dead because of *my* people. *We* killed him. We are just fortunate that we get to take out two of the empire's most powerful playing cards along with him."

You're only a card Cora. A tool.

"I will be used no longer." My voice burned. "I do not belong to the empire. Let me join you. Let me fight."

"Then you must prove your loyalty. Here and now."

I blinked. "How?"

West smiled, pleased with my response and turned slowly, his eyes falling on Jordan. "Kill him."

My mouth fell open and I quickly closed it. Kill Jordan? Kill the boy that protected me time and time again? The one that gave me blue flowers and kisses that made my knees weak? The one who hid me in castle passageways? The man that would kill his own father to save me? I carefully concealed my face into stone and steadied my breath. How could I make them see reason and not reveal the panic brewing in my veins?

And where was Faelin?

"Isn't he far more valuable to you alive?"

"Kill him," he repeated. "He is the emperor's son. He must pay for the sins of his father. He must die."

I looked at Jordan, his words and what he already knew sinking in. It was another game. I was a pawn. And I would have to make an impossible choice. But it would be mine.

He looked at me with nothing but acceptance in his eyes; willing to accept whatever choice I made. Willing to *die* for me if that's what it took. I felt my breath quicken in my chest, my cheeks growing hot as the truth of it landed. Did he deserve to die? Did who his father was justify his death?

"My touch does not hurt him," I admitted. I was already spinning the wheels in my head, searching for how to best handle West. "I can't kill him. He's immune."

West cocked his head. "Then kill him another way." He held a gun out to me. I took it hesitantly in my fingers. He saw me as weak. He believed I'd comply without hesitation. As the Red Reaper, they feared me. But as Cora, I was nothing—just a pawn, a tool, easily manipulated.

I approached Jordan, gun in hand. He sat up a little straighter, his eyes never leaving mine. So blue. So ready to die for me.

I stood behind him and aimed the gun at the back of his head. I could feel the hairs on my body standing up, the snowy breeze on the back of my neck whispering against my skin.

I saw a vision of me in the past. A girl with a crown on her head following orders. A boy standing in front of her telling her everything would be ok.

You won't hurt me Cora.

I imagined myself pulling the trigger, never to see his dimpled smile again, never to tell him how much I hated him again, and I felt sick to my stomach. It felt like shooting myself.

Everyone looked on, waiting.

I met Locke's eyes. I could see the apprehension in them.

I heard a screech from above, saw a flash of red and knew Faelin would help us.

And I knew what I must do. I would go down fighting. I would try to use my strange power and become worthy of their fear.

I made my choice the instant Jordan and I encountered one another in these woods and there was no going back.

Jordan. Be ready.

Before they realized and could act, I absorbed and channeled the fire elemental's power, the flame forming in my hands, and I shot it in the direction of the ice shackles at Jordan's wrist.

Once freed, I pulled the trigger on the gun. A shot hit the burly ice elemental in his shoulder and he cried out in anger as he went down.

Run Cora! Jordan's voice sounded in my head as shards of ice came flying our way. I absorbed them and sent them flying back, hearing the fire elemental cry out as one pierced her chest. Lex and Locke dodged them narrowly. Once again I marveled at how natural it felt to absorb and channel their power, like a dance I learned long ago and knew the steps to.

Jordan fought West, throwing a punch that disarmed him. I'd never seen him fight before. He moved with an agility and strength that rivaled even Locke's. A soldier born and bred.

Faelin soared down, revealing herself at last and as she screeched a ball of flame erupted from her beak and created a wall of fire between us and the Resistance members.

I met Locke's eyes as he shot vines our way, intending to stop us. To stop me. I watched as they twisted and twined towards our feet and I again channeled my power and sent the vines back Locke's direction, watching as they wrapped around him and Lex.

My moves were instinctive, but more naturally honed with Jordan's training.

I grabbed Jordan around the waist, channeling Lex's power to turn us invisible. I took off into the forest trying to get as much distance as I could between the group and us, Jordan's hand in mine.

Flames danced behind us and Faelin screeched again, surging into the cover of the forest.

"Go after them!" I heard West shout in the distance. "Find them! Stop them!"

***

It felt like Jordan and I ran for hours, fueled by adrenaline and the need to place as much distance as possible between us and the Resistance. I knew a few of them were injured, possibly even dead. I knew Locke's vines wouldn't hold him for long, that he would be free of them in no time. I had the feeling he would be the one that West would send after us to finish the job in a cruel sort of joke–if he could get past the wall of fire. And I knew there was no way West would send Lex after us if I could channel her power and stay hidden.

After a short distance I no longer could channel Lex's power and we were fully visible again. Now we needed to rely on our own strength.

"Where is Faelin?"

Darkness surrounded us now and the cold bit into my skin, the snow sticking to my cheeks as it fell.

"I told her to stay away. I sent her somewhere she will be safe."

"Where do we go?"

"I know a place," Jordan said, releasing my hand at last. His face was bruised, bloodied, broken, but life lit up his blue eyes. Nothing else mattered. He was alive. His eyes avoided my own, the heaviness of the day falling between us. "We can't slow down. We need to keep going. They can't be far behind."

I nodded and we continued on, our boots crunching gently in the snow.

"If you truly hate me...why didn't you shoot me?" His voice finally broke the uneasy stillness between us. He already knew the answer of course, but this was the game he and I played. Dancing around words we wouldn't say. Truths that felt too new and raw.

He knew exactly how I felt about him, despite my lies.

I felt a pang and regretted my earlier choice of words, but there would be a better time for that discussion later. "Why didn't you shoot *me*?" I countered, thinking of that day in the woods not long ago where I was staring down the barrel of his gun and he didn't pull the trigger.

He smiled back at me, disarming like the first time he did so.

"I decided that you were right. And that I didn't want to be a pawn for a different army." I made my choice. When it came down to it I would not be forced to kill to prove my loyalty. My loyalty could not be bought. "What happens now...with the empire? Now that your father is..." I couldn't finish the words, the image of the emperor fresh in my mind again. His empty eyes. And I realized there was so much I never got to ask him, so much left unanswered.

"My brother will be made emperor." His eyes were glassy.

"You have a brother?" I cocked my head, but I felt relief that it wouldn't be Jordan. "Why don't I remember him?"

"He's been in Alexandria. Courting one of the princesses there. I'm sure the wedding will be moved up promptly now. He's older than us. He didn't have the same relationship with you as I did. I think father tried to keep him distant from you, from what was happening with the war."

"And your brother...is he just as bloodthirsty for power as your father?"

"Time will tell. But there may be a chance to influence him. He respects my leadership of the soldiers. I was always the son raised for war. Jem was raised for politics and to take over the throne. He may listen to me." There was a faraway sadness in his eyes and I wondered at the relationship he held with his brother. "But it may be too late to turn the tide. So much damage has already been done. And he will be surrounded by my father's advisors. Once one has power how can you expect them to willingly give it up? The empire may be too far gone."

"I don't believe that."

Jordan turned his eyes to mine, an amused smile playing on his lips, but before he could speak he was suddenly thrown back against a tree, vines winding around his middle relentlessly. He struggled against them.

I could have absorbed Locke's power and shot it right back at him.

But I was disarmed. Distracted.

Fueled by hope.

Locke stood a short distance away from me, his silhouette like a dark shadow against the trees.

He simply stared at me and I at him.

Two soldiers on opposing sides.

Two pawns in a war.

Two people who never stood a chance.

I saw it now.

I saw clearly and Jordan's words came back to haunt me.

"It will never happen. Not the way you think. You are of more value to them dead. They will never take the time to properly train you. They fear you. They will never understand you."

I knew Jordan was there. Knew he could hear every word as he fought against the vines, but I needed to know. I needed to hear it from Locke.

"So once you knew who I was...that I was the Red Reaper...was that the end of it for you? Did I imagine all of it? That you felt something for me?" I could see the way my words dug into his skin and burrowed there.

His cheek twitched and still he held my eyes as he took a step closer.

"I thought you said my past didn't matter to you."

His chest rose and fell slowly. Another step closer.

"We are not afforded the same luxuries of normal people Cora. This is a war. Sacrifices have to be made."

"And I'm the sacrifice." I said it as a fact, not a question.

"What we *want* is the sacrifice." His words cut me even deeper. "This is bigger than you and me."

"I thought we wanted the same things." My voice broke slightly.

I took a step back from him and watched as his hand went to his dagger hilt.

"You intend to kill me?"

I stared into the same green eyes I once thought I would drown in, but now I saw only darkness, determination. It was sad, I thought, how wars could drive people to impossible decisions. How he felt as if he didn't have a choice.

"Him." Locke's eyes went to Jordan. "I have to kill him. He's the emperor's son."

"He's not next in line to rule!"

"But he's an heir. If not his brother it would be him. We have to end this war at the root."

Hold on Cora. I'm half way through these vines.

200

I looked at Jordan, his hand moved slightly and I realized he must have a knife on him.

"Once he's dead, come with me. Join the Resistance." His eyes were pleading.

I narrowed my eyes. "I won't let you kill Jordan."

He shook his head. "What are you saying?"

I lifted my chin. "You will have to kill me first."

He gave me no choice.

I calculated how fast I could pull my gloves off...

Touch his skin.

And then I felt sick to my stomach at the thought of killing him to defend Jordan.

Could I do it?

Would I do it?

And the sickening realization that Jordan knew.

He tried to warn me this would happen.

And I didn't listen.

Locke's hand tightened around the dagger.

I tried again. "You don't have to do this, Locke. You don't have to be who they want you to be. What if..." my voice trailed off in thought, in delusion, "we run away from all of this. If you feel anything for me...tell me now. Better yet...tell me you feel nothing for me."

He came closer and I let him.

"Cora! No!" I could hear Jordan yelling at me, but I ignored him.

He wrapped his arms around me...

And I let him.

It felt so good to be in his arms, to feel the warmth of his body.

I felt hopeful.

"I feel everything for you," he whispered into my hair and I felt myself relax into the words, the truth of them. I inhaled his earthy scent, pulled back to look into his green eyes and cupped his face gently with my gloved hands. "But he has to die."

He released me and headed for Jordan again, his dagger ready.

With seconds to act, I touched his arm, gently, and it gave me enough time for him to pause and turn back to me. I stared into his eyes, trying to memorize the exact shade of green.

"I want you to know," I said, making my decision as my gloved hands went to his face again, "I loved you."

And then my lips were on his. Skin against skin.

He kissed me back, his hand on my back clutching me tighter to him.

I could already feel the tears slipping down my cheeks warm and wet. Feel the immense sorrow and shame that erupted in my heart.

Silencer.

I opened my eyes and saw a trickle of blood form near his eye, but I wouldn't let him go. I couldn't let him harm Jordan. My fingers clenched around his back. His body fought me, rejected me, as if he finally understood the dangers of my touch. And his eyes told me he knew exactly what my intentions were.

Then I felt a searing pain in my abdomen.

I didn't even register the fact that he stabbed me or that Jordan yelled my name, until I looked down...saw the dagger in my stomach...his hand holding the blade...the blood that was drip drip dripping down onto the snow staining it red, and then looked back up and into his eyes.

They were burning, tears mixed with blood.

"I loved you too."

I saw us by the Tree of Life. I saw the vines holding my arms up above my head, my waist pulled tightly to the tree. And then I heard him ask the words, *"Do you trust me?"*

I saw him in the woods, his gloved hands at my waist.

"...you'll have a place there."

Felt his whispers against my skin.

I could still feel his kiss on my lips.

I felt like I broke into a million pieces when he drew the knife out, more blood splattering onto the snow.

My heart went with it.

22

I once wondered if time mattered, meant anything, when it was stolen from you. When you couldn't remember. When you lost it...what is left?

If time ceased to exist...I still did.

In between a place of life and death.

In a place where all that I had time to do was think.

Think about my life.

My choices.

All that I had yet to do, experience, and all the time that I wasted being meek and relying on other people to save me.

All the time I spent letting other people tell me who I was and what I was made for.

All the time I allowed others to use me and then discard me when I served my purpose, or became too much of a threat.

I thought about all of it as I lay there in the snow.

I felt numb to the point where I no longer registered the cold.

Funny how someone so deadly and so feared could be undone by a simple dagger.

I stared up into the dark expanse of sky and waited.

Waited for it to end.

It was snowing, large flakes in all shapes and sizes.

I wondered how long it would take for the snow to cover me.

How long before people would forget me and I would simply become an urban legend.

A story passed down to the generations about the empire's Red Reaper and how many lives she took, only to be bested by her enemy, a man she once loved. A warning to never fall in love with a Gifted.

Just like The Heartless Prince.

I was a story now.

And my story…Cora's story…was over before it even began.

Before my eyes closed and I succumbed to the darkness, I heard the soft step of hooves and saw the silhouette of a horse, its horn angling toward me.

***

I opened my eyes, the faint memory of someone calling my name echoing in my mind, warm hands pulling me up from the snow and into their arms.

I was no longer held hostage by the time in between forgetting and remembering.

I could feel my toes again.

I could feel heat around my body, comfort.

I was wrapped in a large blanket and laying on a couch.

A large fireplace cracked in front of me. I watched the flames lick and dance at the wood as I slowly remembered.

I couldn't remember coming here.

But I did remember Locke's last words to me.

I felt the weight of his betrayal. The weight of my own.

Someone moved next to the fireplace. A figure sitting in a rocking chair, his hands in his hair. But now he looked up and relief flooded his face at the sight of me.

He wore black cargo pants, black boots, and a white tank.

I would recognize that golden hair and those blue eyes anywhere.

Jordan.

We stared at each other from across the room, twin ghosts. Shells of the people we once were. Dancing shadows. Only this time his face was not bruised and bloodied, he was perfectly healed.

"Where am I?" I whispered, my throat dry.

His eyes dimmed. "Somewhere no one will find you. You're safe. I promise. No one knows about this place but me."

"How did you...? How did I...?" I wondered at why I no longer felt like I had a stab wound. There was no pain in my abdomen at all. "I'm not...dead?"

He swallowed and I could see the pain in his eyes. "I thought you were. I..." he took a shuddering breath. "If he stabbed you in the right place...you would have been." His words gave me a false sense of hope. "I couldn't make it to you in time. Faelin came back for us."

He closed his eyes, lost in the memory. "And then a Unicorn found us," he went on. "He healed you. And me as well. He wouldn't leave your side and he seems very protective of you." My eyes widened in realization and I wondered if it was Arthur. "He's outside. I don't think he's going anywhere."

He leaned back in the chair and put his hands on his knees. I could see the tension in his forearms. Seeing this much of his skin put me right back in the tent, my fingertips trailing down his chiseled abdomen. He looked devastatingly strong, honed and bred for the life of a soldier. But I didn't know if even *he* was strong enough to keep the empire from finding me if they decided they wouldn't let me go. Or the Resistance for that matter now that I knew they wanted me dead.

And if being almost dead taught me anything, it was that I no longer wanted to rely on someone else to save me. Or protect me.

"What happened? After?"

He left the rocking chair in one fluid motion, going to his knees on the floor beside the couch and he carefully took my hand in his. Warm. Understanding.

A muscle in his cheek twitched and his lips parted.

He looked at me. Really looked at me.

"Cora..." his voice was genuinely laced with empathy. And then a moment later more quietly, "I'm sorry you had to do that. I know how you felt about him."

"But you knew?" My voice felt like an accusation in the darkness. I didn't mean for it to, but it did all the same. "You said something before...about his intentions. But you didn't want to tell me because you knew." I shuddered, my eyes closing.

He sat back on the floor, drew one knee up, and wrapped his hands around it. "I was already the bad guy to you Cora. I knew that if I made him the bad guy you would never believe me. You wouldn't have listened. You needed to see for yourself."

I couldn't deny the truth of his words.

"I knew when it came down to it...he would always choose the Resistance first. Over you." He let out a sigh. "If he didn't run off...and you weren't nearly dead...I would have ended him for what he did to you." He flexed his hands in front of him and I could feel the anger brimming like a live wire beneath his skin.

"He's alive?" I felt a spark of relief.

His eyes flared. "He won't be if I ever see him again."

"I didn't want to kill him." My voice came out void, broken. "I didn't have a choice. He didn't either. I guess this means he and I are enemies now."

"There will always be those that want to kill me simply because of who I am."

I lifted my chin to meet his gaze. "And I won't let them."

He let out a shuddering breath and I waited for him to speak, but he remained silent. Something weighed on him heavily, I could feel it.

I looked around the room the best I could despite the darkness.

I could see a wooden dining table and chairs when I looked behind the couch. A small kitchen. It was a cozy little space. Not a speck of red in sight. A vase with familiar blue flowers sat on the table.

"This is yours?"

He nodded, a few pieces of hair falling lazily into his eyes. He swept them away with his hand. "I bought it years ago. Told no one about it. I always wanted...hoped...to have my own private getaway. Somewhere no one could find me if and when I made the choice to walk away."

"Walk away?" I raised an eyebrow.

"From the empire. From my father. From all of it."

"Are you saying you no longer support the Arias empire?"

"If we are being honest–I haven't supported the Arias empire for a very, very long time, Cora. And you are the reason for that. But I couldn't walk away...until I knew you were safe. As long as he had you...I couldn't walk away. And as long as they made me forget...well...that just prolonged everything further." His throat bobbed. "When everything happened in the last few days...when I heard word that he was coming back to the base to get you and take you back to Sageburn...I knew it was time."

"What were you going to do? How were you going to stop him?"

I was failing to understand.

"I was going to take you away before he got to the compound," he said. "But I couldn't risk telling you and having General Bel find out. But then he came early. I wasn't expecting him so early." He closed his eyes again. I knew he must feel as overwhelmed by the events of the day as I did.

"No one knows what happened to us. I imagine they will find my father's body, if the Resistance doesn't broadcast it to the world that they killed him first. Everyone will assume that we are either dead or taken captive by the Resistance. And the Resistance will believe that Locke killed you."

He looked like an avenging angel sitting on the floor, the orange glow of the fire behind him, the only sounds were his voice and the faint crackle of the fire wood. He steadied himself and looked into my eyes and I once again thought it unfair how disarming his face was.

"You could have obeyed your father. But you chose to protect me instead." I let the words settle between us, knowing I'd also made the choice to protect him when the Resistance wanted him dead.

He nodded, understanding in his eyes. "When you first came to the compound I didn't fully remember you. I knew you as the Red Reaper. I knew you as someone my father used to torture me and train me." I felt myself still at his words. At the memories he must have of me that I had not even tapped into yet. "I still don't remember everything. I only have flashes and glimpses of memories I've garnered from myself and from you. And over the last few days they keep coming, more and more of them." His eyes were glassy. "And the more I remembered...the more I knew I couldn't let them have you. Hurt you."

My chest rose and fell with his words. I didn't know if I could ride these emotional waves. I felt like I was on a train about to career off the tracks. To lose Locke–having him choose the Resistance over me–to needing to reconcile the fact that the memories I kept having were of the man sitting on the floor in front of me–a man willing to walk away from his empire to protect me.

I couldn't take it.

"I don't expect everything to be the same between us Cora." I closed my eyes and my mind flashed to his lips on my own.

Tell me again that you hate me and don't want me.

"I know that you want to shed your past and create a new future. But if you let me...if you trust me...I will help you create whatever you want. I will help you find the answers to all your unresolved questions...about who you are...where you came from..." he paused, still capturing my eyes with his own. "Or...if you want to walk away. Disappear. Start over. And never see me again...I care about you enough to let you go. I meant it when I said your story is not over...and you get to decide how it unfolds."

Tears were falling down my cheeks hot and fast. I couldn't help it.

"Jordan," I said hesitantly. "I don't hate you."

Our hands interlocked. His eyes met my own. "I know."

23

Three days later and just as Jordan promised, no one has bothered us. No one knows where we are. No one has come knocking. He's left a few times to gather food, wood, other supplies, but his absences are always short.

Every time he leaves I feel empty, panicked–until the very moment he walks back through the door again.

Despite his promises that I would be safe, that no one would suspect anything–I kept waiting for it to happen. For someone to come and laugh at the fact that I thought I could hide. That I could escape. For the Resistance to find us. Or for the empire to take me back.

I kept waiting for someone to tell me it was a joke. A dream.

But with every day that passed and no one came...I began to feel lighter. Less anxious. It felt like a stretch to trust Jordan after everything that happened with Locke, but the history between us made it impossible not to. I knew–he would always choose me.

And it killed me that Locke wouldn't.

I spent most of my time in solitude. I sat by the fireplace and I thought. I thought of all the possibilities of what my life could look like now. What did I want it to look like? And then when thinking became too much, too overwhelming, I read books I found lying around, mostly poetry and history.

Anything to get my mind off of the decision that I needed to make.

Jordan always gave me space, but he was always close by. Sometimes he would sit beside me on the couch and read too. Or he would go in the kitchen and cook us a meal or clean around the cabin. Sometimes he would go outside and I would hear him chopping firewood.

But he was so quiet. Eerily quiet.

I knew he was waiting for me to give him an answer.

To decide what I wanted.

Did I want to disappear and start over without him?

Did I want to revisit my past and find out exactly who I was?

Did I want his help?

And did I still want to find my sister? Did she even exist?

And then I would start the cycle all over again of sitting on the couch by the fireplace and staring into the flames...thinking...but going around in circles.

I wondered how long before he would grow tired of my silence, of my inner angst, before he would demand a decision from me. But he didn't.

There was a part of me that missed that cocky man in the tent who told me exactly how I felt, who saw right through me. The man that wouldn't let me sit in denial, who claimed my lips with his own. I craved that distraction now. A sign that I didn't imagine the moment between us.

I was a tangle of thoughts and emotions. I couldn't tell up from down, but I knew I needed to make a choice. This was my life to lead.

And I was done making decisions based on what other people wanted from me.

Jordan insisted that I take his bedroom and he slept on the couch. The distance again felt awkward, but necessary. The moment we experienced when he chose me over his father, and I chose him over the Resistance, over Locke, had changed us both.

His bedroom filled the entire upper floor, along with a nicely sized bathroom. The bed was large and I felt like I was sleeping on clouds when I sunk into the mattress. The bathroom housed an incredible claw foot bathtub. But my favorite part of the bedroom was the view.

Full glass pane windows, along with wide double doors that opened up to a large balcony, gave a sprawling view of the canyons, rows upon rows of trees, and the snow tipped mountains in the distance. Mountains that I knew housed Sageburn on the other side, but from up here it all felt so far away. Like it could never touch me again.

And then that got me thinking about how what happened to me could easily happen to someone else. The empire would find someone new to be their puppet. Someone new to control and inflict pain and death on innocent people.

And I wondered if there was any way I could stop it?

I had always thought of my power as a curse, not a Gift.

But then I remembered Jordan's comment about me learning to control it. That if I learned not to fear it, it was possible I wouldn't hurt anyone. And when I considered that my power might become something I could control, I felt hope.

What if I could use it for good?

What if it didn't have to be the Resistance versus the empire?

What if I could create something new? A new movement where those that wanted peace from both the Resistance and the empire could work together?

Could we have enough sway to end the war?

To stop the empire?

My head was spinning with the possibilities, but I at last knew what I wanted to do.

And at the end of the day, it was my decision.

My freedom of choice.

And I prepared to tell Jordan.

***

I stepped outside the cabin and watched as the snowy mist danced across the canyons. The view here was gorgeous, all mountains and snow capped trees. I made my way down the steps and towards the small stable where Arthur stood.

He looked as majestic as the first time I saw him, black shining fur, a spiraling opalescent horn. His eyes found mine and he let out a small whinny. His eyes were bright jewels, blue like Jordan's.

"We meet again brave one."

I held up a hand and laid it gently on his face. *"Thank you for saving me Arthur."*

"I simply returned the favor."

"Would I have died if you didn't?"

"Hard to say." He whinnied again. *"Do humans often stab one without the intent to kill?*

I lowered my gaze. *"It wasn't a human that did it."*

"Ahhh. I feel your pain, young one. You've endured much."

I stroked his back. *"What will you do now?"*

He nudged me with his snout, warm and wet. *"If you are willing, I pledge myself to you as your familiar. To fight for you, to protect you, and to guide you."*

"I'm truly of Wisterian blood then? I'm not a human?" It was time for me to accept the truth of who I was.

"Have you doubted? Your blood calls to me brave one. Your heart is strong and loyal. Magic flows through your veins, stronger than any I've encountered in my 500 years."

"500 years? Surely you can't be that old Arthur!"

"I've seen many Kings and Queens rise and fall. And empires as well. This empire will be no different, if those brave enough continue to fight. Will you fight young one?"

I pondered his words, my hand falling to the gleaming dagger on my hip.

"You are afraid only because you let them tell you who you are and what you are capable of. When the time comes you will remember the truth of your heritage. And no one will be able to stop you."

"Why can't you tell me who I am?"

"The only one who can tell you who you are...is yourself. You must accept it brave one. And keep that one close," his blue eyes fell on Jordan who stood on the steps of the cabin, his hands in his pockets, watching us curiously. *"He will keep you safe. He is your greatest ally. His heart is loyal to you."*

***

I told Jordan I was ready to talk.

He sat on the couch in front of me. I stood in front of the fireplace.

I gazed out the living room windows, taking in the view of the trees and mountains, watching as the sun began setting over them painting the sky a fantastic shade of pinks and oranges.

Jordan rested his hands on his thighs, but I watched as his fingers flexed in front of him. For as composed as he was most of the time, I was beginning to learn and memorize his tells. He was nervous.

He wore his usual cargo pants and a blue shirt that matched his eyes, it made them distractingly brighter, more alluring. I tore my gaze away, trying to focus.

I cleared my throat and folded my hands together.

"I've been thinking and I know what I want to do."

He stilled. He breathed steadily, but I could feel the tension, the waiting. He braced himself for me to tell him goodbye, I could feel it. I could feel his emotions slipping through as much as he tried to tether them.

I could feel him more easily as the days went on and the more time we spent with one another. I read his feelings and sometimes even his thoughts when he wasn't careful. I wondered if he did the same to me or if he did his best to stay away from my unpracticed mind.

He once said that I could learn to control my powers, that I didn't have to hurt anyone when I touched them. And that I could learn to guard my mind against other empaths like him.

I wanted to learn.

He let out a breath slow and steady and ran a hand through his blonde waves slowly. Another tell. "I'm listening."

I bit my lip. "I never want anyone else to have to go through what I did. I never want someone else to be under the control of the empire. Or the Resistance for that matter. I was never given a choice. And I don't know why. I don't know when or why my life was ripped away from me." I sighed. "But I want to find out. I want to be brave enough to go back to the past. To discover who I was, who I am. And then decide how that will impact my future. But not only that..."

His eyes were fixed on my face, hanging on every word.

"I want to learn how to control my powers. I don't want it to be a curse anymore. I never want to unwillingly hurt someone else with my touch again. I want to become strong and be able to defend myself. And I want to use my powers to help others that are oppressed by the empire."

He was nodding, realization dawning on his face.

"I want to fight back. I don't want to walk away and disappear from history just to become another story passed down over time. I want to create a new movement between the people in the Resistance and the empire that want something different. Those that want a free future. That want peace. To exist among humans and Gifted alike."

I breathed out a sigh feeling the truth of the words. "That's what I want."

He smiled softly, but it didn't quite reach his eyes yet. He waited.

"And I want your help Jordan. I need your help." He blinked and the smile crept up and his eyes widened. "I want you to teach me how to use my power. I want you to help me answer the questions about who I am. And I want you to help me create this new movement." I felt my voice crack. "And I'm scared to do it without you."

He stood now. I lifted my chin to meet his face, his eyes. They were shining. He glowed like a lightbulb, but he hesitated, waiting for me to reach out to him. To let him in.

I took his hands in my own, a silent truce. An understanding.

And his arms wrapped around me strongly.

I breathed a huge sigh of relief, not realizing how much I'd been holding in, carrying, the last few days as I made this decision about my future.

And I wrapped my arms around his waist and back and let myself lean into his chest, feeling the warmth and strength there. And as he held me I could feel our emotions melding together, our memories dancing together. Puzzle pieces, riddles, and unfinished rhymes.

And then he shared a new one with me.

A memory I'd yet to remember.

We are in the garden again. We've snuck out and we know it won't be long before they come to find us and separate us again. Make me go back to my chambers alone and make the Prince promise again that he will stay away from me.

We have minutes maybe.

We sit on the ground against the fountain, our knees touching.

"Father says if I keep being a nuisance he's going to do something I won't like." *His voice is low and quiet in the moonlight.* "I have a feeling he's going to use his mind tricks on me. Make that scary General he has walking around all the time make me forget you the way she always makes you forget me."

I squeeze his hand.

"He says I'm too obsessed with you. That you're not mine to worry about. That I can't possibly love you. But he also knows I'm the only one you listen to." *He sighs and lifts my chin up with his finger so I can meet his eyes.* "If something happens...I want to tell you a story. And how about...if I ever forget you...you tell me the story so I remember again? Ok?"

I nod.

"Let's call it The Heartless Prince. And it's a story about us, but of course we can add and embellish some other details so if the story is ever shared...no one will know it's about me and you. They will think it's made up, rumors. How's that sound?"

I nod again.

"So the story goes like this...there was once a Prince who would never settle down. He broke hearts, but vowed to never love one. But then one day...he met a Gifted. And he fell madly, head over heels in love with her. He loved her so much that he left his empire...his homeland...to run away with her."

I smile. I liked the story already.

"And so now the Prince is used as a warning for those young and naive to stay away from the mountains. To stay away from Wisteria. Because if they are not too careful, they too could be lured in by a Gifted and fall in love. And that would be very dangerous."

"And this Prince?" *I ask.* "He would really run away from his home, give up everything, for this girl?"

"He would always choose her first. Over anything and everything."

He brings his lips close to my ear and whispers, "I will always find you. And if you ever find me...tell me our story...and someday we will run away together."

I felt my arms wrap tighter around his waist as the memory faded and I felt wet tears on my cheeks. I thought of all the times I remembered the story of The Heartless Prince. All the times I'd shared it, but always felt like it was meant for me, a secret I kept close to my heart.

Because it was never meant for anyone else.

It was ours.

"I told you I would always find you," he whispered the words into my hair and I shivered as his fingers skimmed the sides of my stomach.

I couldn't keep denying it.

He loved me.

He would always choose me.

And I knew for certain...

Whatever happened next...

We were going to finish the story...

Together.

TO BE CONTINUED...

The story continues in 2026.

If you loved this book please consider leaving a review on amazon or goodreads. Thank you!

ACKNOWLEDGEMENTS

It's hard to put into words the many thanks I have for all that helped make this novel possible. I've wanted to write and publish my novels since I was eight years old – this is a life long ambition.

Thank you to the many teachers I've had over the years that told me I was meant to write.

I spent so much time pouring into this book. When you write a book it is all consuming mentally and emotionally (if you're a writer you know). Hours upon hours not only writing, but re-writing, and then editing, and then editing some more.

I am grateful to my husband and my children for being understanding and knowing when mommy is on her computer she's writing. Although my kids are too young to read this book, I appreciate their enthusiasm and excitement for the fact that "mom wrote a book".

I am grateful to Becca @beccaleighedits for doing a manuscript evaluation for me and giving me much needed insight into my novel and what could make it better. I highly recommend her services.

I am grateful to my friend Robyn for being the first person to read this book (the very first unpolished draft) and still telling me how much she loved it.

I am grateful to my parents Pauline and David for reading the final draft and championing it. Your encouragement means the world to me and gave me the confidence to get this book out into the world.

And lastly – thank you to the writing community I've found on social media, especially Tik Tok – you all are the best and I can't wait for you to read The Heartless Prince.

PLAYLIST

I personally love when authors include what songs or artists they listened to while they wrote their book. Here are mine:

1. "Once Upon A December" Emile Pandolfi

2. "I Hate It Here" Taylor Swift

3. "Warm Blood" Carly Rae Jepsen

4. "Once Upon A Dream" Lana Del Rey

5. "There Will Come Soft Rains" Katharine Petkovski

6. "Crush" (acoustic version) Jennifer Paige

7. "What If We Could" Blue October

8. "Treacherous" Taylor Swift

9. "Iris" Jada Facer

10. "Terra's Theme" TPR & Roxane Genot (original by Nobuo Uematsu)

11. "The Prophecy" Taylor Swift

12. "Crush" Ethel Cain

13. "Love Like Ghosts" Lord Huron

14. "Kingdom of Burmecia" TPR (original by Nobuo Uematsu)

15. "What Was I Made For?" Billie Eilish

16. "Magic Isn't Real" Blue October

17. "I Scare Myself" Beth Crowley

18. "Transatlanticism" Death Cab For Cutie

19. "Strangers" Ethel Cain

20. "The Night We Met" Lord Huron

21. "Broken" Noelle Johnson

22. "Aria Di Mezzo Carattere" TPR & Roxane Genot (original by Nobuo Uematsu)

23. "Dangerous Hope" Beth Crowley

ABOUT THE AUTHOR

Geneva Cerrato lives in southern California with her husband and 4 children. When she's not reading or writing, she loves to cook, go to Disneyland, or spend time with her community on social media.

You can connect with her on IG or Tik Tok @authorgenevacerrato